Code Name Lucifer

Advance Praise

'A thrilling, high-octane adventure, *Code Name Lucifer* explores the complexities of global espionage from an Indian perspective. Thorat and Rodrigues masterfully capture the tension of covert operations and the humanity of their characters. The interplay between duty and personal struggles makes this book stand out, providing readers with a compelling, unputdownable experience.'

Col Hunny Bakshi, VSM (Retd),
former commander, Covert Ops

'*Code Name Lucifer* delivers an intense, action-packed narrative that blends intrigue and suspense. Thorat and Rodrigues skillfully and brilliantly weave a tale of covert operations, deadly missions, and moral dilemmas. A gripping read for thriller enthusiasts, with well-developed characters and a fast-paced plot that keeps you hooked till the last page.'

Anand Ranganathan, scientist and author

'An intriguing premise with a fresh angle on counterterrorism.'

Ashwin Sanghi, author

'*Code Name Lucifer* is a gripping narrative that delves into the shadowy world of counterterrorism, exploring the thin line between justice and vengeance. When a covert team is formed to eliminate global terror masterminds, the enigmatic leader, Lucifer, takes center stage. Operating in moral ambiguity, Lucifer confronts geopolitical intrigues, personal betrayals, and the cost of relentless pursuit. Combining psychological insights and high-stakes operations, the book examines the scars left by terror and the resilience of the human spirit. With sharp storytelling and intense drama,

Shirish Thorat and Savio Rodrigues weave a tale that questions how far we must go to preserve our nation.'

Lt Gen. Shokin Chauhan (Retd), chairman,
Ceasefire Monitoring Group (Northeast)

'*Code Name Lucifer* is a heart-racing thriller filled with action, espionage, and complex characters. Thorat and Rodrigues craft a gripping story of dark secrets and covert missions that will keep you guessing. With its fast pace and unexpected turns, this book is an absolute page-turner for thriller aficionados.'

Maj. Gen. G.D. Bakshi (Retd), SM VSM

'An expertly crafted espionage thriller, *Code Name Lucifer* delves into a world of danger and deception. Thorat and Rodrigues master the balance between heart-pounding action and character development. The book's fast-paced narrative, alongside its thoughtful exploration of moral ambiguity, makes it an outstanding addition to the genre.'

N.K. Sood, author and former R&AW officer

'The book is a chilling reminder that India is at war and the frosty peace is the result of bold decisions and bloody action carried out by unknown soldiers. Their story showcases a new Bharat that refuses to be a victim but a nation that wants to forge its own narrative in the unequal world.

Kartikeya Sharma, deputy managing editor, News9

Code Name Lucifer

A Story of the Unknown Gunmen

Shirish Thorat

and

Savio Rodrigues

ISBN: 978-93-6547-575-3

First published in India 2025
This edition published 2025

BluOne Ink Pvt. Ltd
A-76, 2nd Floor, Sector 136, Noida
Uttar Pradesh 201301
www.bluone.ink
publisher@bluone.ink

Printed and bound in India by Thomson Press India Ltd.

Kali and Occam are imprints of BluOne Ink

To the unknown gunmen—our friends

Contents

Prologue

You don't know me. You shouldn't know me. And honestly, you probably wouldn't care to know me.

I came into being because some are called to play the role of an angel while others embrace the identity of a devil. These roles are not just assigned; they are woven into the very fabric of existence itself. In a universe where light and darkness are eternally intertwined, both play their parts in a grand and tragic theatre.

She sends an angel to build dreams and instil hope, to guide the lost and comfort the weary. The angel's light is soothing, illuminating the paths of the righteous, nurturing life and fostering kindness. But She also sends a devil to orchestrate chaos, to unleash wrath upon the unsuspecting. The devil's work is subtle, insidious, a whisper in the ears of men that ignites their darkest impulses. It is this darkness that reveals the true nature of light.

Without the devil, would you ever believe in the angel—or, for that matter, in God? The angel's goodness becomes meaningless without the devil's malevolence to contrast it. It is in the heart of darkness that we find the roots of faith; it is the devil who gives the angel its purpose.

I work for Her. She assigns me tasks that Her angels cannot undertake, bound as they are by their perceptions of righteousness and the need to be seen as doing good. Angels wear their halos with pride, basking in the adoration of humanity, their every action scrutinized by the lens of morality. They cannot afford the luxury of ambiguity, for they exist to be the embodiment of hope. I, however, have always operated with the understanding that a devil is destined for darkness.

In this world, rife with diabolical geopolitics, ruthless economic interests, and the perverse machinations of promiscuous men and women, a nation cannot rely solely on its angels. It needs a legion of devils—agents of mobocracy to spread lawlessness, to stir revolutions that destabilize economies, societies, and governments threatening its existence. The fabric of civilization is delicate, and sometimes it requires a devil's touch to unravel it, to expose the vulnerabilities that lay hidden beneath the surface.

I am one of the Fallen Angels, a devil in Her service. She named me Lucifer. The name itself carries a weight, a legacy that is both revered and reviled. It is a name that elicits fear and fascination in equal measure. She tells me I am her most prudent, deceptive, ruthless, and merciless devil. I believe Her. I work for Her. I am alive because of Her.

Once I, too, was an angel. I believed in goodness, in playing the great game of global capitalism under the principles of fairness, truthfulness, and mutual cooperation. I wore my halo with pride, convinced of the righteousness of my mission. I sought to illuminate the darkness, to bring warmth where there was coldness, to inspire change where there was despair. In my innocence, I thought I could create a better world.

But light, as you might have realized, is merely the absence of darkness. Biblically, Earth was formless and void, darkness hovering over the deep, until God said, 'Let there be light.' This act of creation was not just a divine command, it was a profound revelation of the duality of existence.

I learned early that living in the light is an illusion; it's a fantasy spun by those dreamers who convince themselves that the light is the reality of their world and that darkness is dispelled by its glow. They cling to their beliefs, creating a narrative that fits neatly into their understanding of the universe. They forget that darkness is an ever-present force, lurking just beyond the edges of their perception, waiting for the right moment to reclaim its place.

'Hello, darkness, my old friend'—it's more than just a lyric; it's the truth. Darkness is an old friend, always present. Light merely conceals it. In the absence of scrutiny, the shadow thrives, and therein lies the irony: the very light that was meant to guide also blinds.

I was commanded to jump from heaven into hell. She knew that my nation did not need me as an angel—there were plenty of them basking in the light, some flitting in the shadows, but few willing to dwell in the darkness. She sought someone she could trust to traverse that abyss. She said, 'The war we fight is not in the light, nor in the shadows, but deep in the darkness. To win, we need an angel to fall, to become a devil that roams in the night.'

So I jumped, I fell into darkness and became a fallen angel, cloaked in the same shadows that I had once sought to dispel.

In the darkness, there is no right or wrong, no good or bad, for light does not expose one's actions to moral scrutiny. The absence of judgement allows for the freedom to act without constraint. In this realm, the only purpose of an action is to achieve a desired result—no matter how horrific, amoral, or unscrupulous it may be. The ends justify the means.

As I navigated this new reality, I encountered others like me, those who had also traded their halos for horns. We were a brotherhood of sorts, united in our shared understanding of the world's darker nature. We understood that in the pursuit of a greater good, sometimes sacrifices must be made. We were the architects of chaos, the instigators of turmoil, the whispers in the ears of the powerful who had grown complacent in their righteousness.

As I delved deeper into this realm, I began to realize that darkness is not merely a void to be filled, it is a force with its own agency and desires. It is seductive and intoxicating, offering freedom from the constraints of morality that bind so many. I found power in this newfound understanding, a strength that came from embracing my role as a devil. I was no longer confined by the limitations of light; I was free to act, to achieve, to conquer.

In the darkness, I discovered allies among those who had long been cast aside by society—the outcasts, the rebels, the mavericks, and the disillusioned. They were eager to join me in my crusade, to embrace the chaos I promised. Together, we formed a coalition of the forgotten, a movement born from the ashes of betrayal and despair. And so the dance began. I was both the puppet and the puppeteer, manipulating the strings of chaos while simultaneously becoming ensnared by my own creations. The world around me shifted like a living entity, a chaotic symphony where I played the leading role.

In the shadows of this new world, I gathered allies—men and women who had tasted the bitterness of oppression and longed for the sweetness of freedom. They were weary but resolute, and hungry for change. Together, we forged a bond stronger than blood, united by our shared vision of a future free from the shackles of tyranny. In their eyes, I was not a devil but a beacon of hope, a figure to rally behind in the fight against the darkness that had consumed us for too long.

With each passing day, our movement gained momentum. We became a force to be reckoned with, striking fear into the hearts of those who had once looked down upon us. We disrupted their carefully curated narratives, tore down their monuments of power, and illuminated the shadows where they had hidden their sins. I orchestrated acts of defiance—strikes, protests, cyberattacks—each one a meticulously planned endeavour designed to destabilize the status quo.

I was the shadow that moved unseen, the whisper that turned friend against friend. In this dance of deception, I played my role flawlessly, earning the trust of those in power while plotting their downfall. The world was a chessboard, and I was the master strategist, moving pieces with calculated precision.

But even the most carefully laid plans are susceptible to disruption. As our movement grew, so did the forces aligned against us. They began to counter my every move, deploying their own shadows to snuff out the light we had ignited. The dance became a deadly game of cat and mouse, and I was no longer sure who was hunting whom.

In the midst of this turmoil, a chilling realization struck me: the darkness I had embraced was not simply a weapon;

it was a living, breathing entity with its own desires and ambitions. It had become clear that the more I revelled in the chaos, the more it consumed me. The boundaries between my angelic past and my devilish present began to dissolve, leaving only a fractured reflection of who I once was.

Had I fallen too far? I don't know, but in this ever-shifting landscape, I am prepared for whatever lies ahead. I am no longer merely a fallen angel; I am darkness itself.

1

The Research

The fluorescent lights flickered above Dr Ananya Sharma's cluttered desk, casting a sterile glow over the stacks of papers and books that surrounded her. As a post-doctoral student of security and conflict studies at Jawaharlal Nehru University, she often found herself lost in a labyrinth of data, theories, and the haunting narratives of terror that shaped her country. Today, however, was different. Today was the culmination of years of research, late nights, and relentless passion for unearthing the truth behind the scars etched into the fabric of Indian society.

Ananya adjusted her glasses and took a deep breath, steadying herself before diving into the final stretch of her work. Her thesis, titled 'The Persistence of Grief: Understanding the Psychological Impact of Terrorism on Indian Society', was due at the end of the week. The pressure to encapsulate years of research, interviews, and analysis into a concise yet impactful paper weighed heavily on her. It was not just an academic endeavour; it was a personal mission to shed light on the lingering scars that acts of terror leave on the psyche of individuals and communities.

She clicked on the document titled 'Final Draft' and began reading, her eyes scanning each line for clarity, precision, and depth. But her mind raced beyond the words on the screen, recalling the stories she had heard—parents mourning their children, survivors haunted by the sound of explosions, and families torn apart by a single moment of violence. Each case study was more than data; it was a testament to resilience and a reminder of the unending cycle of loss.

As she continued, the weight of her own emotions crept in, mixing with the academic language. Her thesis wasn't just about understanding grief; it was about confronting it, giving it a voice, and perhaps finding a way to heal.

Ananya had grown up in a modest, middle-class family in Khadki, Pune, where the occasional crack of gunfire or the low rumble of detonating explosives from the nearby ammunition and ordnance factory were part of the backdrop of her everyday life. To most, these sounds were mere echoes, routine tests that faded into the distance. But for Ananya, they evoked darker thoughts, shadows cast by the tales of terror and bloodshed her parents shared—a grim reality they had witnessed firsthand during the 2002 Gujarat riots.

Those stories were more than just recounting of past horrors. They had become markers in her young mind, each one etching a deeper understanding of human cruelty and its unending recurrence. She grew up hearing of bombings in crowded markets, of train compartments set ablaze, and of communities that had once coexisted turning on each other with savage ferocity. The brutality was not confined to history books; it was alive, coursing through the streets and seeping into daily conversations, always just a step away from home.

The question that haunted her was why. Why did such violence continue to erupt, generation after generation? It persisted like an untreated wound in the nation's soul, festering without healing, leaving scars that refused to fade. It was this very question that had shaped her life's path, driving her to seek answers through her research. She wanted to understand the persistence of grief and, perhaps, to find a way to help India confront and heal from its darkest memories.

As Ananya penned the introduction, her thoughts wandered back to the day her path was set in motion. It was a rainy afternoon in 2014, and she was transfixed by the heart-wrenching news coverage of the Peshawar school attack, where 132 children had lost their lives in an act of incomprehensible brutality. The grief in the parents' voices, their cries cutting through the air like raw wounds, and the devastation etched into their eyes were images that refused to fade. The world seemed to pause in horror, and yet, even as time moved forward, the pain remained, lingering in the aftermath like a shadow that could not be shaken.

Those scenes haunted her. The senselessness of the violence stirred something deep within—a resolve to seek answers, to understand why such tragedies continued to occur and why the wounds they left behind were never fully addressed. The Peshawar attack became a turning point, igniting a desire not just to study the psychological impact of terrorism but to also explore how unresolved trauma rippled through society, altering the collective psyche of a nation.

With renewed focus, Ananya returned to her paper, determined to weave the threads of her research into a compelling narrative. The crux of her work exposed a harsh and unsettling truth: despite the countless terrorist attacks that had scarred Indian soil, many of the planners and masterminds remained beyond the reach of justice. It was as though the perpetrators had slipped through the cracks, while the victims were left to carry the weight of loss and unanswered questions.

She had meticulously compiled a list of significant incidents from the past four decades, a chronology of trauma that spanned generations. The 1984 anti-Sikh riots, where thousands were massacred, and the justice system that had faltered in the aftermath. The 1993 Bombay bombings, a coordinated series of explosions that shattered lives and trust in a city already struggling to heal from the riots of the previous year. The 2001 Parliament attack, a brazen assault on the very heart of Indian democracy, and the 2016 Uri attack, which reignited fears of conflict along a volatile border.

Each entry in her research was more than just a historical statistic; it was a narrative of grief and resilience, a story of families torn apart and communities that had to rebuild amidst the ashes. Her work sought to give voice to those stories, to make the world see the human cost of terror and the wounds that remained unhealed.

Ananya wrote about the psychological impact on survivors and families of victims, detailing the long-lasting effects of trauma and grief. She cited interviews with psychologists, victims' families, and community leaders, weaving their voices into her narrative. The anguish of those left behind was palpable in her words. 'For many families, the violence did not end with the death of their loved ones. It lingers in their memories, affecting their daily lives and their ability to trust the world around them.'

She delved into the concept of unresolved grief—a phenomenon where individuals and communities could not find closure due to the absence of justice. 'When perpetrators remain unpunished,' she wrote, 'the pain and anger transform into a collective wound, festering and leading to a cycle of violence.'

As she articulated her findings, she considered the broader implications for Indian society. She examined how the unhealed wounds from these tragedies contributed to a pervasive atmosphere of fear, distrust, and anger. 'This persistent grief not only impacts those directly affected but also engulfs the entire nation, shaping its social fabric and political discourse.'

Ananya presented her analysis of the sociopolitical ramifications of terrorism, arguing that unaddressed trauma could lead to radicalization and a desire for revenge among the younger generation. She quoted a study that showed how unresolved grief could manifest in extremist ideologies, fuelling cycles of violence that spanned generations. The words of a young victim's brother echoed in her mind: 'I don't want revenge; I want justice. But every day that goes by without accountability, my heart grows heavy with anger.'

With every page she completed, Ananya felt a mixture of hope and despair. She hoped her research would shine a light on a neglected issue, prompting policymakers to recognize the importance of addressing not just the immediate security threats but also the underlying psychological impacts of terrorism.

After hours of fine-tuning her arguments, she finally reached the conclusion of her paper. Ananya's heart raced as she typed the final lines. 'If we wish to heal as a nation, we must acknowledge the pain of our past and actively pursue justice for the victims of terror. Only then can we hope to move forward, united and resolute.'

With a sense of accomplishment, Ananya saved the document and prepared to submit it to her supervisor. As she clicked 'send', an uneasy feeling settled in the pit of her stomach. She couldn't shake the thought that her research might become more than just an academic exercise. What if it caught the attention of those in power? What if her words ignited a fire that could change the course of national security policy?

Days turned into weeks, and Ananya returned to her routine, attending lectures and conducting interviews for her ongoing research. She had almost forgotten about the paper when she received an unexpected email from her supervisor. It read: 'Ananya, your paper has caught the interest of several departments within the government. I've forwarded it to the Intelligence Bureau for review. They believe your insights may be invaluable.'

Her heart raced. The Intelligence Bureau? The weight of that realization was both exhilarating and terrifying. Ananya had hoped her research would contribute to the discourse surrounding terrorism in India, but she had never anticipated it would reach such heights.

As she lay awake that night, her mind swirled with possibilities. What if her research could lead to a real change in how the government addressed terrorism? What if it could help prevent future attacks? But with those thoughts came a new layer of anxiety. She couldn't shake the feeling that she was about to be thrust into a world of shadows—one that she had only studied from a distance.

Little did she know that her work would soon intertwine with a covert mission led by a man known only as Lucifer, a figure operating in the depths of secrecy and moral ambiguity.

2

The Bureau's Interest

The air inside the Intelligence Bureau (IB) headquarters was thick with tension. It was a place where information was currency and trust a rare commodity. Agents moved through the labyrinthine halls with purpose, their expressions a mask of determination. In this world of shadows and secrets, every whisper could signal the difference between life and death.

In a dimly lit conference room, a group of high-ranking officials gathered around a polished oak table. The walls were adorned with maps, photographs, and reports detailing the latest intelligence on terrorist activities both within and beyond India's borders. At the head of the table sat Rajesh Khanna, the director of the IB, a man known for his keen instincts and a reputation for being unyielding in his pursuit of justice. His piercing eyes scanned the room, assessing the faces of his trusted colleagues.

'Gentlemen,' he began, his voice steady, 'we have a situation that requires our immediate attention.' He gestured to a projector screen where Ananya's research paper, 'The Persistence of Grief', was displayed. 'This paper has crossed my desk, and I believe it warrants a deeper investigation.'

As the projector illuminated the room, Rajesh highlighted key sections of Ananya's paper. 'Her analysis of unaddressed grief in the wake of terrorist attacks is compelling. She articulates how the lack of accountability fosters a breeding ground for anger and radicalization, particularly among the youth. This is not just a psychological assessment; it's a strategic insight into how our adversaries could exploit these wounds.'

The room was silent, each official absorbing the weight of Rajesh's words. Nandita Sharma, a seasoned analyst known for her sharp intelligence and dedication to work, leaned forward. 'Director, while the paper is well-written, it raises several concerns. If the public becomes increasingly aware of these unresolved issues, it could lead to unrest. We've seen similar patterns in other nations where the populace has demanded justice.'

Rajesh nodded. 'Exactly. And that's why we need to be proactive. Ananya's insights could be pivotal in shaping our approach. If we can identify the root causes of this grief and address them head-on, we might thwart the potential for future radicalization.'

As discussions unfolded, Rajesh proposed an ambitious initiative. 'I suggest we initiate a covert operation to track down those responsible for the major terrorist attacks that have taken place over the last forty years. We'll compile a list of individuals—regardless of their age, nationality, or the potential geopolitical fallout—and neutralize them. This will send a clear message: If they attack us, we will go after them, no matter the cost.'

A murmur of agreement rippled through the room, but there were also expressions of concern. Arjun Singh, a seasoned field operative, raised an eyebrow. 'Director, this could provoke an international incident. We must consider the implications of such actions. Not only could they alienate potential allies but they might also rally anti-India sentiments abroad.'

Rajesh met Arjun's gaze with unwavering confidence. 'I understand the risks, but we must also consider the current state of our security. We cannot afford to wait for justice to be served through conventional means. We need to act decisively before these grievances lead to more violence.'

Nandita interjected, her voice steady. 'Director, perhaps we could approach this with a dual strategy—pursuing justice for the victims while simultaneously investigating how these terrorist networks operate. We could utilize Ananya's research to engage with communities affected by violence and begin a dialogue that might heal some of these wounds.'

Rajesh considered her suggestion. 'That's a valid point,' he said after a few moments. 'However, we need to proceed with caution. This operation must remain under wraps. No one outside this room can know of it. We'll initiate an informal inquiry into Ananya's background. If she's as insightful as her paper suggests, we might want her involved in a more formal capacity.'

The room buzzed with discussions on how to proceed. Rajesh ordered his team to conduct a thorough background check on Ananya Sharma, focusing on her academic work, personal life, and any affiliations she might have with activist groups or non-profits. He wanted to ensure that bringing her into this operation would not pose any risks.

Nandita made a mental note to go through Ananya's past publications and academic contributions, and look for her opinion on terrorism and national security. 'If she's going to play a role in this operation, we need to understand her mindset fully,' Nandita said out loud.

As the meeting concluded, Rajesh felt a surge of optimism. Ananya's research could be the key to not only addressing the psychological ramifications of terrorism but also understanding the tactical moves needed to counter them. This was not merely an academic pursuit; it was a matter of national security.

'Let's meet Dr Ananya. Nandita, set up a meeting with her soon,' Rajesh instructed.

3

Convergence of Minds: Meeting Dr Ananya

The sun had just risen over South Block, casting a warm glow on the grey concrete buildings that housed India's intelligence agencies. Inside the dimly lit conference room of the IB, Rajesh sat at the head of the table, meticulously reviewing the latest reports. A sense of urgency filled the air, intensified by the recent resurgence of terrorist activities across the nation.

Rajesh was a man of few words, but his piercing gaze and commanding presence spoke volumes. His reputation as a shrewd strategist was well-known among his peers. Today, however, his mind was preoccupied with one particular report that had crossed his desk: the findings of Dr Ananya Sharma.

As he contemplated the implications of her findings, the door swung open, and Research and Analysis Wing (R&AW) Chief Devendra Joshi entered the room. His tall, lean frame and sharp features made him an imposing figure. Devendra had a reputation for being direct and unyielding, qualities that had served him well in the cutthroat world of intelligence.

'Rajesh, we need to discuss the implications of Dr Sharma's research,' Devendra stated, taking a seat across from him. 'The psychological impact of terrorism is becoming increasingly evident, not just on individuals but on societal structures as well.'

Rajesh nodded, appreciating Devendra's promptness. 'I was just going over her thesis. And have even discussed it with my team. It's clear we're not just facing a threat to our physical safety; the emotional and psychological scars are deepening too. We need a strategy that addresses this. I have invited Dr Ananya for a discussion. She should be arriving anytime now.'

'I agree,' Devendra replied, leaning forward. 'The rise in extremist ideologies and recruitment into terrorist organizations can often be traced back to untreated trauma and collective grief. If we can address these underlying issues, we might be able to mitigate future threats.'

Before Rajesh could respond, there was a knock at the door. It opened to reveal Dr Ananya Sharma herself. She was dressed in a simple, professional outfit, her hair tied back neatly. There was a mix of nervousness and determination in her eyes. The two men gestured for her to take a seat, and she settled in, clutching a folder of her research materials.

'Thank you for inviting me,' she began, her voice steady but laced with tension. 'I understand there's significant interest in my thesis.'

'Indeed,' Rajesh said, his tone softening. 'Your work has caught our attention. We believe it can play a crucial role in how we address the psychological fallout from recent terrorist activities.'

As Dr Ananya Sharma sat across from IB Chief Rajesh Khanna and R&AW Chief Devendra Joshi, she felt the weight of her research pressing on her shoulders. This meeting was critical; they were not just her superiors in the intelligence community but also key players in shaping India's counterterrorism strategy. She took a deep breath, steeling herself to convey the essence of her thesis.

'Thank you both for meeting with me today. My thesis focuses on the psychological impact of unresolved grief on communities affected by terrorism,' Ananya began, her voice steady yet passionate. 'In my research, I argue that when acts of terror occur, the absence of accountability for the perpetrators creates profound emotional scars that extend beyond the immediate victims to entire communities.'

Rajesh leaned in, intrigued. 'What do you mean by "emotional scars"?'

Ananya continued, 'Terrorism is not just about physical violence; it deeply affects the psyche of individuals and communities. People experience a range of emotions—grief, anger, fear, and confusion. When these feelings are left unaddressed, they can fester, leading to cycles of violence and even radicalization. I have documented numerous case studies that illustrate how unresolved grief can manifest into collective trauma that drives communities towards violence or extremism.'

Devendra furrowed his brow, considering her words. 'So you're saying that without accountability, we risk creating a breeding ground for future terrorism?'

'Exactly,' Ananya affirmed, encouraged by their engagement. 'When communities feel that justice has not been served, it breeds a sense of helplessness. This emotional turmoil can lead to feelings of betrayal and anger towards the state and its institutions. In my thesis, I detail how these emotional landscapes can influence people's perceptions of security and their willingness to support extremist ideologies as a means of seeking retribution.'

Rajesh nodded, processing the implications of her findings. 'How do you propose we integrate this understanding into our current counterterrorism strategies?'

Ananya shifted in her seat, feeling the urgency of the conversation. 'We need to acknowledge the psychological dimensions of terrorism in our operational frameworks. By implementing community engagement initiatives that validate the experiences of victims and their families, we can foster resilience. This means not only addressing the immediate threats posed by terrorists but also working to heal the communities left in the wake of these attacks.'

'Could you give us some practical examples?' Devendra asked, his analytical mind eager for tangible solutions.

'Certainly,' Ananya replied. 'We can establish support networks that include psychological counselling and community forums where individuals can share their experiences and feelings. This could be coupled with public acknowledgment from the government, recognizing the pain and trauma that these communities have endured. Additionally, integrating local leaders into these efforts could help in rebuilding trust between communities and the authorities.'

Rajesh leaned back in his chair, contemplating her suggestions. 'And how do we ensure this approach doesn't dilute our operational efficacy against active terrorist threats?'

Ananya had anticipated the concern. ‘That's a valid question. The key is to maintain a dual focus. We must continue with decisive actions against terrorist networks while addressing the underlying grievances that fuel extremism. This can be communicated as a comprehensive strategy to both the home minister and the prime minister, showcasing that we are not only a reactive force but also proactive in securing long-term peace.’

Devendra interjected, ‘You're suggesting a narrative that emphasizes strength in both our operations and our compassion?’

‘Exactly,’ Ananya affirmed. ‘If we can present a united front that incorporates both strategic action against terrorism and psychological healing for communities, we can begin to shift public perception. This will not only reassure the citizens of India that their government is committed to their safety but also counter the narrative that leads individuals toward extremism.’

Rajesh looked at Devendra, a spark of understanding passing between them. ‘Dr Sharma, your research might just provide the crucial insights we need to evolve our strategies. The path ahead is complex, but we need to blend our tactical responses with a genuine commitment to healing. If we can frame our approach to show that we are tackling the roots of the problem, it will lend credence to our operational goals.’

Ananya felt a surge of hope as she recognized the shift in their perspectives. ‘If we can work together to create a framework that addresses both immediate security concerns and the psychological impact of terrorism, we could potentially create a more resilient society.’

Rajesh and Devendra nodded, a newfound resolve evident in their expressions. 'Let's prepare a comprehensive presentation for Aditi,' Rajesh said. 'We'll need to outline how we can operationalize these ideas while ensuring we remain vigilant against threats.' Aditi Mehra, India's National Security Advisor (NSA), would have to be convinced of their plan.

As the meeting concluded, Ananya felt a sense of purpose. Her research was more than just an academic exercise; it could play a vital role in shaping a more holistic approach to counterterrorism in India. By bridging the gap between psychological understanding and operational strategy, they could forge a path that led not only to safety but also to healing—a path towards a stronger, more united India.

After Dr Ananya's departure, Rajesh and Devendra sat back, the silence in the room underscoring the gravity of their next steps. Her insights on the psychological aftermath of terrorism had challenged their conventional focus on operational tactics. But now, they needed to merge those insights into a practical strategy that addressed the urgent need for action.

Rajesh broke the silence, his voice measured. 'Devendra, we need to make sure our strategy is airtight. We can't just go in with a broad idea of addressing the psychological impacts. It needs to be woven seamlessly into our core objectives—neutralizing the immediate threats and restoring public confidence.'

Devendra leaned forward, his expression serious. 'I agree. We need a two-pronged approach that keeps our primary focus on eliminating the terrorists, but also incorporates measures that address the psychological landscape left in their wake. The key is to present it as a complementary strategy—not a shift away from our hardline stance, but an expansion of it.'

Rajesh nodded. 'Exactly. The first step is to lay out a series of targeted operations to hit back at the terror networks. We need to coordinate with all intelligence units to identify key targets and act swiftly. These strikes will send a clear message that we're on the offensive.'

'Phase One,' Devendra said, 'will be built around rapid-response operations—neutralizing high-value targets, disrupting supply chains, and dismantling cells. But we can't just stop there. We need to show that our actions are eradicating threats and also creating conditions for long-term security.'

Rajesh added, 'That's where the second phase comes in. We position it as a follow-up to our tactical successes. We should call it "Operation Twin Shield"—combining direct military action with measures to stabilize and rebuild the communities most affected by terrorism. People need to know that we're not only fighting terrorists but also protecting and healing our own.'

Devendra's eyes narrowed in thought. 'So, Phase Two would involve deploying psychological and community support initiatives along with our tactical operations. We'll use Ananya's insights to guide the framework. Her research could be instrumental in establishing local support systems to help civilians cope with the trauma. The aim would be to strengthen the community's resilience, which will, in turn, enhance overall security.'

Rajesh pulled out a notepad and began jotting down the main elements. 'All right, here's how we can structure it. Phase One focuses on the tactical elimination of threats—

taking down leaders, disrupting financial networks, and preventing future attacks. Phase Two will engage local communities, using intelligence and psychological support to build networks of vigilance and trust. We'll make it harder for extremists to find sympathizers or operators.'

Devendra nodded, a determined look on his face. 'I'll start working on the operational details for Phase One, including target prioritization and inter-agency coordination. We need a comprehensive list of targets, a timeline for executing strikes, and contingency plans for potential escalations. At the same time, I'll get in touch with our foreign allies for intelligence sharing. Any information that can help us tighten the noose is valuable.'

Rajesh agreed. 'Meanwhile, I'll refine the outline for Phase Two with Ananya's input. We'll draft an integrated framework that combines psychological outreach with intelligence efforts. It's not just about providing counselling or support—it's about creating a network that actively contributes to our intelligence-gathering capabilities. We need to identify potential risks before they materialize.'

'Exactly,' Devendra said. 'We'll make sure that any community engagement measures also serve our broader counterterrorism goals. It's about using every tool at our disposal to not just fight back but to create an environment where terrorism can't thrive.'

Rajesh looked at his watch. 'We need to get this in front of the NSA within forty-eight hours. Aditi will expect a detailed, actionable plan that aligns with the government's overall strategy. We can't afford any gaps or loose ends.'

Devendra stood up, determination etched across his face. 'We'll make sure we're ready. I'll brief my team, and we'll start prepping for the meeting with Aditi. We need her on board, fully convinced that Operation Twin Shield can deliver immediate results and set a foundation for lasting security.'

Rajesh rose as well. 'Let's do this. We'll meet Aditi with a comprehensive plan for neutralizing terrorists and addressing the deeper issue of community resilience. If we can get her buy-in, it will set the tone for our briefing with the home minister and the prime minister.'

As they left the office, the path ahead was clear. The plan was about eliminating threats and reshaping the landscape of counterterrorism in India. It was time to prove that they could combine strength with strategy—sending a message to both the terrorists and the people of India that the authorities were not only prepared but also determined to protect the nation on all fronts.

4

Meeting with the NSA

As Rajesh and Devendra began drafting their plan of action, the atmosphere in the office shifted from one of scepticism to focused determination. Both men understood the stakes at play. They were not merely tasked with fighting a war against terrorism; they were responsible for safeguarding the very fabric of Indian society. If they could successfully tackle the threats and simultaneously promote healing and resilience, they might turn the tide in a conflict that had caused untold suffering for far too long.

Devendra felt a renewed sense of purpose as they worked, fuelled by the knowledge that they were embarking on a mission to not only combat terrorism but to also restore hope to a nation grappling with grief. The balance was delicate, but if they could navigate it skilfully, they might just pave the way for a more secure and unified India—a nation capable of rising from the ashes of violence and despair, stronger than before.

As Rajesh and Devendra finished refining their plans, the gravity of their next meeting loomed large. They were set to brief the national security advisor on their operational strategies and the evolving framework for addressing the psychological impact of terrorism. This meeting was pivotal, as Aditi would subsequently relay their findings and proposed actions to both the home minister and the prime minister.

Rajesh glanced at the clock on his office wall, the seconds ticking away as he considered the weight of their responsibility. 'Devendra, we need to ensure that Aditi is fully on board with our strategy. Her support will be crucial when she presents this to the home minister and prime minister. If we can secure their backing, we can move forward with authority.'

Devendra nodded, adjusting his tie, a gesture of anxiety masking his determination. 'Absolutely. Aditi has a sharp mind and a firm grasp of the larger picture. If we can convince her of our combined approach—blending psychological initiatives with decisive operational tactics—we'll stand a better chance of gaining the political will necessary for effective action.'

As they made their way down the corridors of the IB, the weight of their discussions hung in the air. Both men understood that the stakes had never been higher; the nation's security and public trust were on the line. The recent surge in terrorist activities had heightened tensions, and there was an urgent need to reassure the public that the authorities were doing everything in their power to protect them.

They arrived at Aditi's office, a well-appointed room filled with subdued tones of decorum and professionalism. Aditi, a woman known for her no-nonsense approach and incisive intellect, was already seated at her desk, reviewing some documents. As Rajesh and Devendra entered, she looked up, her expression shifting from concentration to one of welcoming acknowledgment.

'Good to see you both,' she smiled, motioning for them to take a seat. 'I trust you've been making progress?'

'Indeed,' Rajesh replied, taking a deep breath. 'We have developed a comprehensive strategy that not only targets the operational aspects of combating terrorism but also addresses the psychological impact it has on our society.'

Aditi's interest piqued. 'That sounds promising. The psychological fallout from terrorism has long been overlooked, and integrating that with our operational goals could be groundbreaking.'

Devendra leaned forward, eager to outline their approach. 'We've identified the necessity of not just eliminating the threat but also restoring faith and resilience within communities affected by these acts of violence. The people of India need to feel safe, and we must work to rebuild that sense of security while maintaining a strong stance against terrorism.'

'Let's hear the details,' Aditi encouraged, her tone serious. 'We need to ensure that any actions taken are effective and also maintain the integrity of our national security strategy.'

Rajesh and Devendra exchanged glances, both aware of the potential for their ideas to clash with more traditional approaches. But they pressed on, outlining their plan to tackle the immediate threats while simultaneously preparing a framework for community engagement and support.

As they spoke, Aditi listened intently, occasionally interjecting with insightful questions or observations. 'You're proposing a multifaceted approach, which could be effective. But I need to understand how you plan to communicate this strategy to the home minister and prime minister. They need clear, actionable items.'

Rajesh nodded, prepared for this line of questioning. 'We intend to present a dual narrative—one that highlights our commitment to decisive action against terrorists while also emphasizing our recognition of the psychological scars these attacks leave on our society. It's crucial to show the leadership that we're addressing the whole issue, not just the symptoms. That's why we recommend Operation Twin Shield.'

Aditi's gaze sharpened as she considered their proposal. 'That's a solid angle. The prime minister is particularly sensitive to public sentiment right now. He needs to project strength, and if we can frame our strategy to include psychological resilience alongside operational success, we might just have a compelling narrative.'

Devendra interjected, 'Additionally, we plan to highlight the role of community support in bolstering national security. Engaging with the local population will create a network of vigilance and trust, making it harder for terrorists to operate unnoticed.'

Aditi nodded, the gears of her mind clearly turning. 'This is starting to come together. I can see the value in your approach, but we'll need to present it in a way that stresses the urgency of immediate action against terrorists. The home minister will want to see results, and the prime minister will want to reassure the public that we're in control.'

As the meeting progressed, Aditi challenged their ideas, probing for weaknesses and demanding clarity. Rajesh and Devendra found themselves defending their approach but also adjusting their narrative to better fit the expectations of the higher echelons of power.

Finally, after an intense discussion that lasted nearly an hour, Aditi leaned back in her chair, her expression one of contemplative approval. 'I believe we have something here that could resonate with the leadership. I'll take your proposal to the home minister and the prime minister. But I need you both to prepare a comprehensive presentation outlining our strategy, focusing on both the operational and psychological aspects. And bring Dr Ananya to the meeting.'

Rajesh exhaled, a sense of relief washing over him. 'We'll have it ready. Thank you, Aditi. Your support is crucial for us.'

As they left Aditi's office, Devendra felt a renewed sense of purpose. They had laid the groundwork for a strategy that could change the narrative around terrorism in India. Now, it was time to rally the political machinery to support their efforts.

'The next steps are critical,' Rajesh said as they walked through the corridors. 'If we can align the NSA with our objectives, we can create a united front. Our next meeting with the home minister will be pivotal. We must present a coherent and compelling case.'

Devendra agreed, already mentally drafting the necessary points for their presentation. 'We need to ensure that they see the value in addressing both the immediate threats and the long-term implications of terrorism on our society.'

Together, they prepared for the next phase of their mission, determined to forge a path that combined decisive action with a commitment to healing. The journey ahead was uncertain, but their resolve was unwavering.

5

From Bureau to High Command

Ananya awoke the next morning with the sun casting golden rays through her window, illuminating the chaos of her apartment. Papers were strewn across her desk, reminders of her academic life that felt increasingly distant. The events of the previous day played over and over in her mind—the invitation to join a covert operation and the intense conversation with Rajesh Khanna and Devendra Joshi. She had spent the night wrestling with her conscience, weighing the implications of her decision.

After a long shower, she dressed in a crisp white blouse and dark trousers, trying to cultivate an air of professionalism. Ananya knew she was stepping into a world governed by protocols and power plays, one where the stakes were as high as they could get.

As she made her way to the IB office, a sense of trepidation hung in the air. The fortified structure loomed over her like a guardian of secrets, and she steeled herself for the day ahead. She arrived to find a small team waiting for her in the conference room, their expressions a blend of curiosity and scepticism.

Rajesh was already present, his expression serious as he gestured for Ananya to sit. 'Welcome, Dr Sharma. Thank you for agreeing to be part of this initiative. We're convening a briefing today with the national security advisor and the prime minister. It's crucial that you are well-prepared for this discussion.'

Ananya nodded, her stomach tightening at the mention of the NSA and the prime minister. 'What can I expect from this meeting?'

'Expect the unexpected,' Rajesh replied, his tone lightening slightly. 'The NSA operates in a different league. They have their own agenda, and political manoeuvring is part of the game.'

Just then, the door swung open, and in walked Devendra, his presence commanding the room. He exchanged brief nods with Rajesh before fixing his gaze on Ananya. 'Ready for your debut?' he asked, a hint of amusement in his eyes.

'I suppose so,' Ananya replied, trying to match his confidence.

Rajesh leaned forward, his expression serious once more. 'This meeting is more than just an introduction; it's about establishing your role within the operation. They will want to know how your research ties into our strategy. Be concise and forthright.'

Ananya swallowed hard, the reality of her involvement sinking in. 'What if they disagree with my conclusions?'

Devendra interjected, 'Then you defend your position. Remember, your expertise is what brought you here. Trust your research.'

Moments later, Ananya found herself seated across from National Security Advisor Aditi Mehra, Prime Minister Ashok Singh, and Home Minister Dinesh Patnaik.

The two women were a study in contrasts: Ananya, with her sharp features and intense gaze, exuded a commanding presence, while Aditi, with her calm demeanour, radiated an air of authority tempered by a sense of approachability.

'Dr Sharma,' Aditi began, her tone direct, 'your research has caught our attention. We're in need of insights that will shape our response to terrorism, especially in light of recent events. What makes your findings essential for our mission?'

Ananya took a breath, feeling the weight of the room's scrutiny. 'My paper examines the psychological impact of unresolved grief on communities affected by terrorism. It argues that the absence of accountability for perpetrators leaves deep scars that can breed cycles of violence. Understanding these emotional landscapes can inform our strategies for counterterrorism.'

The prime minister nodded, his brow furrowed in thought. 'We need a strategy that not only addresses immediate threats but also seeks to heal the underlying wounds in society. Your research aligns with that vision.'

As the discussion progressed, Ananya found herself immersed in a complex web of political dynamics. Aditi and PM Singh exchanged insights about previous operations and their outcomes, highlighting the risks associated with retaliation without proper intelligence. Ananya listened intently, her analytical mind absorbing every detail.

'What are the key factors we should consider in this operation?' Aditi asked, turning her attention back to Ananya.

'Understanding the profiles of individuals involved in terrorism is crucial,' Ananya responded confidently. 'Many are products of their environments, driven by grievances that extend beyond ideology. We must approach them not just as enemies but as individuals whose narratives can be analysed for potential pathways to disengagement or retribution.'

Aditi's sharp gaze held Ananya's as she absorbed the information. 'And how do you propose we address those narratives while executing a counteroffensive operation?'

Ananya hesitated, considering her response carefully. 'By utilizing intelligence-gathering methods that reveal the motivations and connections of these individuals. If we can understand their pain, we can craft a story that appeals to those still on the fence. But we must also communicate our resolve: If we are attacked, we will retaliate.'

Singh leaned back in his chair, his expression contemplative. 'What you're suggesting is not merely an operation; it's a paradigm shift in how we view our enemies. It's about building a narrative that contrasts our response with their grievances. But it also puts us in a vulnerable position. How do we maintain the balance between understanding and action?'

'I believe that's where my involvement can be pivotal,' Ananya replied, her voice steady. 'I can help articulate that narrative, ensuring it resonates not only with our agencies but also with the public. We can cultivate an understanding that encourages resilience rather than fear.'

Devendra watched intently, nodding in agreement. 'We need to frame our actions as proactive and protective rather than retaliatory. The public must see that we are acting not out of vengeance but out of necessity.'

Aditi's expression shifted to one of approval. 'Very well, Dr Sharma. If you can assist in shaping this strategy, your role will be crucial.'

As the meeting concluded, Ananya felt a mix of exhilaration and trepidation. The prime minister thanked her for her insights, and as they exited the room, she couldn't help but notice the glimmer of possibility in the air. This was more than just an opportunity; it was a responsibility that weighed heavily on her shoulders.

Devendra walked alongside her, an approving smile on his face. 'You handled that well. Your insights will guide us as we prepare for the next steps in this operation.'

'Thank you,' Ananya replied, still processing the gravity of her involvement. 'But I'm also aware of the challenges ahead. Balancing understanding with the need for action is a delicate matter.'

'Welcome to the world of national security,' he said, a hint of amusement in his tone. 'Just remember, every choice you make will have consequences, and you must be prepared to face them.'

As Ananya left the headquarters, she felt a newfound sense of purpose. She had crossed a threshold into a realm where her research could have real-world implications, and the political landscape was far more intricate than she had imagined. But with that purpose came a sense of foreboding; the stakes were high, and she could feel the shadows of past decisions creeping closer.

Little did she know that the political manoeuvring within the government would soon intertwine with her personal journey, complicating her mission in ways she could never anticipate. The operation to address the festering wounds of grief and trauma was about to commence, but the path forward was fraught with challenges that would test her ideals, her alliances, and, ultimately, her resolve.

As Dr Ananya left the room, her presentation still lingering in the air, the prime minister leaned back in his chair, his gaze shifting towards Aditi. His eyes asked the unspoken question: What next?

Aditi caught his look and gave a small nod. 'Mr Prime Minister, the first objective we discussed—neutralizing active threats—is crucial to demonstrating our resolve and regaining the public's trust. While Dr Ananya's insights into the psychological impact of terrorism are invaluable, people need to see immediate, decisive action. If we're to stem the growth of terrorism, we must make a clear statement that we will not tolerate any threat to our nation's security.'

The prime minister's expression was stern but focused. 'How do we proceed then? We need a plan that not only targets the terrorists but also ensures that these actions resonate with the people—so they know the government is working to keep them safe.'

Rajesh leaned forward, taking the cue to elaborate. 'Sir, we've structured our approach into what we're calling "Operation Twin Shield". The first phase will involve a series of high-precision strikes against identified terror networks, leadership figures, and infrastructure. Our aim is to dismantle their capabilities, disrupt their operations, and send a strong signal. We've already begun gathering intelligence on key targets, and coordination with allied agencies is underway to ensure swift action.'

Devendra picked up from where Rajesh left off. 'We've also engaged our partners abroad to cut off the financial and logistical lifelines of these groups. Our intelligence suggests that crippling their resources will significantly reduce their ability to plan and execute further attacks.

We're prioritizing high-value targets and critical nodes within their networks. This is to create a ripple effect that will weaken the overall structure of their operations.'

The prime minister's eyes narrowed with interest, and he turned to Aditi again. 'And the psychological aspect? How do we tie Dr Ananya's insights into this strategy?'

Aditi gave a slight smile, knowing this was where the operation could truly set itself apart from conventional counterterrorism measures. 'Mr Prime Minister, this is where Phase Two of our plan becomes essential. While Phase One focuses on taking out the immediate threats, Phase Two will integrate psychological outreach and community support initiatives. We'll collaborate with local leaders, civil society organizations, and even mental health professionals to engage the affected communities. Dr Ananya's thesis highlighted how the persistence of unresolved grief can foster resentment and, eventually, radicalization. We'll address this by providing psychological support and, more importantly, by making the community an active participant in countering extremist narratives.'

Rajesh added, 'The communities most affected by terrorism will be brought into the fold not just as recipients of aid but as partners in our strategy. The message will be clear: The government stands with them, not just to avenge but to heal. We believe this will help foster resilience, making it harder for extremist groups to exploit the scars left behind by their violence.'

Home Minister Dinesh Patnaik who had been listening intently, leaned forward. 'How will this be communicated to the public? People need to feel this, not just see it on the news.'

Devendra nodded in agreement. 'We'll ensure that our actions speak louder than our words. Media engagement will be crucial, but we'll also implement a grassroots-level information campaign in the affected regions. The narrative will focus on the steps we're taking to keep communities safe, backed by visible government presence. Dr Ananya's framework can help guide us in shaping a communications strategy that addresses the underlying fears and anxiety within these communities.'

The prime minister listened carefully, his fingers tapping lightly on the armrest of his chair. 'If we do this right,' he said slowly, 'we can achieve more than just neutralizing terrorists—we can build a foundation for lasting security. But we need to ensure the momentum from Phase One carries into Phase Two seamlessly. I want clear benchmarks for success, both in terms of the operational outcomes and community impact.'

Aditi nodded firmly. 'We'll have a detailed timeline and milestones ready for your review within the next seventy-two hours, Mr Prime Minister. Our strategy will present not just a plan of action but a path forward to assure the nation that we're proactively shaping the future.'

The prime minister's expression softened, his confidence visibly bolstered by the comprehensive nature of the plan. 'Good. Let's ensure that when we strike, we strike hard. But let's also leave a legacy of resilience and hope, not just shattered bodies and broken lives.'

As Aditi laid out her proposal for Phase One of Operation Twin Shield—Operation Black Lotus—she didn't miss a beat when she spoke the words: 'Go Unleash Hell.' She saw the shift in the room immediately; the prime minister's brow furrowed slightly, and the home minister leaned in with piqued interest.

Rajesh and Devendra exchanged a quick glance. The skepticism in their expressions didn't escape Aditi's notice, but it wasn't unexpected. 'I understand your reservations,' she continued, her gaze shifting between Rajesh and Devendra. 'But if we're serious about striking hard and sending a strong message, we need someone who can execute without hesitation. Someone with the experience, audacity, and the right mindset for unconventional warfare.'

'Col Ajay Bakshi,' Devendra said, almost to himself. His tone was laced with a mix of curiosity and caution. 'Lucifer. You're suggesting we let him lead the charge?'

'Lucifer,' Aditi affirmed, her voice calm yet resolute. 'His track record speaks for itself. He's handled some of the most sensitive and dangerous covert operations for us, and his unconventional methods have proven effective in high-stakes situations. We need to hit back hard, hit back where it hurts, and make sure people know we are in control.'

Rajesh leaned back in his chair, a slight frown creasing his forehead. 'He's not exactly known for playing by the book. His methods can be … ruthless.'

'That's exactly why we need him,' Aditi replied, her eyes narrowing slightly. 'The terrorists aren't playing by any rulebook. If we want to outmanoeuvre them, we need someone who understands how they operate—someone who can anticipate their moves and hit them where it'll cripple them most. If there's anyone who can "unleash hell" on our terms, it's Lucifer.'

The prime minister, who had remained silent until now, spoke up, his voice carrying the weight of authority. 'If we proceed with this plan, I need assurance that it won't backfire. We're not just talking about eliminating terrorists; we're talking about restoring the confidence of the people. We cannot afford any missteps.'

Rajesh interjected, 'The key will be in controlling the narrative. While Lucifer carries out the operation, we ensure that the public sees it as a decisive step in their protection, not just an act of retaliation.'

Aditi nodded. 'Precisely. The operation will be as much about perception as it is about action. And Lucifer understands the importance of that balance. If we give him the right directives and put a framework in place, he will deliver. But we will need to keep a close watch and have contingencies ready.'

Devendra, still silent and lost in his thoughts, finally spoke up, 'All right, let's prepare a comprehensive briefing for Lucifer and outline the objectives clearly. We'll also need a detailed framework on public communications and potential fallout scenarios.'

Aditi's expression softened slightly, seeing that the first hurdle had been crossed. 'I'll set up the meeting with Lucifer. We'll get him up to speed and ensure that this operation is executed with precision. This is only the beginning; Go Unleash Hell will be the first wave of Operation Black Lotus, but the strategy will unfold in phases. We need to be prepared for what comes next.'

The prime minister's nod was almost imperceptible, but it carried the weight of approval. 'Then let's move forward. I want progress reports regularly. And make sure that when we strike, we do it with the strength and clarity that leaves no doubt—we are in control.'

'What do we call Phase Two of Operation Twin Shield, if Phase One is "Operation Black Lotus"?' Devendra asked, his gaze shifting to Aditi.

Without missing a beat, Aditi replied, 'Operation White Lotus.'

She let the name linger in the air, explaining, 'While Black Lotus signifies the covert, aggressive strikes and the shadowy nature of our actions in Phase One, White Lotus represents the transition to strategic consolidation and the restoration of order. It's about bringing balance, just like the contrasting colours suggest—moving from chaos to stability, but always with a sharp edge.'

As the meeting ended, Aditi's confidence was palpable. The pieces were coming together, and the time to unleash hell was drawing near.

With that, the meeting adjourned, and the officials exited the room one by one. As the door closed behind them, the prime minister's words echoed in their minds—this was about more than just stopping the terrorists. It was about restoring faith in the government's ability to protect its people and sowing the seeds of unity and strength in the face of terror. For Rajesh, Devendra, and Aditi, the real work was just beginning.

6

Enter Lucifer

The shadows loomed long in the dimly lit room, a stark contrast to the bright lights of the conference room where Ananya and the high command strategized. Lucifer, known only by that name, sat alone in a sparsely furnished safe house on the outskirts of Delhi, the walls lined with maps and photographs of targets. Each image told a story of pain, loss, and unresolved justice. Here, the weight of his mission pressed heavily upon him, stirring memories he had fought hard to bury.

Once a decorated officer in the Indian Special Forces, Lucifer had carved out a reputation of a man who operated in the shadows, taking down threats without a trace—a ghost and devil. His real name, his past, and even his face had been shrouded in layers of secrecy. Only a handful of individuals in the intelligence community knew who he truly was; Aditi Mehra, the NSA, was among them. They shared a history that was forged in the fires of high-stakes operations and unyielding trust.

As he stood before a map of India, punctuated by red pins marking recent terrorist activities, his mind drifted back to the early days of his career. The first mission had been a test of character, a turning point that had led him down this dark path. He had witnessed the brutalities of war firsthand and experienced the destruction wrought by those who would harm innocents. Each act of violence had etched itself into his psyche, fuelling a resolve that had only grown stronger over the years.

His phone buzzed, breaking the silence. Aditi's name flashed on the screen, and he answered immediately, the urgency of her voice palpable even through the static. 'Lucifer, we're moving forward with Operation Black Lotus. I need you to assemble a team of operators, your Fallen Angels. We have a list of targets, but I want you to focus on those who have eluded justice for far too long.'

'Understood,' he replied, his voice steady but intense. 'Do we have a timeline?'

'The plan is to act swiftly, but we must remain discreet. We want to minimize collateral damage and keep our movements off the radar of other intelligence agencies. You know what's at stake,' she emphasized, her tone serious. 'Our enemies are watching.'

Lucifer felt a thrill of adrenaline course through him. The prospect of going after the architects of terror, of finally bringing justice to those who had suffered for decades, ignited a fire within him. 'I'll find the best operators, serious skills, high resilience, the ones that don't need micromanagement.'

'Good. Choose wisely. I trust you to make the right call,' she added, her voice softening for a moment. 'And remember, we're in this together.'

As the call ended, he felt the weight of her trust. It wasn't just a mission; it was personal—a chance to reclaim the lost lives of his team to bring them out of the shadows to the light.

Lucifer knew that for Operation Black Lotus to succeed, he needed more than just capable operators; he needed people who were personally invested in the mission, individuals whose motivations aligned with the ruthlessness required to 'Go Unleash Hell'.

The names on his shortlist stood out for their skills and mindset. Vicky Sampath, code-named Heracles, and Sheetal Thukral, known as Jezebel, were the obvious primary choices—each with their own unique talents and reasons for taking on this dangerous endeavour. An operation of this scale couldn't be executed without them.

The recruitment took place at a covert safehouse in the foothills of a remote mountain in the quiet and uninhabited village of Sattari, a place far from prying eyes yet easily accessible. Lucifer arrived first, his presence commanding as always, dressed in a simple pale blue shirt and tan chinos. The dim lighting of the room cast shadows across his face, making his intense gaze even more formidable. As he waited for Heracles and Jezebel to arrive, he reviewed their profiles once more, not because he needed to but because he liked being reminded of what his crew was capable of.

Heracles was the first to enter. The door creaked open, and Vikram strode in with a calm and confident demeanour. Standing just under six feet, he was muscular but lean—a result of years of deployment in the 2nd Paras. His eyes habitually scanned the room before settling on Lucifer, whom he acknowledged with a respectful nod.

'Lucifer,' he greeted, his voice gruff but measured.

Lucifer gave a slight nod in return. 'Heracles. I trust you know why you're here.'

Vikram's lips curled into a faint, knowing smirk. 'If it involves taking down scum, I'm all in.'

'Good,' Lucifer said, gesturing to a chair. 'Take a seat. We'll get started once Jezebel arrives.'

Moments later, Sheetal Thukral stepped through the door. She wore a casual black jacket and jeans, but her eyes sparkled with the sharpness of a mind always at work. Her reputation as Jezebel preceded her—a cyber-intelligence prodigy who had once taken down an entire rogue syndicate's network with nothing but a laptop and an encrypted flash drive. She exchanged a quick glance with Heracles before turning her attention to Lucifer.

'Nice to see you in person, Lucifer,' she said, a hint of dry humour in her tone. 'I was starting to think you were a myth.'

Lucifer cracked a rare smile. 'Well, the stories aren't too far off. Now that you're both here, let's get down to business.'

He laid out a map of the region on the table and began briefing them. 'Operation Black Lotus—our first objective is to neutralize multiple high-value targets. These are terrorist cells operating with impunity, exploiting the chaos in our political landscape. We're not just here to dismantle their operations; we're here to crush the spirit of those who think they can escape justice.'

Lucifer's finger traced several red marks on the map, each representing a confirmed or suspected terrorist hideout. 'Heracles, you'll be leading the ground teams for these three targets,' he said, tapping the map with precision. 'Expect armed resistance and multi-layered security. Use your judgement, but remember that our aim is not just to kill but to also gather intel that can take us to the leadership chain. That means taking the occasional prisoners and subjecting them to implemented interrogation.' Lucifer paused and then continued, 'I will have experts on standby for that.'

Vikram leaned in, scrutinizing the locations. 'Understood. I'll need the best assault team for this, and a mandate of expediency to deal with any threats along the way. There won't be time for permissions and after-action reviews.'

Lucifer's eyes glinted. 'You'll get what you need. Bureaucracy has no place in hell.'

Turning to Sheetal, he continued, 'Jezebel, you'll handle the cyber warfare side of things. We need their communications systems penetrated and primed for disruption. Also, make a full appraisal of their security systems, construct a blueprint for rendering them neutral, and rig for catastrophic failure. Make it look like their networks were hit by rival factions—leave a digital trail that leads them on a wild goose chase. We want them paranoid, divided, and unable to trust even their own resources.'

Sheetal nodded, already mentally mapping out her strategy. 'I can breach their mainframes, open back doors, and do a data dump and exit, laying down some digital breadcrumbs. By the time they realize what's happening, it'll be too late.'

Lucifer placed two folders on the table—one for each of them. 'Inside are the specifics on your targets, including personal backgrounds and last known movements. There's also intel suggesting that some of these individuals have deep connections within political circles. We'll use that information to trace the money and logistics behind these operations.'

Heracles picked up his folder, flipping through the pages. 'So, we're taking out the cells while you pull at the strings leading back to their financiers?'

'Precisely,' Lucifer confirmed. 'This operation is about sending a message to the puppet masters as much as it is about eliminating the foot soldiers. If we can cripple their funding and expose their connections, the entire network will begin to unravel.'

Sheetal glanced at Heracles, then back at Lucifer. 'And what about collateral damage? There's bound to be civilians in some of these locations.'

Lucifer's expression hardened. 'Our orders are clear. We avoid unnecessary casualties. But if it comes down to a choice between risking lives and securing a mission, you do what you must. The terrorists made their choice when they decided to target innocents. Now, we show them the consequences.'

There was a brief silence as the weight of Lucifer's words settled in. Both Heracles and Jezebel understood the gravity of the mission—it wasn't just another operation; it was a declaration of war against those who thought they could bring terror to any doorstep without repercussions.

The briefing concluded, but Lucifer's gaze lingered on his new recruits. 'Remember, we're not just fighting terrorists; we're fighting the rot that enables them to exist. Stay sharp. Trust no one but each other. And above all, practice field discipline every second from this moment onward.'

As Heracles and Jezebel left the room, they felt a palpable shift in the air. They were no longer operators on a mission; they were instruments of retribution, the tip of the spear that Lucifer had begun to forge. The hunt had begun, and with every step closer to the first target the storm of Operation Black Lotus would gather momentum.

7

Lucifer Recruits His Ratpack

Lucifer knew that recruiting the right people would be the most critical part of Operation Black Lotus. The team needed to be a perfect blend of skills, determination, and disillusionment with the system. He had already selected Heracles and Jezebel, who would be his second and third in command. Now, it was time to reach out to others who could fill out the ranks of what he called his Ratpack. But in the world of shadows, they would be known as the 'Fallen Angels'.

Together with Heracles and Jezebel, Lucifer began contacting each of the shortlisted candidates. He used encrypted channels and clandestine meeting spots to gauge their interest, assessing their skills and motivations. The Fallen Angels were not merely operators; they were individuals whose principles and anger aligned with the team's mission of delivering retribution outside the bounds of traditional law.

Lucifer's recruitment drive for his Ratpack continued as he and his trusted lieutenants, Heracles and Jezebel, scoured through the final list of candidates. The narrowing down had been ruthless, with each individual's skill set, background, and psychological profile rigorously assessed.

Lucifer knew the stakes were too high for half measures; Operation Black Lotus needed a team that operated outside conventional norms but with an unflinching commitment to justice.

Their next steps involved making contact with the chosen recruits, each of whom had retreated into the shadows after being discarded by the system they had once served. Lucifer, Heracles, and Jezebel reached out through various discreet channels, using encrypted communication and trusted intermediaries to set up the meetings. Each of these encounters would be a test, not just for the recruits but for Lucifer as well, to determine if they were ready to commit to a cause that defied bureaucratic and political agendas.

The first meeting took place in a nondescript warehouse on the outskirts of Delhi, where Aarav 'Shade' Mehta had been laying low since his dismissal from the intelligence community. Lucifer arrived with Heracles, and as they approached Aarav's scepticism was evident. He scanned them warily, arms crossed over his chest.

'So, the great Lucifer has come to enlist a disgraced analyst?' Shade said with a smirk. 'You must be desperate.'

Lucifer's eyes hardened. 'Not desperate. Determined. We don't recruit the dismissed; we recruit the disillusioned. There's a difference. You've seen the inefficiencies firsthand. You know the cost of hesitation when red tape is involved. We offer you a chance to be part of something where your skills won't be wasted—where you can truly make a difference.'

After a tense pause, Shade's shoulders relaxed slightly. 'All right, I'm listening.'

Next was Sofia 'Raven' D'Souza. Her meeting was arranged in the back room of a café in Goa, far from the digital haunts where she usually lurked. Jezebel handled this one, knowing that Raven's disillusionment with the system mirrored her own experience.

As Jezebel explained the mission, Raven tapped her fingers against the table, her sharp gaze fixed on Jezebel. 'You're telling me you want me to hack into the kind of systems I've spent years avoiding just to stay off the radar?'

'Yes,' Jezebel replied, unfazed. 'But this time, it's for something bigger than us. We're going to expose the rot and tear it out by the roots.'

Raven's lips curved into a sly smile. 'You had me at "tear it out". Count me in.'

Irfan 'Spectre' Khan met them in a cramped apartment in Delhi, where stacks of surveillance footage filled the space. Lucifer could tell from the outset that Irfan had never stopped working, even if the system no longer paid him.

'We need eyes everywhere,' Lucifer said bluntly, as Heracles outlined the kind of surveillance network they planned to build. 'You've already been doing the job of an entire agency here, but without the backing to actually make a difference.'

Irfan leaned back in his chair, folding his arms. 'And what makes you think this time will be different?'

'Because this time,' Lucifer replied, 'we don't answer to anyone but the mission.'

The recruitment drive continued in this manner, each encounter unique, each recruit a puzzle piece that fit into the grand picture Lucifer was assembling.

Neha 'Wraith' Singh, with her background in strategy, met them in an abandoned factory in Punjab. Her anger simmered just beneath the surface, but Lucifer knew that it could be channelled into something much more potent.

Ajay 'Viper' Rao agreed to meet in an isolated forest in Maharashtra, his instincts still those of a soldier. When Heracles laid out the plan, Ajay's nod came before they were even finished. 'I've been waiting for a fight like this.'

Meera 'Dove' Verma was found training in a makeshift gym in Uttar Pradesh. Her intensity during the brief sparring session with Heracles convinced Lucifer that she belonged with his Ratpack.

Raza 'Ghost' Malik made contact through a series of dead drops in Kashmir, finally agreeing to a face-to-face meeting under the cover of the night. His quiet determination spoke more than words ever could.

Nisha 'Hawk' Qureshi, with her aggressive combat style, was brought on board after Lucifer and Jezebel demonstrated the need for a more direct approach in some situations. Her bluntness was refreshing. 'If we're going after them, we don't stop until the last one falls.'

Dev 'Inferno' Choudhary, the explosives expert from Rajasthan, was lured out of self-imposed exile with the promise of striking back against those who exploited chaos for personal gain.

Farah 'Tempest' Kaur, who had become a master manipulator in the world of communications, met them in a quiet town in Punjab. Her skill at controlling narratives would be vital to the operation's success.

Zaid 'Falcon' Ahmed, now using his aerial reconnaissance skills for less noble causes, agreed to rejoin the fight after Lucifer showed him a target list that included the names of those who shut down his missions.

Leila 'Scarlet' Gill, a mysterious young lady from Haryana, excels in espionage, seduction, and psychological warfare. Her sharp intellect and deadly charm make her an indispensable member of Lucifer's team.

Lastly, Tariq 'Grim' Iqbal, whose talents in psychological operations had once turned the tide of conflicts, found his purpose rekindled when Lucifer told him, 'This time, we're writing our own playbook.'

With the recruits assembled, Lucifer, Heracles, and Jezebel briefed them on the mission. Operation Black Lotus was more than just a covert action plan; it was a declaration of war against a system that allowed terrorism to thrive under the guise of diplomacy and procedural limitations.

Lucifer stood before his Ratpack, the room dimly lit but charged with a sense of purpose. 'You've all been cast aside by the very institutions you once served,' he said, his voice steady and commanding. 'But it's not your skills that were the problem; it's the lack of willpower from those above. This is our chance to correct that, to be the sword that cuts through the layers of corruption, hesitation, and cowardice. Our target is clear, our methods will be unconventional, and our objective is simple—eradicate the threat before it grows. There are no rules here, only results.'

The room fell silent with shared understanding. These men and women had found a cause that resonated with their individual experiences, a mission that gave their fractured pasts a unifying direction. Lucifer saw the fire in their eyes, and he knew that they were ready.

Operation Black Lotus was officially underway, and a new chapter in the war against terrorism was about to be written—one that would not be dictated by the rules of engagement but by the determination of those who had nothing left to lose and everything to gain.

8

Erase the Past

With the team of thirteen fully assembled, Lucifer felt a sense of satisfaction and pride. This group was unlike any he had seen before—a perfect blend of expertise, tenacity, and, most importantly, a shared sense of purpose. Each member had been carefully selected for their unique skills and unyielding spirit, ready to challenge the established order.

The abandoned warehouse echoed with the muted sounds of anticipation as the members of the Ratpack gathered, ready to embark on a mission that would redefine their lives. Sunlight streamed through broken windows, casting long shadows across the makeshift operational hub. Dust motes danced in the air, a fitting metaphor for the lives they were about to leave behind. Each member understood that the path they were about to tread on was fraught with danger, yet the collective desire for justice burned brighter than the fear of what lay ahead.

Lucifer stood at the centre, his presence commanding and eyes sharp as he surveyed the assembled team. This was no ordinary mission; it was the culmination of months of planning and strategy, a carefully crafted response to the terror that had plagued their homeland for far too long. Each member had been meticulously selected, their skills honed through years of experience in the field.

'Welcome, everyone,' Lucifer began, his voice steady and authoritative. 'We are going to deliver a series of spectaculars. This team is more than a collection of individuals; we are a maverick force united by purpose. We are here to erase the past—not just our own but the very narrative of terror that has been imposed upon us.'

He gestured toward the first group, known as the Seers, specialists in intelligence gathering and target identification. They were the backbone of their operation, responsible for analysing data, monitoring communications, and tracking movements to uncover terrorist networks.

Shade, a tall man with sharp features and an intense gaze, stepped forward to represent the Seers. His analytical prowess had earned him a reputation for missing no detail. 'We will sift through mountains of data to paint a clearer picture of the enemy,' he assured the group. 'No piece of information will go unnoticed under my watch.'

Beside Shade stood Grim, whose psychological insights complemented Shade's analytical skills. 'Understanding the enemy's motivations is as critical as knowing their whereabouts,' Grim added, his voice steady. 'With the right psychological profiling, we can predict their movements, anticipate their actions, and, ultimately, dismantle their networks from within.'

Lucifer nodded approvingly. 'Together, you will form the eyes and ears of our operation. Your insights will guide our actions, and your intelligence will keep us one step ahead.'

Next, Lucifer turned to the Shadows, the team specializing in surveillance and planning. Operating in the background, they would gather intel and lay the groundwork for every mission.

Spectre stepped forward, his demeanour calm and collected. With extensive experience in surveillance techniques, he had earned the respect of his peers. 'I'll create detailed operational plans that account for every possible scenario,' Spectre assured the team. 'Our missions will be meticulously planned, and I won't leave anything to chance.'

Ghost, the infiltration expert, stood beside Irfan. 'I can identify vulnerabilities in enemy defenses,' he said confidently. 'I'll slip in and out undetected, gathering intel that others might overlook.'

Completing this section was Raven, the team's brilliant hacker. 'I'll access their digital systems, find hidden secrets, and disrupt their communications,' she promised, her fingers twitching as if already typing away at a keyboard. 'They won't know what hit them until it's too late.'

Lucifer smiled. He liked the slight arrogance; it was the hallmark of the consummate professional. 'Your ability to operate discreetly will be invaluable. You'll ensure our actions remain in the shadows until it's time to strike.'

Finally, Lucifer turned to the Reapers, the execution team responsible for carrying out their missions with speed and precision. This was the core of their operations—the muscle behind their plans.

Viper, the formidable leader, stepped forward. He was known for his tactical brilliance and decisive action. 'I'll coordinate our missions, ensuring we strike swiftly and efficiently,' he asserted, his voice carrying authority. 'We'll leave no trace behind, just the results of our work.'

Standing with Ajay were Dove and Nisha 'Raven' Qureshi, both fierce warriors in their own right. Dove, with her combat training and focus on precision, stated, 'I'll make sure that we handle any opposition with speed and effectiveness. There's no room for hesitation.'

Nisha, known for her relentless approach to close-quarters combat, added, 'And if things get messy, I'll be there to clean it up. We'll ensure our enemies never see us coming.'

Lastly, Inferno rounded out the Reapers, overseeing explosives and technical operations. 'I have my dets and specs ready, Boss. We got all sorts of noises' he said, enthusiasm gleaming in his eyes.

As the team prepared for the next phase, each member understood the importance of severing ties with their previous lives. They were leaving behind not just their jobs but the identities they had held for years. This was a rebirth into a world of shadows and uncertainty.

As the sun dipped below the horizon, casting an orange glow over the abandoned warehouse, the Ratpack gathered for the first time in their operational hub. The atmosphere was thick with anticipation, a sense of purpose hanging in the air as Lucifer prepared to present their objectives for the first phase of Operation Black Lotus.

'Phase One was about gathering our team and assessing our capabilities,' Lucifer began, his voice steady and commanding. 'Phase Two will focus on our first mission—targeting the leaders of the terrorist cells that have slipped through the cracks of bureaucratic oversight.'

As he detailed the plan, the room filled with a palpable excitement. Each member understood the risks but also the power of their combined skills. 'We are not just fighting a war against individuals; we're dismantling an entire infrastructure that feeds off terror and chaos,' Lucifer stated, his intensity infectious.

He paced slowly, ensuring he made eye contact with each member. 'Our targets are not just names on a list; they are the architects of suffering, the masterminds behind the attacks that have claimed innocent lives. We will show them that we are not merely a response to their actions—we are a reckoning.'

Lucifer laid out the details of the operation, speaking in clear, concise terms. 'Shade and Grim, you'll be responsible for gathering intelligence on our first target, a high-ranking leader of a terrorist cell operating out of the region. We need to know his habits, his network, and how best to approach this.'

Shade nodded, already scribbling notes in his notebook. 'We'll begin monitoring his communications and tracking movements. With Grim's insights, we can determine when he'll be most vulnerable.'

'Good,' Lucifer replied, moving on to the Shadows. 'Spectre, Ghost, and Raven, you will lay the groundwork. Surveillance is key. Ghost, you'll need to identify access points for infiltration, while Irfan develops the operational plan. Sofia, you'll provide technical support by accessing their communications and any data that might help us.'

Spectre leaned forward, a fire igniting in his eyes. 'We'll create a comprehensive plan that details every movement, every contingency. There won't be room for error.'

Raven smirked, confidence radiating from her. 'And I'll have their systems down before they even know we're there.'

Lucifer turned his attention to the Reapers. 'Viper, you'll lead the execution of the mission. I trust your instincts to adapt under pressure. Dove and Nisha, you'll be prepared for close encounters, while Inferno will oversee any demolitions necessary to ensure our escape routes remain clear.'

Viper smiled, a fierce determination shining through. 'We'll strike swiftly and leave no trace behind. They won't even know what hit them.'

'Remember,' Lucifer added, his tone growing serious, 'we are not just seeking revenge; we are dismantling the very infrastructure that supports this cycle of violence. Every action we take must serve that purpose.'

The Fallen Angels had gathered, and Operation Black Lotus was up and running.

9

The Training Begins

As the sun began to rise over the abandoned warehouse, the crew gathered for the first day of training under Lucifer's command. The atmosphere buzzed with anticipation and resolve, a palpable sense of purpose radiating from each member. They were ready to transform their individual skills into a cohesive fighting force capable of executing Operation Black Lotus with precision.

Week One: Foundations of Teamwork

Lucifer stood at the front, exuding confidence and authority. 'Today marks the beginning of our transformation from a group of lone wolves into a finely tuned unit. Each of you brings unique skills to the table, but success will depend on how well we integrate those abilities. We are not just individuals; we are a team.'

The training schedule was rigorous, designed to push their limits and forge trust among the members. The first session focused on team dynamics. Heracles took the lead, emphasizing the importance of communication and collaboration. He organized a series of exercises that required each member to rely on one another, simulating real-life scenarios where their lives might depend on their teammates' instincts.

'Pair up and navigate this obstacle course blindfolded,' Heracles instructed, demonstrating the first task. 'You'll have to rely on your partner's voice to guide you through. Trust is the foundation of our success.'

As they stumbled through the course, laughter and shouts filled the air, breaking the initial tension. The exercise forced them to communicate clearly, each member learning to articulate their thoughts and trust their partner's judgement. Jezebel paired with Ghost, her sharp wit contrasting with his quiet confidence. They quickly found their rhythm, guiding each other through the course and reinforcing their bond.

Week Two: Combat Training

With the foundations of teamwork laid, the focus shifted to combat training. Viper took the lead, ready to impart his extensive knowledge of tactical manoeuvres and close-quarters combat.

'Combat is not just about brute strength; it's about strategy, timing, and knowing your opponent,' he stated, demonstrating various hand-to-hand techniques. Each member paired off to practice, focusing on speed, precision, and control.

Dove excelled in this environment, her natural instincts and combat experience shining through. She quickly became a mentor to the others, especially to Nisha, who had a propensity for aggressive tactics but lacked the finesse Meera brought to the training.

'Control your aggression,' Dove advised during a sparring match. 'It's not just about overpowering your opponent; it's about knowing when to strike and when to retreat.'

Week Three: Tactical Exercises

The third week brought a shift to tactical exercises, focusing on planning and executing mission scenarios. Heracles divided the team into smaller groups, assigning them specific objectives they would need to accomplish under simulated conditions.

'Each team will develop a plan to infiltrate a target location, gather intelligence, and exit without being detected,' he instructed. 'You'll have to rely on the strengths of your teammates to succeed.'

As the teams discussed strategies, Raven emerged as a critical thinker, her background in hacking and surveillance lending itself well to crafting detailed plans. Working with Grim, they identified potential weak points in security and devised clever methods to bypass them.

'Let's create diversions using the local terrain and digital signals,' Raven suggested, her eyes alight with excitement. 'If we can confuse their surveillance, we'll have a clearer path.'

The teams executed their plans with varying degrees of success, allowing for constructive feedback. Lucifer observed from the sidelines, impressed by their creativity and adaptability. He called the teams together to discuss their experiences, encouraging them to share insights and learn from one another.

Week Four: Real-World Simulations

With the foundational skills developed, the team was ready for real-world simulations. The Ratpack would conduct a series of missions designed to mimic the challenges they would face in the field.

'Today, we're simulating a high-stakes operation,' Lucifer announced, his voice resonating with authority. 'You'll be tested on your ability to think on your feet, adapt to changing circumstances, and execute your plans under pressure.'

As the team moved into the field, they found themselves in a controlled environment set up to replicate a hostile zone. Obstacles were strategically placed, and actors posed as guards and civilians, creating an immersive experience that would test their resolve.

As they navigated the simulation, each member had the opportunity to shine in their respective roles. Spectre expertly observed and reported on enemy movements, while Ghost slipped through the shadows, gathering intelligence without being detected. Meanwhile, Nisha showcased her combat skills, effectively neutralizing threats with precision.

However, the simulation wasn't without its challenges. When a surprise element—an explosion—was introduced, chaos erupted. The team quickly fell into their training, instinctively working together to regroup and adapt their plan on the fly.

Week Five: Leadership and Decision-making

As the training approached its conclusion, the focus shifted to leadership and decision-making. Lucifer emphasized the importance of not just following orders but being proactive in difficult situations.

'Leadership is about making tough choices and being accountable for them,' he explained. 'In the field, there won't always be time for discussion. You must be able to make decisions based on the information available.'

He organized a series of scenarios where members had to step up and take charge. Each member took turns leading their team through various challenges, with others assessing their performance.

Heracles observed as Dove took the lead during one scenario, showcasing her ability to keep her cool under pressure. 'We need to split into two groups. One will create a diversion while the other retrieves the intel,' she instructed, her tone confident and clear.

As training progressed, the team members grew closer, sharing their experiences and motivations. Bonding sessions during downtime allowed them to connect beyond their skills, fostering a deeper sense of trust and loyalty.

On the last evening, they gathered around the daily campfire, beers and brews in hand, sharing stories of their pasts. Shade spoke about his experiences as a whistleblower, while Wraith opened up about the ethical dilemmas that had plagued her career.

The evening ended with a sense of unity, reinforcing their commitment to one another and their shared mission. They understood that they were not just fighting for justice; they were fighting for each other.

Lucifer looked at his crew and smiled in satisfaction. He never needed this training period to improve their skill sets; that was just an excuse. What he needed was the bonding of these men and women into a highly functional unit and the training had helped him achieve that. He had a talented group five weeks ago, but now he had a team.

10

The Hunt for Muzzamil Khan

The hunt for Muzzamil Khan began months before the warm waters of the Indian Ocean washed over the white sands of the Maldives, hiding the sinister preparations that were unfolding. For years, Muzzamil had remained an elusive ghost, slipping through intelligence nets and vanishing whenever the heat drew too close. His role as one of the masterminds behind the 26/11 Mumbai terror attacks made him a high-value target for numerous intelligence agencies, but it was his ability to blend into different locales—whether war-torn mountains or luxurious urban hideaways—that made him such a formidable fugitive.

Rumours of his presence had surfaced in various places: Pakistan's Federally Administered Tribal Areas, Dubai's upscale Jumeirah neighbourhoods, and even the slums of Karachi. Each time, the Ratpack had found themselves a step behind, but the trail had left clues—small and disconnected—that eventually painted a pattern. The latest lead, pieced together through electronic intercepts and covert human sources, suggested that Muzzamil had made his way to the Maldives. He had found refuge in the very place people came to escape, using the cover of luxury resorts and private villas to obscure his true identity.

The Maldives, a paradisiacal archipelago known for its stunning beaches, high-end resorts, and coral atolls, was not the kind of place one would expect to find a man like Muzzamil Khan. But for someone needing to remain under the radar, its secluded islands, accessible only by boat or seaplane, offered an ideal temporary sanctuary. The very isolation that attracted tourists also made it difficult for law enforcement or intelligence agencies to conduct operations without arousing suspicion.

After the 26/11 terror attacks, the Maldives had emerged as a strategic hideout for Lashkar-e-Taiba (LeT) operators seeking refuge from international scrutiny. Its vast network of remote islands and atolls provided a perfect sanctuary for militants to evade detection, using the region's bustling tourism industry as a convenient cover for covert movements. The nation's relatively lax security protocols and porous borders further enabled the operators to establish safe houses, regroup, and plan future operations without drawing attention. The scenic beauty of the Maldives hid a darker reality, as terrorists exploited the geography to maintain anonymity and build connections across the Indian Ocean, posing a persistent threat to regional security.

Lucifer knew this would be no ordinary hunt. Muzzamil Khan was a high-profile international terrorist. His death would not go unnoticed, and the ramifications would reverberate across intelligence communities globally. They had to be surgical in their approach—quick, decisive, and clean.

Lucifer and his top operators, Heracles and Jezebel, laid out the strategy with meticulous precision. Their sources had tracked Khan to a small town on one of the larger islands, where he was believed to be staying under the guise of a businessman. They had learned his routine: shopping, office, trips to the capital city of Male, movements to a villa that appeared to be privately rented, and interactions with a limited circle. Security around him was tight but not excessive, designed to blend in rather than stand out. This routine, however, also presented a vulnerability.

Surveillance confirmed that Muzzamil had a consistent pattern of visiting a kebab shop in the town square at midday, often picking up a meal before heading back to his rented villa. He always travelled in a black SUV, accompanied by a driver and a bodyguard. Lucifer decided to strike there, where the risk of collateral damage would be minimized. Besides, the location offered multiple egress routes to the jetty where a speedboat would take the team to the airport.

The plan was simple: execute a precision attack with likely zero collateral damage, ensuring that Muzzamil and his two associates were taken out quickly and without drawing unnecessary attention. The use of a motorcycle was deliberate; it would allow the shooters to move in and out swiftly, taking advantage of the traffic to blend away after the hit. They had chosen a two-man team for this operation, code-named 'Shade' and 'Ghost', because of their expertise in close-quarter combat situations.

The sun beat down harshly as midday approached, the scent of grilled meat wafting from the kebab shop mixing with the salt air. Tourists wandered about the town square, taking in the sights, snapping photos, and browsing shops. To them, it was just another beautiful day in paradise. But for the Lucifer's Ratpack, it was a perfect day for hunting.

Muzzamil's black SUV pulled up outside the kebab shop as expected, stopping in the shaded area adjacent to the outdoor seating. Muzzamil sat in the back seat, his burly form barely contained within the vehicle's cramped space. His driver, a young Pakistani with military experience, remained in the front, while the bodyguard, an Afghan veteran, kept a watchful eye on their surroundings.

From a nearby alley, Shade and Ghost observed the scene, awaiting the right moment. Ghost had a Tavor X95 with a custom-built suppressor in a plastic shopping bag, a thirty-round magazine and a bullet in the chamber. He flicked the safety and began to take long and slow breaths, his eyes widening as a natural reaction towards situation awareness. He had a spare magazine in his jacket because you never knew when things could go south. Shade carried a Sig Sauer handgun chambered for 9mm ammunition tucked away in his waistband. A woman in a burka walked past the SUV, holding her young child's hand, and the moderate midday traffic offered enough cover for their approach. The timing was perfect.

The motorcycle started from its parked position just beyond the square, the driver weaving smoothly through the light traffic, coming to a stop a few meters from the SUV. Ghost, the pillion rider, dismounted with an easy, practised motion and gently squeezed the trigger, sending out precise bursts of 5.56 ammunition. The muted crack of the bullets went through the windshield completely masking the sound of the actual gunfire.

The burst of gunfire was brief, accurate, and lethal. Muzzamil was the first to go down and slumped forward in the back seat as the bullets ploughed into his head and chest. The driver and bodyguard took double taps through their faces. Ghost walked calmly to the rear and pumped in two more bullets into Muzzamil Khan's head, and rummaged and collected the cell phones and wallets of all occupants of the SUV and a laptop that was on the rear seat before walking back to the waiting motorcycle with unhurried steps. The pair sped off, merging seamlessly into the traffic that encircled the town square.

The entire action lasted slightly over a minute, leaving behind a faint smell of cordite, three dead bodies, and the kebab seller's dumbfounded stare. It was a full two minutes before the pedestrians realized what had happened.

The immediate response was confusion and panic. Onlookers rushed to the SUV, some hoping to offer aid while others scrambled to find cover, fearing that another wave of violence might follow. It took a while for local law enforcement to arrive, secure the scene, and push back the growing crowd. By that time, a speedboat was well on its way to the airport, and the weapons, clothes, and ammo resting at the bottom of the Indian Ocean. The smoking burnt-out frame of the motorcycle would be found the next day.

News of the attack spread rapidly, reaching international media outlets within hours. 'High-ranking L-e-T operative Muzzamil Khan assassinated in the Maldives,' the headlines read. Speculation swirled around the identities of the assassins, with some reports suggesting rival factions within the terror organization, while others hinted at the possibility of a covert operation by an unknown special forces unit.

Lucifer and his team had achieved their first goal: a clean, efficient kill with zero collateral damage. But while the operation itself was a success, the consequences of Muzzamil's death rippled far beyond the atolls of the

Maldives. Intelligence agencies worldwide took note of the precision with which the hit had been carried out, seeing in it the hallmarks of a highly trained and well-organized group.

Col Ajay Bakshi observed the fallout with a sense of grim satisfaction. The death of Muzzamil Khan sent a clear message: those who orchestrated atrocities against innocents would not find peace, no matter how far they ran or how well they hid. It was a message that resonated in the corridors of power as well as in the back alleys where terror was bred.

Yet, for Lucifer, this was just one more step in a longer war. The Ratpack had carried out its first strike and the operation had just commenced. As the team regrouped to plan their next move, he knew they would need to stay one step ahead at all times. With each successful mission., confidence could mutate to over confidence and complacency, and that could be fatal. There had to be a balance between assurance and doubt—besides insecurity made for better performance.

In Islamabad, the deputy chief of the ISI walked down the corridor to his boss's chambers, in his hand a hastily put together file of the Muzzamil assassination. An analyst had numbered and labelled the file with a white chit on it with the script 'Khalaayi makhlooq'. This translated to 'unknown gunmen' and this was the file placed on the desk of the ISI chief. Over the next months, this file would get thicker, much thicker.

The unknown gunmen—a shadowy collective—feared for their precision and unpredictability. Whispers of their existence spread through intelligence circles—tales of their cold efficiency hinting at a dangerous new threat.

11

Operation Black Lotus: Strike One—The Aftermath

Within hours of the news hitting international media, an emergency meeting was called at South Block. Present in the room were Prime Minister Ashok Singh, NSA Aditi Mehra, IB chief Rajesh Khanna, and the head of R&AW Devendra Joshi. The home minister and the minister for external affairs were also present.

Prime Minister Singh and Home Minister Patnaik listened intently as Aditi briefed the room on the operation. 'The first strike was a success,' she said. 'Muzzamil Khan was taken out with zero collateral damage. The operators executed the mission precisely as planned.'

The PM's face remained expressionless, his fingers drumming softly on the table. 'And what's the response on the ground?' he asked, turning his gaze to the R&AW chief.

'Local authorities in Maldives are treating it as a gang-related execution for now,' the R&AW chief replied. 'There is no direct link back to us. Our contacts in the region have confirmed that the Maldivian police have not yet identified Muzzamil as the deceased, but that won't take long.'

The prime minister nodded. 'Good, keep an eye on developments, particularly on our neighbours and their patrons,' an obvious reference to Pakistan, Bangladesh, China, and the USA.

Aditi stepped forward. 'With your permission, sir, I suggest we prepare for the next phase of Operation Black Lotus. The devices we gathered during the strike have been examined and we have actionable intelligence. The Fallen Angels are ready to proceed.'

The prime minister's lips curled into a faint smile. 'The first strike may have gone unnoticed, but the rest will not. We must prepare for the possibility of diplomatic consequences in case that happens.'

At the R&AW headquarters, the response to Muzzamil's death was a mixture of satisfaction and trepidation. The agency's analysts had long tracked Muzzamil's movements, providing key intelligence that facilitated his elimination. But with satisfaction came concern—Operation Black Lotus was now in motion, and the stakes were incredibly high. The murmurs among senior officers reflected the gravity of the situation; many had only heard whispers of the operation's existence and even fewer knew the details. The common refrain was a question: How far would the government go to pursue this shadow war?

At the IB, the mood was more cautious. While they appreciated the success of the mission, some officers expressed unease about the potential blowback. The bureau had always been risk-averse when it came to international operations, particularly in the Indian Ocean region, where a misstep could severely damage India's diplomatic ties with nations like the Maldives, Mauritius, and Sri Lanka. Rajesh, in particular, raised concerns during the emergency meeting.

'Madame Aditi,' he began, 'I understand the need for decisive action, but we must be prepared for the fallout. The LeT and its affiliates will retaliate. And if we're linked to this, it will be a significant escalation.'

Aditi was firm in her response. 'We have taken every precaution to ensure our involvement remains secret. Lucifer and the Ratpack are trained to operate incognito for extended periods. Besides, I have deniability protocols in place—at its worst they can be written off as a bunch of rogue mercenaries operating for some unknown paymaster. There is no trail linking us to Muzzamil's death, and the operators know the risks. We have anticipated potential blowback from LeT, but we cannot afford inaction. These individuals are responsible for the deaths of thousands of our citizens and soldiers. Letting them continue to operate freely is not an option.'

The IB chief understood the play and was content that he had placed on record his misgivings. A career officer, he had learnt the CYA (Cover Your Ass) rule long ago. The stakes of Operation Black Lotus went far beyond a single kill. If uncovered, this covert war would set off a chain of political and diplomatic repercussions that could destabilize relations across South Asia, the Middle East, Europe, and the Americas. Despite this, there was an unspoken agreement in the room: the operation had to continue, no matter the risks.

Prime Minister Singh was not a man who made decisions lightly, and authorizing Operation Black Lotus was one of the most difficult choices of his political career. He had come to power with a mandate to strengthen

India's national security and had promised the families of 26/11 victims that justice would be served. Yet, delivering on that promise was not easy in a world where terrorist masterminds were shielded by borders, power play, and hegemony.

The prime minister's mind went back to the images of 26/11, the burning Taj Mahal Palace Hotel, the massacre at Chhatrapati Shivaji Terminus, and the faces of the families who had lost loved ones. He thought about the Parliament attack, the 1993 bombings, the downing of the Kanishka aircraft, the Akshardham attacks, and so many others. The memory hardened his resolve. He knew that this operation had to be more than a symbolic act; it had to be the start of a relentless campaign to dismantle terror networks that had eluded justice for far too long. It was to offer closure to a nation nursing decades-old wounds that were and are still festering.

After the emergency meeting, he sat down with NSA Aditi in his office, away from the formalities and procedural constraints of the larger gathering. 'This is your operation, Aditi. It's your vision that brought us this far. We've just taken a bold step. I need to know—do you believe we can see it through?'

Aditi met his gaze without hesitation. 'Yes, sir. We have the right team, the right intelligence, and the right strategy. Lucifer and the Fallen Angels will not stop until every one of these targets has been neutralized. This is just the beginning.'

Prime Minister Singh nodded. 'Then make sure it stays that way. We can't afford to lose control over this narrative. The media is already speculating. Keep our allies informed, but only to the extent necessary. We must ensure that the leaks do not come from our side.'

Within hours of Muzzamil Khan's death becoming public news, whispers began to emerge in media circles and among political insiders. Some in the intelligence community leaked details that suggested the killing was not random but part of a covert agenda driven by New Delhi. Theories proliferated across news channels and social media, hinting at a secret operation to avenge the 26/11 attacks and dismantle terror networks.

Speculation grew that Prime Minister Ashok Singh had personally sanctioned the operation and was being supported by a handful of trusted advisors, including NSA Aditi. The term 'Operation Black Lotus' had not yet surfaced in the media, but the murmurs of a shadowy programme targeting high-profile terrorists gained traction. Journalists with contacts in the intelligence services began dropping hints that this was just the beginning, suggesting that other LeT operators were likely to meet the same fate.

The opposition party in Parliament wasted no time in questioning the government's alleged involvement in extrajudicial actions. The leader of the opposition, Pawan Malhotra, took the opportunity to attack the prime minister during a televised debate, stating, 'If these reports are true, it would mean that our government is conducting assassinations on foreign soil. This is a dangerous precedent. We are a democracy, not a rogue state.'

The Prime Minister's Office maintained a careful silence, neither confirming nor denying the allegations. Instead, they let the media wander in a fog of uncertainty, which only fuelled more speculation. It was clear that the operation was not meant to be known, but the success of Phase One had emboldened whispers in the corridors of power. Some saw it as a bold move, while others worried that it would escalate tensions with Pakistan.

Among those who were aware of the covert operation, NSA Aditi's role was seen as pivotal. She was viewed as the architect of Operation Black Lotus and its driving force. She had convinced Prime Minister Singh to authorize the operation despite the inherent risks, and her influence was growing in the intelligence community. Some called her ruthless, others hailed her as a strategic genius who was taking the fight to the enemy on India's terms.

In private conversations, officials within the Ministry of External Affairs speculated about how long such an operation could remain covert. There was a growing realization that while initial successes might be kept under wraps, it was only a matter of time before the larger scope of the operation became apparent to foreign governments and the global intelligence community.

Meanwhile, Aditi was well aware of the speculation surrounding her. She had cultivated a reputation as a sharp and decisive strategist who did not shy away from making difficult decisions. But she also understood the dangers of being too visible in her role. She kept a tight lid on details, sharing information on a strict need-to-know basis even within her own team. The goal was to strike at the terrorists' hearts while keeping the operation invisible until the job was done.

Back in the shadows, Lucifer and his unit were already preparing for the next phase of Operation Black Lotus.

Muzzamil Khan's elimination had been a resounding success, but it was just the beginning. They knew the risks would increase with every move they made. The team operated under the knowledge that if they were ever captured or killed, their government would disavow them. In espionage parlance they were NOCs—non-official covers.

As they reviewed intelligence for the next strike, Lucifer brought the team together in a briefing room at their Sri Lankan safe house. 'We've made a statement,' he said, glancing at each team member. 'But now the real work begins. Our next target is another high-value individual. The longer we wait, the more they'll prepare. We have to act fast but without fault.'

Lucifer had already selected the next target: Sajid Mir, a high-ranking LeT member and the principal architect behind the 26/11 terror attacks. The sheer brutality and scale of the attack, which left 166 people dead, had put Mir high on Lucifer's priority list. This kill list was known only to Lucifer, who determined each target with calculated precision, and Sajid Mir's name had been on it for a long time. His role in coordinating the 26/11 operation had made him a symbol of terror and impunity—someone who had escaped justice for far too long.

Tracking Sajid Mir had always been a challenge for international intelligence agencies. Despite being one of the world's most wanted terrorists, his whereabouts remained elusive. Pakistan had long denied his presence within its borders, and official records conveniently omitted any trace of him. Even those who managed to catch a glimpse of his shadow encountered only dead ends and stonewalling. For Lucifer and the Ratpack, the hunt for

Mir represented more than just targeting an individual; it was a direct challenge to a network of protection that had shielded him for years.

The team understood that standard tactics would not be effective in locating and neutralizing Mir. With Jezebel's expertise in deep cover operations, they devised a plan that would pierce the layers of secrecy surrounding him. Their strategy went beyond conventional intelligence and targeted weak links in the networks that Mir depended on. They began infiltrating the low-level operators and informants connected to his security apparatus, unravelling the web of disinformation that had kept him hidden. For Lucifer, this mission was not just about retribution but also about sending a clear message: even the most protected terrorists could not escape the reach of the Fallen Angels.

As Lucifer briefed his team on the details, each member understood the stakes were higher than before. They had just set the tone for Operation Black Lotus, but now they had to sustain the momentum. Every operation had to be executed with the same precision and deniability, and each target taken down had to further the goal of dismantling the entire terror network.

Operation Black Lotus was now truly underway. With the death of Muzzamil Khan, the line between conventional military action and covert warfare had blurred, leaving the world to wonder just how far India would go to eliminate its enemies.

Inside the government, the tension was palpable. There were those who fully supported the operation, convinced that it was the only way to bring closure to the families of the victims and to send a strong message to Pakistan.

Others worried about the potential repercussions if the operation were uncovered. In the intelligence community, the murmurs of Operation Black Lotus grew louder, and so did the curiosity about who would be the next target.

As for Lucifer and the Ratpack, they embraced the silence that came with their work. They were warriors in the shadows, moving forward on a path few dared to tread, armed with the knowledge that they were the tip of a spear thrust into the heart of terror. With each strike, they sent a message: there would be no sanctuary for those who sought to harm their homeland.

The covert war had begun, and it would be fought in the shadows, with no medals or public accolades for the soldiers who carried it out. For Lucifer and his team, it was a mission with no end in sight—only a relentless pursuit of justice. And as they prepared for the next strike in Karachi, one thing was certain: Operation Black Lotus was just getting started.

12

The Hunt for Sajid Mir

It wasn't until late 2023 that the Ratpack received credible intelligence confirming Sajid's location: Central Jail at Dera Ghazi Khan in Pakistan. The information suggested that Mir had been placed there under an assumed identity, ostensibly to keep him hidden while satisfying international pressure to show action against terrorists.

To many, the idea that a man like Sajid Mir could be touched within the fortified walls of a high-security Pakistani prison seemed ludicrous. But to Lucifer and the Ratpack, it presented a unique opportunity—a challenge that could be met with cunning and precision. Killing Mir in an overt manner would trigger a diplomatic firestorm, so the approach had to be subtle, untraceable, and definitive. Lucifer's plan was to eliminate Mir through a method that would make his death appear as a natural occurrence, or at least an accident.

Lucifer understood that to take down Sajid Mir, conventional methods would not suffice. They needed a solution that could penetrate the prison's layers of security without raising alarms. After evaluating various options, they decided on a lethal but sophisticated method:

a binary toxin. This poison, harmless when delivered in two separate parts, would become deadly only when both parts came into contact inside Mir's body.

The binary toxin would be introduced in two stages. The first part would contaminate his skin cells through an indirect method, ensuring that it remained in his system for up to ninety days without causing harm. The second part would be administered via his water supply, ensuring that the poison would activate once he came into contact with it. The intricate planning and patience required for such an operation made it a challenge fitting for the team.

The first step was finding a way to introduce the initial part of the binary poison into Mir's food. They identified the cook who handled meals for the high-profile prisoners in Central Jail. A man in his late forties, he had been working at the jail for years and was known to be a meticulous but unremarkable employee. He wasn't the kind of person who drew attention, which made him a perfect conduit for the operation.

Leila Gill, one of the unit's most skilled operators, took on the role of infiltrating the cook's life. Posing as a relative of a prisoner who frequently visited the jail, she befriended him over several weeks. With her charm and a fabricated backstory, Leila slowly won the cook's trust, often bringing him small gifts and chatting with him during his breaks. Over time, their conversations grew more personal, and she subtly introduced the idea that she could help him make some extra money on the side.

With the relationship established, Leila moved to the next phase of the plan. One day, she invited the cook to meet her outside the prison, ostensibly to discuss the side work she had mentioned. During this meeting, she subtly introduced the first part of the toxin by gifting him a bottle of aftershave lotion. The primary toxin was designed to transfer onto his skin cells and hair through simple contact. The cook, unaware of what was happening, continued with his life as usual, but now he was unknowingly carrying a lethal substance.

The toxin in his skin cells and hair was not dangerous to him directly but would transfer to anything he touched—specifically, the food he prepared. Over the following days, the toxin found its way into Sajid Mir's meals, embedding itself into his system. Once there, it remained dormant, waiting for the second part of the poison to activate it.

The Ratpack now faced the challenge of introducing the second part of the toxin into Mir's environment without detection. Unlike the first phase, which had relied on human contact, this phase would require a more calculated approach. The team identified the water pipe that supplied the cell block where Mir was being held. The plan was to inject the second component of the poison directly into the water supply, ensuring that when Mir came into contact with the water—whether while washing his face, taking a bath, or even rinsing his hands—the poison would activate.

Heracles took charge of this stage. He arranged for a maintenance worker on the prison's payroll to be temporarily replaced by a Fallen Angel disguised as a technician. The infiltration was timed perfectly, aligning with a scheduled inspection of the prison's water system. Grim, posing as the technician, managed to access the pipe that led directly to Mir's cell. There, he injected a calculated dose of the secondary toxin into the water, ensuring it was sufficient to activate the first toxin but not potent enough to be detected by standard water quality tests.

That humid afternoon Sajid Mir returned to his cell after a routine morning with the rest of the inmates spent under the watchful eyes of the guards. The heat had been oppressive, and Mir headed to the small bathroom attached to his cell to freshen up. As he splashed water onto his face, the two toxins mixed within his skin cells, initiating a chemical reaction that unleashed a deadly neurotoxin into his bloodstream.

Mir's death was not dramatic; it came as quietly as the toxins that had infiltrated his body. After a few minutes, he felt a strange tingling sensation spreading across his limbs, followed by a sudden, overwhelming weakness. As he staggered towards his bed, his vision blurred, and he struggled to catch his breath. The toxin attacked his nervous system, causing paralysis before he could cry out for help. Within minutes, he was lying motionless on the floor of his cell, the life draining from his body.

The guards found him hours later during their evening rounds. An initial assessment suggested that he had suffered a sudden heart attack, a plausible explanation for a man of his age and lifestyle. The prison authorities, eager to avoid any controversy, did not conduct an in-depth investigation. The cause of death was recorded as 'natural causes', and the matter was swiftly closed.

The final step of the operation was to eliminate any loose ends. Lucifer had always taken pride in his follow-up and thoroughness, and this mission was no different. The cook, now a liability, was the last piece of the puzzle. Leila arranged for his abduction by luring him to an isolated apartment and the cook was never seen again. The prison officials noted his absence and informed the ISI who put two and two together. But without any evidence they could do nothing—evidently, this was another addition to the file on the unknown gunmen.

From the NSA's point of view the operation was a resounding success—a high-profile target had been eliminated with surgical precision, and there was no evidence to trace the act back to them. Lucifer's angels had once again proven that justice could be delivered, even in the most fortified of places.

News of Sajid Mir's death quickly spread across intelligence circles and the global media. Though officially it was reported as a natural death, speculation arose about the possibility of foul play. The timing, coupled with the mysterious circumstances of his demise, led many to believe that a clandestine operation had been carried out after the killing of Muzzamil Khan. Fingers were once again pointed at India, but the lack of evidence linking the country to the incident left these accusations hanging in the air.

For Lucifer and the team, the hunt for Sajid Mir was more than just the elimination of another target; it was a statement. It reinforced the message sent with the killing of Muzzamil Khan—that there was no safe haven for those who harboured terrorists. The unit could strike anywhere, even within the guarded walls of a Pakistani prison, and leave no trace behind.

As Sajid Mir's body was lowered into the earth, the legend of Lucifer and the Fallen Angels grew. Their shadowy existence continued to fuel speculation and fear, ensuring that their enemies could never rest easy. For those who had blood on their hands, the clock was already ticking.

13

Operation Black Lotus: Strike Two—The Aftermath

The death of Sajid Mir followed a familiar pattern that was hard to ignore. Like Muzzamil Khan, he had evaded justice for years, shielded by his powerful connections within Pakistan's intelligence and security apparatus. Both had managed to stay out of reach despite being on international watchlists, leading many to believe they were untouchable. Now, however, they had met their end in quick succession, leaving intelligence agencies scrambling to piece together the puzzle. Was there a coordinated effort underway to take out these figures? And if so, who was behind it?

Both operations had been carried out with precision and minimal collateral damage, suggesting a level of planning and execution that went beyond the capabilities of ordinary criminal elements or rival terror groups. In Mir's case, the apparent 'natural causes' of his death within a high-security jail added a layer of intrigue. Speculation was rife that his demise had been orchestrated through an undetectable means, such as poison, delivered in a manner that would leave no trace.

Rumours spread quickly across intelligence networks. The operations did not fit the typical methods of existing groups like Mossad, who were known for their targeted killings. This was different, shrouded in a level of secrecy and surgical accuracy that left almost no trace. Suspicions began to focus on India, given the nature of the targets—both men had been involved in attacks against Indian civilians and military personnel. The timing suggested that this was not a coincidence, and international agencies began piecing together what little evidence they could find.

At the CIA headquarters in Langley, Virginia, Director William Burns convened a sensitive compartmented information facility (SCIF) meeting with his senior analysts. The agency's concern was growing; two known terrorists had been killed in what appeared to be well-coordinated assassinations, yet no one had claimed responsibility. Their initial suspicions leaned towards an Israeli operation, but the profiles of the targets and the absence of any trace led them to reconsider. The most plausible theory pointed to India—a country with a strong motive for revenge after the Mumbai attacks and a history of covert intelligence operations.

'Start digging,' Burns instructed the analysts. 'Coordinate with our assets in the field and the South Asia desk. I want to know if this is coming out of New Delhi, and if so, who's behind it.'

Across the Atlantic in London, MI6 had similar concerns. As the UK's Secret Intelligence Service probed the details surrounding the deaths, they too noticed a peculiar signature—a pattern that suggested state sponsorship but without the usual fingerprints. Their operators began reaching out to contacts in India, trying to understand if there was any chatter on the ground that linked these operations to a rogue unit or an official task force.

In Pakistan, the ISI was facing the brunt of the embarrassment. The fact that Sajid Mir, a high-ranking LeT operative, had been eliminated on their soil was a direct affront to the agency. General Farooq Hussain, the ISI chief, was furious. He had no doubt that the Indians were behind this. He quickly authorized a counter-operation to gather intelligence on Indian networks, activating several sleeper cells and mobilizing political assets sympathetic to Pakistan. It was time to put pressure on India and expose whoever was carrying out these attacks.

As international attention focused on India, Prime Minister Ashok Singh called for a high-level meeting with NSA Aditi, Home Minister Dinesh Patnaik, and the chiefs of IB and R&AW. The atmosphere in the conference room at South Block was tense. The stakes had escalated after Sajid Mir's death, and there was growing concern that the operation's cover might soon be blown.

Aditi began the briefing. 'We anticipated a reaction after Muzzamil Khan's elimination, but Sajid Mir's killing has accelerated the chatter among international agencies. The CIA and MI6 are actively probing us, and the ISI is more certain than ever that we're behind this. There's also increased scrutiny from their assets in India. They're looking for any indication that we sanctioned these hits.'

Prime Minister Singh leaned forward, his face grave but resolute. 'We knew the risks when we green-lit Operation Black Lotus. Our objective remains clear: eliminate high-value targets who continue to orchestrate terror against our people. We need to stay ahead of this. What's the status of our cover?'

The R&AW chief, Devendra Joshi, spoke up. 'So far, we've maintained plausible deniability. However, given the sophistication and international profiles of the targets, it won't be long before agencies like the CIA start piecing together circumstantial evidence. We need to anticipate their moves.'

Home Minister Dinesh Patnaik added, 'The domestic front is also becoming trickier. While public sentiment leans towards applauding these actions—what they're calling the work of the 'Unknown Men'—we're seeing murmurs in political corridors suggesting that the government is sanctioning extrajudicial killings. Our opponents are using this to fuel allegations about violations of international law.'

Aditi's voice was calm but firm. 'It's vital we control the narrative. We need to leverage the ambiguity. Let the media and the people continue speculating about who is behind these killings. At the same time, I've instructed our disinformation units to plant counter-stories implicating rival terrorist factions. It will add layers of misdirection.'

The prime minister nodded. 'We need to stay the course. But be prepared for blowback. If any definitive link emerges, it could lead to diplomatic consequences. We've got to maintain our operational tempo while shielding our involvement. Now, let's discuss the next strike.'

Meanwhile, in the media and across social networks, the legend of the 'Unknown Men' was growing. Headlines speculated about a covert group targeting terrorists with impunity. Some called them vigilantes; others saw them as government-sponsored assassins. It was whispered that the prime minister himself had sanctioned a secret task force to carry out these missions, with National Security Advisor Aditi Mehra as the operation's mastermind.

Editorials praised the audacity of what was happening, pointing out that India's enemies were being hunted down no matter where they hid. In contrast, some critics argued that the approach was reckless, pointing to the risk of escalating tensions with Pakistan and the potential for backlash from international human rights organizations.

Amidst this cacophony, the Ratpack prepared for their next strike. The whispers in the media only fuelled their resolve; they were a shadowy force operating under the radar, ready to serve justice to those who had escaped it for far too long.

In the wake of the recent killings, the global intelligence community was abuzz with speculation. At the centre of this storm was Tom Harrington, the South Asia bureau head for the *Washington Chronicle*, en route to the Maldives. Tom was not just a journalist; he was a covert operative for the CIA, trained to unearth stories that could shift the balance of power in the region. With the agency's interest piqued, he was tasked with investigating the unfolding narrative surrounding the deaths of Muzzamil Khan and Sajid Mir.

Meanwhile, his colleague Rizwan Siddique was on the ground in Pakistan, combing through leads and interviewing sources connected to the LeT and the broader jihadist network. The objective was clear: find an India angle that could embarrass the Indian prime minister and question the country's role in what appeared to be a series of extrajudicial killings. In a world where information was currency, the revelations of their findings could reshape geopolitical alliances and influence public opinion in ways that went beyond mere reporting.

Arrival in Maldives

The Maldives was a picturesque paradise, but beneath its serene surface lay a darker underbelly that had become a refuge for terrorists in the aftermath of the 26/11 attacks. With the sun setting over the horizon, casting a golden hue on the turquoise waters, Tom stepped off the small seaplane and onto the dock of a luxury resort, the perfect cover for his investigation.

As he made his way to the reception, he could feel the tension bubbling beneath the surface. The murders of Muzzamil Khan and Sajid Mir were creating ripples across international intelligence circles, and the attention of both the media and the governments was focused on India.

'Mr Harrington,' a voice called, interrupting his thoughts. It was an informant he had met in the past, a local with connections to both the hospitality industry and the criminal underworld. 'We need to talk. This isn't just about two dead terrorists anymore.'

Tom nodded, knowing the implications of what was unfolding. 'Let's find somewhere private.'

They moved to a secluded bar on the property, tucked away from the public eye. As they settled into their seats, the informant leaned closer. 'I've heard whispers. The Indian government is behind these killings. They have a shadow team operating in the region, and they're not stopping anytime soon.'

'Shadow team?' Tom raised an eyebrow, intrigued. 'What do you mean?'

'Word is, they're responsible for Muzzamil Khan and Sajid Mir. They're executing targets with impunity, and India is giving them the green light,' the informant said, glancing around nervously as if expecting someone to overhear. 'I was told by my sources that the speedboat that sped away after the Muzzamil hit rendezvoused with an Indian coastguard cutter in international waters.'

Tom leaned back, contemplating the weight of this information. If true, this would make for a compelling story—one that could potentially turn public sentiment against the Indian government. But he needed solid proof. 'Can you connect me with anyone who knows more about this?' he asked, determined to follow this lead.

The informant hesitated, glancing around again. 'I can try. But you need to be careful. People are watching.'

Investigating in Pakistan

Meanwhile, in Pakistan, Rizwan Siddique was deep into his investigation. He had managed to secure interviews with several members of the LeT, each one more paranoid than the last. The mood among them was tense; the recent killings had sent shockwaves through their ranks.

As he navigated the bustling streets of Karachi, Rizwan's mind raced with possibilities. He had learned that the ISI was tightening its grip and activating assets to track down the perpetrators of these killings. They were desperate to uncover the truth, fearing that their own operators might be next on the chopping block.

In a dimly lit café in a less-frequented area of the city, Rizwan met with a contact who had insider knowledge of the LeT's operations. The man, who went by the name of Rahim, had connections to various factions within the group.

'I heard you're looking into the recent deaths,' Rahim said, his voice low. 'You need to know that there are rumours about an Indian hit squad. They've come out of nowhere, executing targets like it's nothing. People are calling them "Khalaayi Makhlooq".'

'Do you have proof?' Rizwan pressed. 'Anything that can tie them back to India?'

Rahim hesitated. 'I don't have hard evidence, but I know people. The whispers are everywhere. If you want to make this known, you'll have to dig deeper. The ISI is actively trying to silence anyone who talks about this.'

As Rizwan sipped his tea, he contemplated his next move. If he could find credible evidence of India's involvement, it would not only elevate his story but also shine a light on the broader implications of such actions.

Back in India

Back in India, the atmosphere was thick with uncertainty. PM Ashok Singh convened a meeting with his top officials in a secure location. NSA Aditi was present, along with the heads of IB and R&AW.

'First Muzzamil Khan, now Sajid Mir. We're gaining momentum, but we're also drawing attention,' Rajesh said, his expression serious. 'The CIA and ISI are closing in. We need to remain vigilant.'

'We can't back down now,' the home minister interjected. 'These were critical targets, and we've dealt significant blows to their operations. But we have to consider the fallout. If the media gets wind of this, it could be a public relations disaster.'

The intelligence chiefs exchanged glances, aware that their covert operations had brought them into the international spotlight. The pressure was mounting, and with Tom Harrington's investigation in motion, they had to prepare for the inevitable questions that would arise.

'Let's focus on controlling the narrative,' Ashok Singh said decisively. 'We can't let the media twist our actions. If they're framing us as a rogue state, we need to counter it effectively. Aditi, get ahead of this story.'

14

The Hunt for Sukhdool Singh

The assassination of Sukhdool Singh, also known as Sukha Duneke, would be a meticulously planned operation that bore all the hallmarks of Col Ajay Bakshi's signature style: precision, stealth, and deniability. Sukha was no ordinary target; he was a notorious gangster on India's most-wanted list, accused of orchestrating a string of criminal activities across Punjab. After fleeing to Canada in 2017 with the help of forged documents, Sukha had continued to extend his criminal empire from abroad, exploiting the safety and relative freedom offered by his new location. To the authorities in India, he was a symbol of how criminals could exploit international borders to evade justice. To Lucifer and the Fallen Angels, he was the next name on their list—a target whose death was long overdue.

Sukha Duneke's criminal career was intertwined with some of the most dangerous figures in the Punjab underworld. His reach extended from drug trafficking to extortion, with ties to local politicians, businessmen, and other gangsters who fed off the region's turbulent criminal landscape. While he may have found relative anonymity and safety in Canada, his activities had continued to resonate back in India, contributing to the ongoing violence that plagued Punjab. Among the most infamous of his alleged connections was the murder of popular Punjabi rapper Siddhu Moosewala, a crime that had sent shockwaves across India and drawn even more attention to the problem of cross-border criminal networks.

In the aftermath of Moosewala's death, the Punjab Police sought custody of another notorious gangster, Lawrence Bishnoi, who was believed to be directly involved in the singer's murder. Bishnoi, a powerful figure with a vast criminal network, presented an opportunity for Lucifer and his Ratpack. The team, led by Heracles, saw an opening to exploit Bishnoi's influence to their advantage. A discreet arrangement was made with Bishnoi's associates, ensuring that his custody would not be handed over to the Punjab Police. In exchange, Lucifer's Ratpack would receive critical intelligence on Sukha Duneke's movements and daily activities in Canada, making it easier to plan his elimination.

Heracles and his team spent weeks shadowing Sukha, mapping his daily routine to identify any potential vulnerabilities. The gangster lived in a quiet residential neighbourhood in Canada, blending in with the local community and avoiding the flashy displays of wealth often associated with criminals of his stature. He had maintained a low profile, rarely venturing far from his home except for the occasional meeting with known associates, which were conducted with utmost discretion. This made tracking him a challenge, as Sukha appeared to be acutely aware of his own precarious situation.

Despite his efforts to live inconspicuously, Sukha was not entirely free from his old habits. Surveillance revealed that he frequently met with members of the Canadian arm of Bishnoi's gang, where he discussed ongoing operations and coordinated the flow of illegal narcotics into India. These meetings were often held at nondescript locations—parking lots, rented warehouses, and even local diners. He always changed locations to avoid a predictable pattern. Yet, Sukha did not realize that Bishnoi's network, now cooperating with Lucifer's team, was also working to map out his every move.

The intelligence gathered by Bishnoi's associates was critical. It revealed that Sukha had a small but consistent routine—he visited a local gym every other day at dawn, followed by a stop at a nearby café for his morning coffee. He also had a penchant for late-night parties at the homes of other expatriates, where alcohol flowed freely, and discussions about past and future exploits were not uncommon. This information was essential for planning the strike. They needed to find a time when Sukha would be least protected, or at least caught off guard.

After extensive surveillance and analysis, the team concluded that the best time to strike would be in the early hours of the morning. Sukha's house, while appearing ordinary, was fortified with security features—motion sensors, cameras, and a reinforced front door. However, it was during his early morning gym visits that his guard would be low. The plan was straightforward: execute him in his own home shortly before he left for the gym, making it look like a hit carried out by rival gang members, thereby adding to the cover story of gang violence.

Heracles orchestrated the operation with the help of Lawrence Bishnoi's gang members, who had already been briefed on the specifics of the mission. The team included two 'handymen'—operators trained in close-quarter combat and quick insertion and egress, leaving little evidence behind. Working with Bishnoi's associates ensured that the team could not only access insider information but also acquire the resources needed to pull off the operation without drawing undue attention.

On the day of the operation, the handymen arrived at Sukha's residence just before dawn, wearing civilian clothes to blend in with the early morning quiet of the neighbourhood. Bishnoi's associates provided them with the access codes to disable the security system, codes that had been obtained through a well-placed bribe to a local security technician who had installed the system.

Heracles and Dove parked three blocks away and approached the house on foot, looking like a couple out for their morning walk. Heracles picked the lock on the back door, allowing them to slip inside without setting off any alarms. The layout of the house had already been acquired, and they navigated the rooms with ease, knowing exactly where Sukha's bedroom was located. They reached his room in seconds, finding the target asleep and completely unaware of the intruders in his home.

The execution itself was swift and merciless. Dove stepped forward, squeezed the trigger on her Colt Woodsman .22 calibre pistol and fired two suppressed shots into Sukha's head. The small calibre round had a low energy cartridge that enabled penetration of the skull but didn't have the power to exit it, therefore ricocheting within the skull, further scrambling the brain and ensuring death.

Heracles, who stood guard in case of any unforeseen interruptions, now stepped forward. They started a quick search of the rooms. They found a laptop and several USBs as well as Sukha's cell phone. Behind a sack of rice in the pantry, they found a duffel bag full of dollars. Fifteen minutes after arriving at the house, the team exited as discreetly as they had entered, leaving behind only a few shell casings and a sense of chaos for the authorities to unravel.

News of Sukha Duneke's death spread rapidly across Canada and India. The media was quick to label it as another instance of escalating gang violence, citing his criminal past and the rising tensions between rival factions in the Punjabi underworld. Pundits speculated that the hit had been ordered by one of Sukha's many enemies, while others pointed to his connections to the drug trade as the most likely motive. Few, however, considered the possibility that the assassination was part of a larger, more covert operation orchestrated from afar.

The elimination of Sukha Duneke marked yet another milestone for Lucifer's Ratpack in unleashing hell, but it also presented a new set of challenges. As more high-profile figures were targeted, the scrutiny around the operations increased. Each kill brought with it the risk of exposure, and Lucifer knew that a single mistake could unravel the entire mission. As he prepared to identify the next target, he understood that they would need to adapt and refine their tactics, employing even greater levels of deception and misdirection.

The next target would have to be chosen carefully, with an eye towards maximizing the psychological impact and minimizing the operational risks. Lucifer began to shift his focus towards individuals who played a less direct role in terror activities but nonetheless posed a significant threat through their financing and logistical support of anti-India elements. The goal was to send a clear message: not just the perpetrators of violence but those who facilitated it would be subject to his team's wrath.

15

Unravelling the Threads

In the heart of Washington, D.C., Tom Harrington, head of the South Asia Bureau for the *Washington Chronicle,* who had just returned from the Maldives, leaned back in his chair, fingers steepled under his chin. He had just come back from an emergency briefing with his contacts, and the news was unsettling. The pattern of recent killings—Muzzamil Khan in the Maldives, Sajid Mir in Pakistan, and now Sukhdool Singh in Toronto—indicated a coordinated effort, one that had caught the attention of several international intelligence agencies.

'Tom, we need to dig deeper,' said Rizwan Siddique, Tom's colleague, who was investigating the story in Pakistan. 'There's a connection here that we're not seeing yet. It feels orchestrated.'

'Orchestrated is right,' Tom replied, pulling up the latest reports on his computer. 'And the name that keeps coming up is Col Ajay Bakshi. He's said to be behind some of the most successful black ops India has conducted in recent years.'

'Lucifer,' Rizwan mused, recalling the name that whispered through intelligence circles like a ghost. 'He's become somewhat of a legend, hasn't he? Known for his ruthless tactics and an uncanny ability to get results. But I believe he retired a decade ago.'

'Yes, and that's what makes him so dangerous,' Tom said. 'The information we've gathered points towards a sophisticated network, possibly led by him or his operators.'

'Let's start digging into Bakshi's background. We need to know who we're dealing with,' Rizwan suggested, already typing furiously on his laptop.

The next few hours were a blur of phone calls and emails, as Tom and Rizwan worked tirelessly to uncover more about Col Ajay Bakshi. They contacted various sources, including former intelligence operators and journalists who had reported on Bakshi's exploits.

'Here's something,' Rizwan said, pulling up an old article. 'There's an informer in Pakistan who worked with him during a counterterrorism operation a few years back. He mentioned Bakshi's ability to connect the dots—he would see patterns where others saw chaos.'

'Patterns ... that's interesting,' Tom said, leaning closer to the screen. 'If Bakshi is behind these operations, it's likely he has a larger strategy at play. And I have a hunch that he is doing this on the behest of the Indian government.'

'Let's reach out to that informer,' Rizwan proposed. 'If he has insight into Bakshi's operations, it could provide us with the angle we need.'

They worked late into the night, their excitement mingling with the tension of their investigation. They secured a meeting with the informer, a nervous ex-operative who agreed to meet them at a discreet location in Lahore.

The Informer's Revelation

The following week, in a dimly lit café on the outskirts of Lahore, Tom and Rizwan met the informer, a wiry man with darting eyes named Bilal. Over cups of steaming chai, Bilal recounted his experiences with Bakshi.

'He's not just a soldier; he's a strategist,' Bilal explained, his voice low. 'Bakshi has a way of thinking three moves ahead. When I worked with him, I saw him operate outside the confines of protocol. He does what needs to be done, no matter the cost.'

'What do you mean by "no matter the cost"?' Rizwan asked, leaning in.

'There's a ruthlessness to him that is ... unsettling,' Bilal continued. 'He doesn't shy away from collateral damage if it serves his purpose. The killings we've seen? It fits his modus operandi. He believes in the end justifying the means.'

'And what about these recent hits? Muzzamil Khan and Sajid Mir?' Tom pressed.

Bilal took a deep breath, glancing around the café as if to ensure no one was listening. 'I can't say for certain, but there's a pattern to these operations. It suggests that Bakshi is eliminating existential threats for the Indian government. Elections are around the corner.'

Death of Sukhdool Singh, Repercussions in Canada

Meanwhile, the situation in Canada was growing more complex. Sukhdool Singh's body had been discovered and the Canadian government was on high alert. Denise Daniel, Canada's external affairs minister, was scheduled for a press conference to address the growing concerns about India's involvement in the murder of a Canadian resident.

As the media gathered, Denise took to the podium, her expression grave. 'We are deeply concerned about the recent extrajudicial killings of Canadian residents on our soil. The murders of Muzzamil Khan in Maldives, Sajid Mir in Pakistan, and now Sukhdool Singh in Canada indicate a dangerous pattern of violence that cannot be tolerated.'

Reporters pressed her for details, and Denise didn't hold back. 'We have credible intelligence suggesting that the Indian government may be behind these operations. These actions violate international law and threaten the sovereignty of our nation and other nations too.'

The backlash to the allegations of Indian involvement in the extrajudicial killings of Canadian resident was immediate and explosive. Social media platforms erupted with discussions, accusations, and debates. Hashtags like #JusticeForSukhdool, #CanadaUnderAttack, and #IndiaExposed trended worldwide as citizens and commentators voiced their opinions.

Speculations about a covert assassination campaign orchestrated by Indian intelligence began circulating rapidly. Users shared theories, memes, and accusations, each more sensational than the last. Twitter threads dissected every piece of available information, while Facebook groups filled with passionate debates about India's alleged involvement, fuelling both outrage and intrigue.

In Canada, the public outcry was palpable. Many citizens, shocked by the possibility of foreign governments conducting operations on their soil, demanded accountability. Activists and civil rights groups began calling for an independent investigation, echoing the sentiments of political leaders who questioned the integrity of the Canadian government's response to what they deemed an assault on national sovereignty.

The situation ignited a complex debate within Canadian society. Some viewed the allegations as a legitimate threat that required a robust response from the government, while others cautioned against jumping to conclusions without sufficient evidence.

Canadian Prime Minister James Arthurton held an emergency meeting with his cabinet to discuss the growing tensions. 'This is not just about the lives lost; it's about Canada's position in the global arena,' he emphasized, making it clear that the government had to act decisively.

As public sentiment grew, Canadian media outlets began featuring experts who weighed in on the implications of such an operation. Some experts likened the alleged actions to historical incidents of extraterritorial operations by various countries, warning that it could set a dangerous precedent and further complicate international relations.

Back in India, the narrative took a different turn. The ruling party's members and supporters took to social media to frame the situation in a light that painted the government as a proactive defender of national interests. Prime Minister Ashok Singh found himself at the centre of a propaganda campaign that portrayed him as a leader willing to take decisive action against terrorism, likening India's operations to the strategic, albeit controversial, measures employed by Mossad.

'India is not afraid to protect its citizens abroad,' read one widely circulated post from a prominent party member. Supporters argued that the government's alleged actions demonstrated strength in a world where terrorism needed to be countered aggressively.

'Why should we apologize for protecting our interests?' another comment read, reflecting a sense of national pride that resonated with many Indians. The media landscape in India echoed this sentiment, with certain outlets highlighting Singh's leadership as a vital bulwark against global terrorism.

Despite this surge in positive perception among the ruling party's supporters, opposition leaders were quick to voice their concerns. They criticized the government for potentially jeopardizing diplomatic relations with Canada as well as of Indians living in Canada, framing it as a reckless manoeuvre that could have far-reaching consequences.

'Are we willing to sacrifice our diplomatic ties for the sake of some shadowy operations?' questioned Pawan Malhotra, the leader of the opposition party. His statement garnered attention and support from various civil rights groups and think tanks who expressed concern over the lack of transparency regarding India's actions abroad.

'There is a thin line between counterterrorism and state-sponsored vigilantism, and it seems this government has crossed that line,' he added, calling for a thorough investigation into the allegations against India.

As tensions escalated, diplomatic relations between Canada and India faced unprecedented strain. Canada's Foreign Affairs Minister, Denise Daniel, issued a statement emphasizing the importance of maintaining international norms regarding sovereignty and the rule of law. 'Canada will not tolerate actions that undermine our safety and security. We are committed to investigating these allegations thoroughly,' she asserted.

The political landscape was further complicated by allegations of leaked documents from within the Indian government, suggesting that some officials were considering a covert retaliatory campaign against Canadian nationals involved in supporting Khalistani movements. This revelation sent shockwaves through diplomatic circles and heightened calls for caution among leaders from both nations.

International observers were keenly aware of the developments, and discussions about the implications of these events emerged in diplomatic circles worldwide. Analysts began to assess how this situation might affect India's standing on the global stage, particularly concerning its relations with Western nations in light of ongoing partnerships and alliances.

Experts weighed in on the importance of maintaining a dialogue rather than resorting to covert actions. 'The world is watching, and how India responds will define its future interactions with not just Canada but with other nations that are grappling with similar issues of domestic and international terrorism,' noted Dr Ashaa Patel, an international relations expert.

The unfolding situation marked a pivotal moment for India's leadership, as Prime Minister Ashok Singh found himself navigating a complex web of internal and external pressures. On one hand, he faced mounting support from hardliners advocating for aggressive counterterrorism measures. On the other, the call for diplomacy and a measured response from opposition leaders and international observers was growing louder.

This dual pressure led to tense meetings within Singh's administration, where discussions centred around how best to address the allegations while preserving India's international standing. Singh knew that a miscalculation could not only result in political fallout but could also have real consequences for citizens, diplomats, and businesses engaged in bilateral relations.

As Singh contemplated his next steps, he realized that how he addressed this crisis would define not only his legacy but also the trajectory of India's foreign policy in a world increasingly defined by complex interdependencies and escalating tensions. But he also knew that Operation Black Lotus was beneficial for India no matter the pressure his government faced at this point.

16

The Shadow of Lucifer

Tom Harrington and Rizwan Siddique sat in a cramped office adorned with maps, photographs, and dossiers back in India at the South Asia bureau office. The soft hum of a nearby air conditioning unit provided a backdrop to their intense discussion about Col Ajay Bakshi, the enigmatic figure whose fall from military grace had drawn them into a labyrinth of shadows and intrigue.

'Look at this,' Tom said, leaning over a stack of files on the cluttered desk. He held up a photograph of a stern-looking man in a military uniform, a young Ajay Bakshi, posing with fellow officers. 'This was before he became Lucifer. Look at the row of medals. This guy was a fricking hero.'

Rizwan nodded, rifling through another file filled with operational reports. 'And now? Now he's a ghost. He operates in the dark, far removed from the principles he once stood for. Something changed him.'

'Something indeed,' Tom replied, pulling out a detailed report of Bakshi's last mission in Kashmir. 'This mission is where everything started to unravel for him. It's crucial we understand the events that transpired. It's the key to deciphering how a decorated officer became a shadow operative.'

The report described the covert operation in Kashmir that had set off a chain of events leading to Bakshi's transformation. The objective had been to extract a high-value target suspected of masterminding several terrorist attacks. However, once on the ground, the intelligence proved faulty.

'His team encountered civilians,' Rizwan said, reading aloud from the report. 'Women and children, not the terrorists they were led to believe would be there. This was a classic case of bad intel that could cost lives—and it did.'

'Bakshi made a choice,' Tom interjected. 'He refused to engage. Instead, he withdrew his team, going against orders from higher command. That's a death knell for any officer's career.'

Rizwan's brow furrowed as he pieced the narrative together. 'And then they court-martialled him for insubordination. He was cleared, but the damage was done. He had shown that he was willing to defy orders to protect the innocent. That is not something the military bureaucracy tolerates.'

'Precisely. It's the nature of the beast,' Tom replied, his voice low and contemplative. 'The military trains its leaders to follow orders. But Bakshi, he learned the hard way that sometimes those orders lead to catastrophes.'

As the investigation continued, Tom and Rizwan dug deeper into Bakshi's post-military life. What they discovered was a man who had effectively vanished from public records. It was as if he had slipped through the cracks of the system he once served. Their research led them to a series of private security firms that employed ex-military personnel, many of whom had come into contact with Bakshi under his new persona.

'Look at this,' Rizwan exclaimed, pointing to a list of private contractors. 'He was advising several firms on counterterrorism operations. It's a common path for veterans, but he took it further. He became the ghost that no one could catch.'

'Just like the myth of Lucifer,' Tom said. 'The fallen angel, now a dark figure who operates outside the law.'

They reviewed the details of his transformation into Lucifer, where Bakshi's reputation morphed from a soldier to a vigilante in the shadows, leading a covert unit known as the 'unknown gunmen'. The NSA had sought him out for a black-ops mission, tapping into his unique combination of skills.

'Here's where it gets interesting,' Rizwan said, highlighting a document that outlined the team's formation. 'Bakshi didn't just recruit any operators. He sought out the misfits, those who had faced similar dilemmas or had been pushed out of the military for various reasons. It was as if he was building a family of misfit mavericks united by a common cause.'

Tom grinned, impressed. 'He created a brotherhood of the disillusioned. But at what cost? Each member carries their scars. They are a force to be reckoned with, but also a powder keg waiting to explode.'

As they delved into interviews with individuals who had worked with Bakshi before, it became evident that his motivations were rooted in a desire for justice. However, the methods employed by the Fallen Angels raised significant ethical questions.

'Some see him as a hero,' one former operative stated during an interview. 'He does what the government can't. He operates without constraints, hunting down terrorists that have slipped through the cracks. But his methods? They're brutal.'

'Brutal,' Tom echoed, flipping through more documents. 'And yet, in this world of moral ambiguity, perhaps that's what is needed. But it raises questions. Is he truly a force for good, or has he become the very thing he sought to destroy?'

Their investigation led them to a meeting with a retired intelligence officer, who had once crossed paths with Bakshi during his days in the military. The officer had watched Bakshi's rise and subsequent fall from grace with a mixture of admiration and concern.

'Bakshi was a good officer, the best,' the retired officer recalled, his voice thick with nostalgia. 'But he was haunted by what he saw, particularly after that mission in Kashmir. He believed he could do better, that he could save lives by taking matters into his own hands. And that's where he lost his way.'

'Lost his way?' Tom questioned. 'Or found a new path?'

'Both, perhaps,' the officer mused. 'He operates in a world that doesn't play by the rules. The lines between right and wrong are blurred. To him, justice is personal now. It's about avenging those who have suffered at the hands of terror.'

The deeper Tom and Rizwan dug, the more they discovered about the duality of Bakshi's character. Interviews with operators who worked on missions with Bakshi as a private military contractor revealed a man of contradictions: ruthless yet principled, calculating yet impulsive.

'Bakshi leads by example,' one operative remarked. 'He's fiercely loyal to his team and has a code, but when it comes to justice he believes in being judge, jury, and executioner.'

'Does he ever question that code?' Rizwan asked, intrigued.

'Not publicly,' the operative replied. 'But there are moments when you can see it in his eyes—doubt, weariness. He knows the darkness he's embracing, but he also believes it's necessary.'

As Tom and Rizwan continued their investigation, they found that Lucifer and his team operated outside the purview of conventional military oversight. Their missions were often untraceable, leading them to engage in questionable tactics that raised red flags in the intelligence community.

'Look at this,' Tom said, displaying a series of reports detailing the operations. 'Assassinations, sabotage, infiltration. They are effective, but the implications of their actions are far-reaching. What happens when they cross a line?'

'Bakshi's ambition might lead to consequences he hasn't anticipated,' Rizwan said. 'If the military can't control him, then who can? He's a wild card, and wild cards can be dangerous.'

Intrigued by the complexities of Col Ajay Bakshi's life, Tom and Rizwan felt a growing urgency to uncover the truth behind his actions. They knew that to understand the full extent of Bakshi's motivations, they needed insider information. Their investigation led them to a contact—a member of one of the teams Bakshi had formed after leaving the military. This contact, operating under the alias 'Viper', was allegedly involved in an operation known as Black Lotus, aimed at disrupting terrorist networks across India.

The meeting was set for a Tuesday afternoon in an inconspicuous café nestled in a quiet neighbourhood on the outskirts of Delhi. Tom and Rizwan arrived early, scanning the area for any signs of surveillance. The café was a modest establishment with a warm ambiance, its wooden furnishings and soft jazz music creating an inviting atmosphere that masked the tension underlying their purpose.

As they settled into a secluded corner booth, Tom glanced at his watch, his mind racing with questions. 'I hope Viper shows up,' he muttered, a hint of impatience creeping into his voice.

Rizwan nodded, his expression a mix of anticipation and concern. 'We need to tread carefully. This is not just about Bakshi anymore; we're dealing with a clandestine operation that could have serious implications.'

Just then, a figure entered the café, dressed casually in dark jeans and a hoodie, with a baseball cap pulled low over his eyes. Tom and Rizwan exchanged glances, instinctively recognizing him as their contact. The man scanned the room before approaching their table, his demeanour calm yet alert.

'Viper?' Tom asked, leaning in slightly.

'Yeah,' the man replied, slipping into the booth opposite them. He looked around cautiously before speaking again. 'We need to keep this quick. My time is limited, and I can't afford to draw attention.'

Rizwan leaned forward, eager to dive into the discussion. 'We want to understand Col Bakshi—why he's continuing to target terrorists for India after everything that's happened. What's his mindset?'

Viper hesitated for a moment, weighing his words. 'Bakshi is driven by a profound sense of justice.

After what happened in Kashmir, he believes he's the only one who can take decisive action. The system failed him, and he's turned to the shadows because that's where he feels he can make a real difference.'

Tom interjected, 'But isn't he playing a dangerous game? Working outside the law can lead to chaos. What if he misjudges a target? It could backfire spectacularly.'

Viper's expression hardened. 'You don't understand. The intelligence we operate on is often flawed. The bureaucracy is slow, and Bakshi knows that. He's seen what happens when you wait too long. Innocents die, and the perpetrators walk free.'

'Doesn't that make him a vigilante?' Rizwan pressed. 'Is he not risking lives, including his own, by going rogue?'

'Maybe,' Viper admitted, his voice lowering. 'But in his mind, he's preventing further atrocities. Every time he eliminates a terrorist, he feels like he's avenging the victims—including those he couldn't save during his military career.'

Tom considered this, his mind racing with implications. 'And what about Operation Black Lotus? What's your role in it?'

Viper's eyes flickered with a mix of pride and caution. 'We're targeting high-profile terrorists who have evaded justice. We're gathering intelligence, planning strikes. It's risky work, but it's necessary. We want to take down the networks that threaten our homeland. I know nothing about it except what Lucifer tells us.'

'Lucifer? Who is that?' asked Tom.

'Bakshi is Lucifer,' Viper replied. Tom and Rizwan looked at each other in amazement.

'What if it leads to unintended consequences?' Rizwan questioned. 'You're playing with fire.'

Viper shrugged. 'Sometimes, you have to embrace the darkness to find the light. Bakshi believes in that philosophy. He's become a symbol of a new kind of warfare, one that operates in the shadows but is still fighting for something real.'

As Viper spoke, Tom and Rizwan exchanged glances, realizing the depth of their investigation had just taken a darker turn. Bakshi was no longer just a rogue operative; he had become a complex figure wrestling with his demons and pursuing what he saw as justice.

Tom leaned back in his chair, his eyes narrowing as he studied Viper's expression. 'You're risking a lot by talking to us,' he said slowly. 'You're revealing details about Lucifer and his team—covert operations, private missions. Why tell us all this? What's in it for you?'

Viper's gaze remained steady, a faint smile touching the corners of his lips. 'I'm a mercenary,' he replied, his tone flat. 'I work to get paid. Information has a price, just like everything else in this line of work. If you're offering something that matches the value of what I'm giving you, I'm not above sharing a few secrets.'

Tom's eyes flickered with suspicion. 'So this is just about money? You're doing this for a quick payout?'

Viper shook his head, his expression becoming more serious. 'Col Bakshi—Lucifer—isn't like me. He didn't start out as a mercenary. He's a patriot. Everything he's done, all the rules he's broken, the blood on his hands—it's because he believes he's fighting for a higher cause. But somewhere along the way, he chose the path of a mercenary, not because he wanted to abandon his ideals but because he found the system too broken to work within it. He's still a patriot at heart, but his methods have changed. He operates in the shadows now, where morality gets blurred and loyalties are flexible.'

Tom leaned forward, his voice tinged with scepticism. 'So why is he still doing India's dirty work? If he fell out with the government, why come back and risk everything to eliminate terrorists for them?'

Viper's gaze hardened. 'Bakshi isn't doing this for the government, at least not directly. He's doing it for the people, for the countless victims of terrorism who never saw justice. He made his choice a long time ago—to become what was necessary to hunt down those who thought they could escape retribution. The Fallen Angels exist because there are some evils that conventional forces can't touch. Bakshi's the kind of man who doesn't need the system's permission to do what he thinks is right.'

Rizwan, who had been silent until now, chimed in, 'But if he's a patriot, wouldn't he have more impact working openly within the government? Or is this just a way to get back at those who betrayed him?'

Viper's jaw tightened, and his voice grew cold. 'Bakshi doesn't care about politics or personal vendettas. He doesn't care who signs the cheques or takes credit for the missions, as long as he gets to strike at the heart of those who harm innocents. The truth is, when the stakes are this high, you can't afford to play by the rules. He learned that the hard way.'

Tom met Viper's gaze, trying to gauge the truth behind his words. 'And what about you? If you're just a mercenary, why are you so loyal to him?'

A hint of a smirk formed on Viper's lips. 'Because I know what he's fighting for. I've seen what he's willing to sacrifice, what he's already lost. There aren't many men who can do what he does and still look at themselves in the mirror. For all his flaws, for all the darkness he's embraced, there's still something noble about his fight. That's why most of the pack follow him. Not because they're paid, but because they believe in the cause. I believe in his cause, but I also believe that my cause as a mercenary is bigger than his. He will do his job and in time people will forget him and his work. I want our work on Operation Black Lotus to be remembered; I want the money and the recognition.' Viper stood up and left the café.

Viper's words left Tom and Rizwan in silence. It wasn't the explanation they expected, nor the black-and-white morality they had been searching for. As they sat in the dimly lit café, they began to see that the story of Lucifer and his team was not just one of mercenaries and shadowy operations; it was a story of men who had chosen a path out of a desperate need to right the world's injustices, even if it meant crossing lines that most would fear to tread.

As the investigation continued, Tom and Rizwan began to piece together the fragmented puzzle of Col Ajay Bakshi. The man they uncovered was not simply a hero-turned-rogue; he was a reflection of a system that had failed him, pushing him into the shadows.

'Lucifer,' Tom mused as they prepared their final report. 'A fallen angel, yes, but also a victim of his circumstances. A soldier who sought justice in a world that often makes that impossible.'

Rizwan nodded thoughtfully. 'The complexity of justice is that it's often intertwined with vengeance. Bakshi may believe he's serving a greater good, but at what cost? The lines have blurred, and in the shadows, he walks a dangerous path.'

As Tom Harrington and Rizwan Siddique sifted through the mountain of information they had gathered on Col Ajay Bakshi, one question loomed larger than the rest: Why was a private military contractor, once scorned by the very system he had devoted his life to, now targeting terrorists on behalf of India?

Tom leaned back in his chair, rubbing his temples in frustration. 'It doesn't add up. Bakshi was court-martialled for defying orders to kill a supposed terrorist target. He had a genuine fallout with the Indian military establishment. So why would he risk everything to continue eliminating threats to India?'

Rizwan, who had been studying a map of Bakshi's known operations, looked up with a thoughtful expression. 'Maybe it's not just about India for him. Perhaps this is about redemption. A way to reconcile with his past mistakes.'

'Redemption?' Tom scoffed. 'By playing the role of a mercenary? That sounds like a dangerous game. The line between hero and villain is razor-thin, and Bakshi seems to be straddling it quite precariously.'

'But isn't that the nature of warfare in the shadows?' Rizwan replied, his tone steady. 'After his fall from grace, he was thrust into a world where the rules are often rewritten. He could see himself as a rogue agent, someone who can operate without the bureaucratic constraints that once stifled him.'

Tom considered this. 'So, you think he's created his own code of honour? A vigilante approach or there is something else, something more personal?'

'Exactly. Bakshi likely believes he's protecting innocent lives by eliminating terrorists who would do harm. He might see his actions as justifiable, even noble, despite the fact that he's operating outside the law.'

Tom frowned. 'But how does that justify working as a private contractor? He's no longer accountable to anyone but himself. What's stopping him from crossing ethical lines?'

Rizwan shook his head. 'Nothing, perhaps. But remember, for someone like him, the thrill of the hunt and the chance to exact revenge may be intoxicating. He could be channelling his anger and disillusionment into a mission that feels right, even if it defies conventional morality.'

Tom stood up, pacing the room. 'And what about the consequences? If he's targeting terrorists indiscriminately, he risks escalating tensions. What if he mistakenly hits an innocent target? It could lead to diplomatic disasters that would haunt India.'

'That's the inherent danger of operating in the shadows,' Rizwan acknowledged, his voice thoughtful as he sipped his coffee. 'But perhaps Bakshi has calculated that the threat of terrorism outweighs the potential fallout of his actions. He might think that if he can eliminate key figures, he's doing a service to his country—one that has failed to protect its own citizens effectively.'

Tom tapped his fingers on the table, his gaze fixed somewhere in the middle distance. 'So, what you're saying is, he's taken it upon himself to act as the judge, jury, and executioner? It sounds like he's operating on the belief that the system itself is the problem—that it's too slow, too corrupt, or just too ineffective to deliver the kind of justice he thinks is necessary.'

Rizwan nodded, leaning back in his chair. 'Think about it. A man like Bakshi, with all his military experience, has probably seen first-hand how bureaucratic red tape can cost lives. If you've witnessed that kind of failure repeatedly, it might start to look like the rules are the enemy. So, you bend them—or you break them.'

'Or you ignore them altogether,' Tom added. 'But even then, it's risky. There's no oversight. What happens when he goes too far? Who stops him if he crosses a line?'

'That's the catch,' Rizwan replied, his tone growing more sombre. 'Without oversight, there's no one to hold him accountable except himself. But maybe he's already accepted that he's a lost cause—damned, in a sense. Maybe, for him, it's not about redemption or revenge but about balancing the scales. If he can save a life here, prevent an attack there, then in his mind, it's worth it—even if it means becoming a monster in the process.'

Tom frowned, the thought weighing heavily. 'So, he's become something like a necessary evil. A man who knows he's already on the wrong side of morality but figures it's a small price to pay if it means stopping people who have no regard for human life.'

'Exactly,' Rizwan said, his eyes steady on Tom's. 'In his view, every terrorist he eliminates is one less threat to the people he's trying to protect. He's not in it for revenge against the military or the bureaucrats who let him down. He's doing this because, in his mind, it's the only way to prevent innocent lives from being lost.'

'But it's a lonely path,' Tom murmured, almost to himself. 'You can't walk that kind of road without losing parts of yourself along the way.'

'True,' Rizwan replied, a hint of sadness in his voice. 'But I don't think Bakshi sees it as losing himself. He sees it as a sacrifice. One that someone has to make, because if no one does, the cycle of violence just keeps going. It's not about legacy or glory. It's about making sure that someone, somewhere, doesn't have to bury a loved one because of another senseless attack.'

Tom sighed, the enormity of it all settling over him like a weight. 'He's embraced the darkness because he thinks it's the only way to fight it.'

'And that,' Rizwan said quietly, 'might just be the most dangerous calculation of all.'

17

The Hunt for Ejaz Ahmed Ahangar

The hunt for Ejaz Ahmed Ahangar, also known as Abu Osman al-Kashmiri, was set in motion with the usual precision. For Lucifer and his cohorts, the path to bringing him down had been fraught with obstacles. Ahangar was a master of evasion, adept at slipping through the cracks and hiding among the mountainous terrain of Afghanistan's Kunar province, where alliances shifted with the wind. He was the recruitment chief for Islamic State's Jammu and Kashmir (ISJK) branch. His connections ran deep through networks of al-Qaeda, ISIS, and various jihadist factions across Central and South Asia.

Sitting in the dimly lit briefing room, Lucifer laid out the details of the mission. His gaze swept over the faces of his team members, who were assembled around the large tactical table. On it lay a map of the Kunar province marked with possible locations and routes. The atmosphere was tense but focused.

'Abu Osman's gotten comfortable,' Lucifer began, his voice calm and measured. 'He thinks he's safe because the terrain is tough and the locals protect him. But he's also become predictable. Our latest intel places him on a specific supply route—one he's used three times in the past two weeks. We're setting up an ambush there.'

Aditi, one of the team's key strategists, leaned in, tapping a marked area on the map. 'We'll need to block the road after his convoy passes a chokepoint here. The IEDs will take out the lead vehicle and halt the convoy in the kill zone. But we need to move fast. The Afghan forces nearby could get curious if they hear the explosions.'

Lucifer nodded. 'Right. We'll have less than five minutes to neutralize the convoy and extract any intelligence before we fall back. Heracles,' he said, turning to one of his senior operators, 'coordinate with the warlord's men. Make sure they're positioned here and here.' He indicated two high-ground vantage points. 'We need their firepower to create enough chaos so that we can close in and take out Ahangar.'

Heracles responded, 'The warlord's been promised a hefty sum for his opium crop in return for his cooperation. He'll have his men ready to go. But if we miss the window…' His voice trailed off.

'There won't be a second chance,' Lucifer interjected firmly. 'This has to be clean and fast.'

The team departed for the operation site, their gear packed and weapons ready. As they travelled towards the mountainous region, Lucifer's thoughts drifted to the mission's significance. Ahangar was not just another target; he was a symbol of the resilience of terror networks that had spilled blood across the region. The man had orchestrated multiple recruitment drives and plots, all from behind a veil of supposed invisibility. For Lucifer, eliminating Ahangar wasn't just about retribution; it was about dismantling a node in a web of evil.

On the evening before the operation, Lucifer gathered the team for a final briefing at their staging area, situated a few kilometres from the kill zone. The setting sun cast long shadows across the rough terrain, and the air was thick with anticipation.

'Remember,' Lucifer said as he looked at each member, 'this is about sending a message. Ahangar thinks he can hide, that the world has forgotten him. We're here to remind him that there is no safe place for those who spill innocent blood.'

Heracles tightened the strap on his vest and exchanged a look with Jezebel. 'If we can get our hands on any communication devices or documents from the convoy, we could uncover more targets,' Heracles said. 'It might give us the edge we need to stay ahead.'

'Agreed,' Lucifer responded. 'But first, we end Ahangar.'

The ambush site was a narrow mountain pass, surrounded by steep cliffs and jagged rocks. An hour earlier, Jezebel and Viper had used a portable drill to make a foot-deep hole in the centre of the trail at the chokepoint and placed the IED. Once the remote was paired, they covered the IED and camouflaged it with gravel and dirt so that it was undetectable. The warlord's men had already taken their positions behind the boulders, their assault rifles trained on the approach path. The Ratpack positioned themselves at strategic points, ready to move in once the IED was detonated. Jezebel had slathered thick grease over the cone-shaped main charge and embedded about two kilograms of twelve-gauge buckshot as shrapnel to rip through anything short of level three armour.

As the sun dipped below the horizon, two SUVs appeared on the winding road. The vehicles moved cautiously, their headlights slicing through the encroaching darkness. Lucifer observed them through the scope of his rifle, waiting for the exact moment. His finger rested lightly on the trigger as he spoke the word into his walkie-talkie, 'Ignite.'

Jezebel, who was stationed near the IED trigger, pressed the detonator. The explosion was deafening as 200 grams of Semtex went off, throwing the lead SUV into the air, flames erupting from its shattered frame. The second vehicle came to a screeching halt, and the occupants scrambled to exit as gunfire erupted from all directions. The warlord's men unleashed a hail of bullets, while the Ratpack targeted the militants with surgical precision.

Lucifer spotted Ahangar crawling out of the wreckage, covered in dust and blood. His eyes met Lucifer's for a fleeting moment—he looked defiant. Lucifer raised his rifle, steadying his aim on Ahangar's chest. But before he could pull the trigger, Heracles beat him to it, firing a single shot that ended the militant's life. Lucifer lowered his weapon and moved towards the wreckage to confirm the kill.

As the team gathered whatever intelligence they could find—cell phones, encrypted hard drives, handwritten notes and maps—the warlord's men secured the perimeter. Lucifer looked down at Ahangar's lifeless body and felt a grim satisfaction. This was not just the death of a terrorist; it was the closing of a chapter in a long, bloody story that had claimed too many lives.

Later that night, as they made their way back to their safehouse, Jezebel broke the silence. 'Do you think it's over?'

she asked, her voice barely audible over the hum of the vehicle.

Lucifer's eyes remained fixed on the road ahead. 'It's never over,' he replied. 'But with every strike, we get to move ahead.'

News of the death of Ejaz Ahmed Ahangar rippled through the intelligence community as well as jihadist networks. As the news spread, so did a cloud of uncertainty and speculation about who was responsible. Some sources attributed the incident to rival jihadist factions vying for power in the region, while others believed it was the result of local tribal conflicts exacerbated by Ahangar's presence. The Afghan government, along with international intelligence agencies, scrambled to piece together the details of what had transpired in the rugged terrain of Kunar. Yet, despite their efforts, there was no trail leading back to Lucifer and his team. Their precision and anonymity remained their greatest weapons, and once again, the world was left guessing.

For Lucifer, this was not just another successful mission; it was part of a broader campaign to send a message. After striking in the Maldives, Pakistan, and Canada, his team had now claimed a target in Afghanistan, marking a geographic expansion of their covert operations. Each assassination added to the legend of the elusive group and its enigmatic leader, leaving intelligence agencies frustrated and militant networks rattled. The pattern was becoming unmistakable—high-value targets with links to terror activities in India were being methodically hunted down and eliminated. So far there was no proof that directly connected the Indian government or any official agency to the killings.

Inside Kabul's intelligence circles, rumours were flying. Some speculated that the hand of a foreign power was at play—possibly a collaboration between Indian intelligence and Western agencies fed up with Pakistan's shielding of terrorists. Others theorized that it was a rogue group of mercenaries driven by ideological motives or personal vendettas. The lack of evidence kept the real story shrouded in mystery. Even those in intelligence circles with knowledge of covert operations were baffled by the sophistication and seamless execution of these assassinations. In this case, the group's ability to operate without leaving a trace was rare, even in the shadowy world of clandestine warfare.

For militant groups like Lashkar-e-Taiba and Islamic State affiliates, Ahangar's death was more than just the loss of a key operative. It signalled that no place was safe, not even in Afghanistan's mountainous strongholds, which had long served as a sanctuary for extremist leaders. The elimination of Ahangar, coupled with recent hits on other high-profile targets, started to sow fear and paranoia within the ranks. Jihadist commanders were suddenly more suspicious of their inner circles, tightening their security and frequently altering their movements. Lucifer's message was clear: the walls that had once protected these figures were now closing in.

The ambiguity surrounding Lucifer's operations fuelled speculation, with journalists and analysts dissecting every detail of Ahangar's last days. Each of the group's strikes left behind the same set of unanswered questions and a growing legend around the team's leader, known only as Lucifer. The absence of any leaks in operations, combined with the precision of their methods, made it nearly impossible for anyone to pin down the group's true identity or motives.

While the Indian government steadfastly denied any association with the alleged Operation Black Lotus, the denials seemed to do little to douse the fire of speculation. Instead, the very ambiguity around the existence of such a covert group fuelled the narrative of a new, assertive India, unafraid to project power and protect its interests beyond its borders. For many, especially in India, the idea of the Fallen Angels taking on enemies of the state—those responsible for heinous acts of terrorism—resonated strongly. The aura of these unknown operators began to symbolize a form of justice that bypassed the sluggishness and red tape of international diplomacy.

18

The Bond of Friendship

The air was thick with tension as Col Ajay Bakshi, known in the underworld as Lucifer, navigated the labyrinthine alleyways of an obscure neighbourhood in New Delhi. He had chosen this desolate location for their meeting—away from prying eyes and listening ears, the perfect backdrop for a conversation that could shape the future of national security. The crumbling walls around him were remnants of an older time, much like the ideals he once held as a military officer.

The dim light of a solitary streetlamp flickered as he approached a nondescript building that looked abandoned. It was a former warehouse, its windows boarded up and its doors bolted shut, except for a single entrance that led to a back room where they could talk without fear of being overheard. It had been several weeks since their last operation, and the success of Operation Black Lotus had stirred the pot—both within the government and in the shadows they inhabited.

National Security Advisor Aditi Mehra was already inside, waiting for him. She was dressed casually, in a dark jacket and jeans, an outfit that belied her status as one of the country's most powerful intelligence figures.

But here, away from the sterile offices and the political games, she was simply Aditi—the woman who had once shared dreams of service and duty with Ajay back in their days at the Indian Military Academy (IMA).

As Ajay entered, he was struck by the stark contrast between the desolate surroundings and Aditi's resolute demeanour. She stood up, her expression a mix of relief and concern as she moved to embrace him. It was a familiar gesture, a reminder of the bond they had forged so many years ago.

'Ajay,' she said softly, pulling back to look into his eyes. 'You chose a hell of a place for a meeting.'

He chuckled, though it didn't reach his eyes. 'Better here than in some sterile government office with walls that can talk. Besides, it's fitting, isn't it? We've been operating in the shadows, and here we can speak freely.'

Aditi nodded, glancing around the dimly lit room. 'It's quiet, that's for sure. And I appreciate the discretion. The fallout from the deaths of Muzammil Khan, Sajid Mir, Sukhbool Singh, and Ejaz Ahangar's death is heating up, and the last thing we need is for someone to connect us to these operations.'

Ajay gestured for her to sit at a makeshift table. 'Let's get to it then. How much heat are we really facing?'

She took a deep breath and settled into her chair, the weight of her position evident. 'The government is feeling the pressure. Khan, Mir, Sukhbool, and Ahangar were major players, and their elimination has triggered alarm bells not just in Islamabad but also in Washington, Ottawa, and London. They're wondering how we got such precise intel. Quiet questions are being asked loudly.'

Ajay's brow furrowed. 'What are they saying? Are they suspicious of our operations?'

'They're not quite there yet, but there are whispers,' she replied, her tone serious. 'Some believe we've crossed a line. The politicians are getting uncomfortable. They want results but aren't willing to face the consequences of our methods. There's talk of restricting our covert operations.'

Ajay's expression was inscrutable, but there was a glint in his eye. 'They should wonder. Khan, Mir, Sukhbool, and Ahangar had evaded every intelligence service for a decade. Now they are dead, and we have more on our list to eliminate. You and I both know that they are threats to our nation. I don't give a damn what Washington, Islamabad, London, or Ottawa thinks. For that matter, I don't think what some of our leaders in India think.'

'True,' Aditi admitted, her voice dropping slightly. 'But it's also brought us under scrutiny. The government is facing questions—publicly, we are supposed to be cooperating with the global community, engaging in diplomatic efforts. Privately, we're eliminating these high-value targets with surgical precision. The line between counterterrorism and covert warfare is becoming blurred.'

Lucifer leaned forward, his voice measured but resolute. 'And that's why Black Lotus exists, Aditi. We aren't bound by diplomatic red tape or bureaucratic incompetence. We do what needs to be done, consequences be damned.'

The ease with which he spoke of eliminating enemies and defying diplomatic norms reflected his transformation from the idealistic officer she had known at the IMA. Back then, Ajay had been one of the academy's brightest cadets, with a passion for justice and a fiery resolve to protect his country at all costs. But after his fallout with the military establishment, his views had hardened. He saw the world in shades of grey now, not black and white.

'Sometimes I wonder if you've completely embraced the darkness, Ajay,' Aditi said, her tone a mixture of concern and admiration. 'I remember a time when you would have fought to do things the right way, to stay within the boundaries.'

'Boundaries are for people who have the luxury of time,' Ajay retorted, a faint smile tugging at the corner of his lips. 'You and I both know that in this line of work, the moral high ground is often a liability. We don't have that luxury, not when our enemies will do anything to destroy us.'

Aditi felt a pang of nostalgia as she listened to him. She thought back to a time when they had been cadets, running drills together, sharing stories of their families and their ambitions. Back then, Ajay's sense of justice had been unwavering, almost naïve. She, too, had been idealistic, determined to rise through the ranks and make a difference, a determination that had only intensified when she had seen the cost of indecision and bureaucracy first-hand.

Their paths had diverged after the IMA. While Aditi had climbed the ladder within the intelligence community, earning respect as a shrewd and unflinching officer, Ajay's career had taken a different turn. His court martial and subsequent departure from the Army had transformed him into something else. Yet, despite everything, she had never lost faith in him. It was why she had reached out to him when Operation Black Lotus was conceived, knowing he would not hesitate to do what needed to be done.

She looked at him now, his rugged face hardened by years of conflict and the scars of battles, both visible and unseen. 'You may not believe it, Ajay, but I still see the same man from our academy days. You've just ... adapted to the world's ugliness in ways most wouldn't dare.'

Ajay's smile faded, replaced by the cold, determined look that had earned him his nickname. 'I adapted because I had no choice. The system doesn't work, Aditi. We both know it. After Kashmir ... I realised that the fight had to be taken outside the confines of protocol. Operation Black Lotus is about results, not red tape.'

Aditi sighed, leaning back in her chair. 'And we are getting results, but we're also burning bridges. The deaths of Khan, Mir, Sukhbool, and Ahangar will draw more than just attention—it will provoke retaliation. There are already reports of increased recruitment efforts by Lashkar-e-Taiba, Khalistani extremists, and Lashkar-e-Jabbar and their affiliates. And then there's the political fallout. Some within the government are uncomfortable with how far we're willing to go.'

'They'll change their tune when another attack is thwarted, or another terrorist is taken off the board,' Ajay replied curtly. 'The team was never meant to be a conventional force. We're scalpels, not hammers.'

The mention of the team brought a subtle shift to Aditi's expression. 'Your team ... they're effective, no doubt. But how long can they keep this up? We're operating in hostile territories, with no official support if things go sideways. One mistake and it's not just the Angels who'll be compromised. It's the entire nation.'

Lucifer's jaw tightened. 'They know the risks. They've all lived with the consequences of doing things by the book and getting burned for it. That's why they're here.

Each of them has their reasons for fighting, for seeking justice on their own terms.'

Aditi nodded, understanding all too well what it meant to live with the consequences of making tough decisions. She had handpicked the personnel alongside Ajay, selecting individuals who had been discarded by the system despite their skills and dedication. Each had a reason for operating in the shadows, for walking the line between patriotism and mercenary work. In a way, these men and women were a reflection of Ajay himself—outcasts with a purpose.

'Still,' she said softly, 'there's a fine line between being a patriot and a zealot. You know that better than anyone.'

Ajay's eyes met hers, a glint of old affection mixed with the hardness of a man who had lost faith in institutions. 'Maybe there is no line, Aditi. Not anymore. Do you think politicians and diplomats have the luxury of staying clean? They don't. They're just better at pretending they do. I'd rather get my hands dirty and know exactly who I'm fighting for.'

Aditi felt the weight of his words, knowing that Ajay had always seen things in stark terms, even back in the academy. But there was a time when she had been able to temper his darker impulses, to remind him that there was still room for principles in a world driven by power. She wondered if he had lost that part of himself entirely or if it was just buried beneath layers of cynicism and experience.

She leaned forward, her gaze unwavering. 'I trust you, Ajay. I trust your judgement, and I trust your team. But I need to know—do you still trust me? This operation, the lives at stake ... it's not just about winning. It's about making sure we're not becoming what we're fighting against.'

Ajay's face softened, the harshness melting away for a brief moment. 'I've always trusted you, Aditi. You're the only one who saw me for who I was, even when I couldn't see it myself. But make no mistake—we're at war, and wars aren't won by playing fair.'

He took a step closer to her, his voice lowering. 'Operation Black Lotus will succeed because we're willing to do what others won't. If that means bending the rules or going off the grid, so be it. We'll cross every line if it keeps the country safe.'

Aditi searched his eyes, finding the same determination that had once inspired her during their academy days, and the same unyielding resolve that had driven him after Kashmir. Despite everything, she knew that underneath the hardened exterior, Ajay still carried the burden of protecting the innocent, even if his methods were more ruthless than they had ever been before.

'Just promise me,' she said finally, her voice barely a whisper, 'that you'll know when to stop. That there's still a line you won't cross, no matter how dark it gets.'

Lucifer's gaze remained steady. 'For you, Aditi, I'll try.'

It wasn't a promise, but it was the closest thing she would get from a man who had long since learned that the rules of war were written in blood, not ink. And as much as she hated to admit it, she needed Lucifer's darkness to shield the light she fought to protect.

19

The Exposé

In a dimly lit office at the *Washington Chronicle*, the air was thick with anticipation. Tom Harrington sat across from Rizwan Siddique. Together, they were about to unveil a story that could shake the foundations of international diplomacy and redefine the narrative surrounding extrajudicial killings. The topic at hand was both explosive and deeply complex: the recent killings of Muzzamil Khan in the Maldives, Sajid Mir in Pakistan, Sukhdool Singh in Toronto, and Ejaz Ahmed Ahangar in Afghanistan. What linked these seemingly disparate incidents was more than just a thread of violence; it was a clandestine operation orchestrated by a shadowy figure known only as Lucifer.

The investigation had begun months earlier, with Tom receiving an anonymous tip about a covert operation referred to as Black Lotus. Initial investigations revealed little, but when an informant known only as Viper came forward, the story took a dark turn. Viper was a member of a group dubbed by some in the media as the Unknown Gunmen or sometimes referred to as the Fallen Angels, a term that sent chills down the spines of those who understood the implications. This organization operated under the radar and was involved in activities ranging from intelligence gathering to direct action against perceived threats to national security. Viper's identity was a tightly held secret, but his information was invaluable, connecting the dots between the killings and the Indian government's covert operations.

As Tom and Rizwan prepared to publish their findings, the tension was palpable. The article painted a chilling picture: these were not mere casualties of conflict; they were targets in a calculated effort by the Indian government to silence and eliminate existential threats. The operators behind the killings were acting under the directive of Col Ajay Bakshi also known as 'Lucifer', the notorious leader of Operation Black Lotus. This clandestine mission aimed to eliminate perceived enemies of the state, with little regard for due process or international law. The narrative was compelling, and as the publication date approached, it felt as if a storm was brewing on the horizon.

On the morning of the release, the *Washington Chronicle*'s website crashed under the weight of unprecedented traffic. News outlets around the globe scrambled to cover the story, and within hours, the revelations began to ripple across the international stage. Social media exploded with reactions, as hashtags like #JusticeForTheVictims and #AccountabilityForIndia trended worldwide. The implications of the story were staggering: the governments of the US, Canada, Pakistan, and the Maldives found themselves on high alert, their leaders convening emergency meetings to address the unfolding crisis.

As the sun set over Washington, D.C., foreign ministries across the globe were inundated with calls demanding accountability. U.S. Secretary of State Jessica Mallory held an emergency press conference, her expression grave as she addressed the nation.

'We take these allegations very seriously,' she stated firmly, her voice steady despite the brewing chaos. 'If these extrajudicial killings are confirmed, we will pursue sanctions against those responsible, regardless of their rank or position. The United States cannot stand by while the principles of human rights are undermined.'

In Canada, Prime Minister James Arthurton convened an urgent meeting of his cabinet. 'We must act swiftly to protect our citizens and uphold our commitment to international law,' he declared.

Meanwhile, in Pakistan, the political climate was volatile. The ruling party faced accusations of complicity in allowing foreign covert assets to operate within its borders. Prime Minister Asad Malik called for an immediate investigation, asserting, 'We will not allow our sovereignty to be compromised. If these allegations are true, those responsible must be held accountable.' The Pakistani military, wary of any encroachment on its authority, echoed similar sentiments, calling for a review of security protocols to prevent foreign meddling.

In the Maldives, where Muzzamil Khan's killing had sparked outrage, President Amina Rahman addressed the nation in a live broadcast. 'We cannot allow our island nation to become a playground for international assassins,' she said passionately. 'We will work with our allies to ensure justice is served. Those who think they can act with impunity will be held to account.' Her words resonated deeply with the Maldivian populace, many of whom had admired Khan for his powerful speeches and teachings on Islam.

Ajay Bakshi sat in the dimly lit confines of his office, the weight of the world pressing down on him like an boulder. The *Washington Chronicle*'s exposé had erupted like a thunderclap, detailing the extrajudicial killings linked to his covert operations. Yet, despite the chaos swirling outside his walls, Bakshi's reaction was one of remarkable indifference. He leaned back in his chair, his expression impassive, as if the storm surrounding him was a distant tempest that would eventually pass.

To Ajay, the article was little more than a collection of half-truths and sensationalism. In his mind, he had acted in the service of his country, executing what he believed were necessary operations to eliminate threats to national security. The term 'extrajudicial killings' rang hollow to him; in the high-stakes world of intelligence and counterterrorism, moral absolutes often blurred. His job was to protect, and sometimes that meant making decisions that would be scrutinized by those who had never faced the complexities of his battlefield.

His indifference stemmed not just from a hardened sense of duty but from an unwavering belief in his mission. Ajay had spent years cultivating a reputation as a decisive leader, someone who operated in the shadows for the greater good. In his mind, the ends justified the means. The public outrage and international condemnation felt like distant echoes, far removed from the realities he navigated daily. He had seen first-hand the devastation wrought by terrorism and understood that, in some cases, pre-emptive measures were necessary to safeguard the innocent.

As reports flooded in about protests across India and calls for accountability from foreign governments,

Ajay remained unfazed. He was a soldier, trained to endure pressure and navigate turbulent waters. While others crumbled under scrutiny, he steeled himself. He understood the implications of the exposé, but to him, it was merely a reflection of a society unaccustomed to the grey areas of warfare. The civilians who protested and the politicians who clamoured for his head were playing their roles in a theatre of politics, oblivious to the grim realities that dictated his actions.

In the face of public outcry, Ajay maintained his composure. He dismissed the idea of a public address as unnecessary; what could he possibly say to those who could never grasp the complexities of his decisions? Instead, he chose to retreat into the operational mindset that had served him well over the years. He began to strategize, thinking of how to weather this storm and continue his work.

The military culture had instilled in him a sense of loyalty and resilience, and Ajay found solace in that. He knew that political tides could shift, that the media frenzy could wane, and that he would still be left with his mission—one that he believed in wholeheartedly. His focus shifted to securing the resources and support he needed to carry on with his operations, convinced that the righteousness of his cause would ultimately prevail.

Ajay's indifference crystallized into a steely resolve. He remained engaged with his team, unyielding in his determination to continue the fight against those he deemed enemies of the state. The exposé, while troubling, became just another challenge to overcome, and in Ajay's world, challenges were meant to be faced head-on, not wallowed in. The colonel was determined to emerge from the shadows, unscathed and resolute, even as the world around him spun into turmoil.

In the halls of power, the Prime Minister's Office was flooded with calls from anxious ministers and party leaders, all demanding an immediate response to the *Washington Post*'s explosive exposé. The revelations had not only shaken the foundations of national security but also ignited a firestorm of criticism that threatened the government's stability. Panic set in as the political landscape shifted beneath their feet, with many officials fearing a loss of credibility on both domestic and international fronts.

The government launched a counteroffensive, quickly labelling the report as 'sensationalist' and 'a smear campaign orchestrated by foreign powers'. In their eyes, it was an affront to India's sovereignty, one that sought to undermine the hard-earned reputation of the nation. An emergency press conference was convened, and the Minister of External Affairs, Dharmendra Shinde, took the podium, flanked by senior officials. The atmosphere was tense, with cameras flashing and reporters clamouring for answers.

'We categorically deny these allegations,' Shinde asserted, his voice tinged with indignation as he addressed the press. He pointedly emphasized, 'India does not engage in extrajudicial killings, and we will not entertain baseless claims that seek to tarnish our reputation.' He spoke with the conviction of a man tasked with defending his country, but even as he delivered his statements, the scepticism in the room was palpable. The denials rang hollow in the ears of many, particularly among the opposition parties, who seized upon the moment to challenge the government's narrative.

The Congress Party, led by the astute opposition leader Pawan Malhotra, capitalized on the outrage. Malhotra's voice boomed in the assembly as he demanded an independent parliamentary inquiry into the alleged operations. 'If our government has sanctioned such actions, it is a betrayal of our democratic principles,' he declared, his rhetoric powerful and persuasive. 'We must hold those responsible accountable, regardless of their rank.' The chorus of calls for transparency grew, and Malhotra's passionate appeal resonated with many, spurring further calls for accountability from both sides of the aisle.

Protests erupted across the country in the days that followed. Activists took to the streets, brandishing placards and chanting slogans demanding an end to the culture of impunity that had allowed such operations to flourish. The air was thick with discontent, and the dissenters rallied around the idea that the government could no longer hide behind a facade of national security. They called for an inquiry, not only into the actions of Col Ajay Bakshi but also into the broader implications of state-sanctioned violence. Their anger was directed at what they perceived as a betrayal of the nation's democratic values, and their numbers grew daily.

Yet, amidst the rising tide of protests and calls for justice, there existed a significant faction that admired the work of Col Bakshi. In military circles and among some segments of the public, Ajay was seen as a protector of the nation, a soldier who had done what was necessary to safeguard Indian interests against a backdrop of international threats. His supporters argued that the nature of modern warfare demanded unconventional tactics, especially in a world fraught with terrorist threats. They viewed Bakshi's operations as strategic moves in a larger game, one where the stakes were nothing less than national survival.

Instead of the article creating an outcry against what some labelled as 'state-sponsored assassinations', it inadvertently showcased India's unseen resolve to deal with existential threats. There was a growing perception that India, like Israel, had reached a point where traditional counterterrorism measures were no longer sufficient, and covert operations targeting high-value threats were necessary. For years, Indian intelligence agencies had been accused of lacking the decisiveness shown by countries such as Israel in dealing with hostile elements. Now, with the stories of the Fallen Angels emerging, many viewed this as India's way of catching up—delivering justice in a more covert but potent manner.

The detailed exposé, intended to pressure the Indian government into reining in the alleged rogue assets, ironically helped build an almost legendary image of Lucifer. Instead of facing backlash, the group found itself at the centre of a narrative where many saw their actions as a bold statement against terrorism. The fact that these missions were carried out with minimal collateral damage further cemented their reputation for precision and skill. The media's portrayal of the Fallen Angels as an elite group undertaking difficult, high-risk operations enhanced their allure, almost glorifying their actions despite the morally ambiguous nature of the missions.

Internationally, intelligence circles and counterterrorism experts debated whether the Fallen Angels were a myth designed to instil fear among terrorists or if they represented a real, unprecedented level of covert capability from India. While the world's governments scrambled to piece together the puzzle of Lucifer's operations, the Indian government's silence only added to the mystique. It was as though the very denials of involvement were part of a calculated strategy, allowing the legend to grow unchecked.

Ultimately, while the *Washington Chronicle* article may have aimed to paint Lucifer and his team as overzealous vigilantes, it instead contributed to a growing legend—a story of India's newfound willingness to confront its enemies wherever they lurked, regardless of borders, with an uncompromising approach to defending its national security.

The aftermath of the *Washington Chronicle* report saw a polarized reaction across Indian media, with television channels taking divergent stands on the revelations concerning Lucifer and the Fallen Angels. On one end of the spectrum, Reporter TV, led by the fiery Arnob Swami, took an aggressively nationalist stance. Swami, known for his combative style and fervent support of India's security forces, dismissed the *Washington Chronicle*'s report as nothing more than an orchestrated attempt to undermine India's fight against terrorism. With characteristic zeal, he extolled Lucifer's unit as unsung heroes who were doing the work that needed to be done to protect the nation. 'Who cares what some foreign journalists think?' he declared in a prime-time broadcast. 'India has had enough of terror attacks, and if Lucifer and his team are taking out those who threaten our peace, then they deserve our support, not condemnation.'

Reporter TV's narrative struck a chord with many viewers who felt a sense of pride in the thought of India taking an offensive stance against its enemies. The portrayal of Lucifer as a vigilante-like figure, who operated in the shadows, to eliminate terrorists captured the public's imagination, with some even comparing the covert operative to an Indian James Bond. The channel's coverage consistently framed the actions of Lucifer and his team as a necessary evil in a world where conventional diplomacy had failed to bring justice to victims of terrorism.

On the other hand, journalists like Ramandeep Desai of Bharat TV offered a more cautious take on the issue, raising concerns about the diplomatic fallout and the potential repercussions for India. Desai questioned whether the glorification of extrajudicial killings could come back to haunt the nation. 'Let's not forget,' he said during a panel discussion, 'that by engaging in such operations, even if indirectly, India is opening itself up to retaliatory strikes. What happens when terrorist groups use this as an excuse to escalate violence against innocent civilians? We have to ask ourselves if this is the right path.'

Ramandeep also highlighted the strain in India's relationships with Pakistan, Canada, the Maldives, and Afghanistan following the killings. He argued that the fallout from these actions could jeopardize not only diplomatic ties but also provoke a cycle of revenge, leading to more lethal terror strikes on Indian soil. His stance attracted support from those who viewed the revelations as a dangerous overreach, potentially endangering more lives than it saved.

The contrasting views on Indian television encapsulated the larger national debate: Was Lucifer a patriot or a rogue?

Within the government, tensions mounted as ministers grappled with how to balance the growing dissent with the need to maintain national security. While Shinde's assurances were intended to quash the uprising, the backlash showed no signs of abating. A faction of the ruling party even quietly applauded Ajay's resolve, believing that the situation could be spun in their favour. Some argued that a show of strength, rather than capitulation to foreign media narratives, would fortify the government's position both at home and abroad.

As the days turned into a cacophony of accusations and defences, the prime minister convened a crisis meeting with key advisors. The conversation was fraught with urgency as they weighed the implications of the exposé and the subsequent fallout. Should they stick to their narrative of denial, or was it time to pivot and acknowledge the reality of the situation? The room was thick with tension, and each leader had a stake in the outcome, knowing that their decisions could redefine the future of the administration. The balancing act between addressing the public's outrage and defending national pride loomed large, setting the stage for a turbulent political showdown.

In the dimly lit conference room of the Prime Minister's Office, the atmosphere was heavy with tension. The prime minister leaned back in his chair, fingers steepled beneath his chin, lost in thought as he processed the whirlwind of events triggered by the *Washington Chronicle*'s exposé. The revelations surrounding Operation Black Lotus had ignited a firestorm of criticism, and the implications were daunting. His instinct was to protect the country's interests, but the public outcry and mounting pressure from opposition parties compelled him to reconsider the operation's continuation.

'Is it time to abort Operation Black Lotus?' he mused silently, the gravity of the question weighing heavily on his conscience. The operation, designed to target high-value threats across borders, had been a hallmark of his administration's counterterrorism strategy. However, the backlash had turned the mission into a political liability, placing the government on the defensive. The prime minister understood that a decision to halt the operation could send shockwaves through the military and intelligence communities, potentially undermining their morale and effectiveness. Yet, the growing chorus for accountability demanded a response that could no longer be ignored.

Realizing the importance of gathering insights from key figures, the prime minister signalled for his aides to arrange an urgent meeting with Home Minister Dinesh Patnaik and National Security Advisor Aditi Mehra. Both were integral to the operational framework that had given rise to Operation Black Lotus, and their perspectives would be crucial in determining the path forward. As he waited for them to arrive, he considered the stakes involved. The success of his government hinged on national security, but the principles of democracy and transparency were equally paramount.

When Dinesh and Aditi entered the room, the tension was palpable. They greeted the prime minister with a sense of urgency, their expressions revealing a shared concern for the fallout from the exposé. After exchanging pleasantries, the prime minister wasted no time in addressing the elephant in the room. 'We need to talk about Operation Black Lotus. The recent reports have put us in a precarious position, and I'm questioning whether we should continue down this path.'

Dinesh, a seasoned politician with years of experience navigating the complexities of governance, took a moment to collect his thoughts. 'Sir, I understand your concerns,' he replied, his tone measured. 'But we must also consider the implications of abandoning the operation. Black Lotus has been effective in neutralizing threats, and stopping it now could embolden our adversaries.'

Aditi nodded in agreement. 'From an intelligence perspective, halting Black Lotus would send a message of weakness. We cannot afford to appear vulnerable, especially when our enemies are constantly seeking to exploit any sign of disarray. However, we need to reassess our strategies and communication regarding the operation. We should not lose sight of public sentiment; transparency is key.'

The prime minister listened intently, weighing their insights. He appreciated the necessity of demonstrating strength and resolve, yet he couldn't shake the feeling that the operation had morphed into something more than a counterterrorism initiative; it had become a political tool, one that was now being scrutinized under the unforgiving spotlight of public opinion. 'I understand the need for strength,' he said finally. 'But we also need to be accountable to our citizens. We must navigate this carefully.'

As the discussion deepened, the prime minister and his advisors brainstormed potential strategies to manage the fallout while considering the future of Operation Black Lotus. They debated how to address the allegations head-on without undermining national security, ultimately concluding that a recalibration of the operation might be necessary. The prime minister knew that any decision he made would resonate throughout the political landscape and beyond, impacting both the administration's credibility and the lives of those involved in the operation.

After hours of deliberation, the prime minister concluded that it would be prudent to adopt a dual approach—enhancing transparency while ensuring that operational capabilities remained intact. The path ahead was fraught with challenges, but the PM understood that the time had come to make a decision that would shape the legacy of his administration. As they left the conference room, a sense of resolve settled over him. He was determined to navigate the complexities of governance with both courage and integrity.

As days turned into weeks, the ramifications of the exposé rippled through diplomatic channels. The United Nations called for an urgent meeting to address the allegations against India. A coalition of nations, led by Canada and Pakistan, pushed for a formal investigation into the killings, framing the issue as one of global importance. The discourse surrounding extrajudicial killings was thrust into the spotlight, forcing governments to reevaluate their own policies on human rights and state-sponsored violence.

20

The Hunt for Ripudaman Singh Malik

Ripudaman Singh Malik's name was synonymous with the 1985 Air India bombing, the deadliest act of terrorism in Canadian history. The bombing of Flight 182 over the Atlantic had claimed 329 lives, most of them Canadians of Indian descent. The bombing's mastermind and those who had financed and supported the attack were long suspected to be among Sikh separatists in Canada advocating for an independent Khalistan. Though Malik had been acquitted of all charges in 2005, the shadow of suspicion never fully left him. Many in the intelligence community, including those in India, continued to regard him as a dangerous person with connections to radical networks.

With his wealth and influence, Malik had fortified his life in Surrey, living behind layers of security that were almost impenetrable. Cameras, guards, and cutting-edge technology protected him from any harm. Yet, despite his fortress-like existence, he had vulnerabilities, as all men do. It was Col Ajay Bakshi, the infamous Lucifer, and his team of battle-hardened veterans who saw Malik as an unfinished chapter in the ongoing story of retribution for the 1985 bombing. The decision to eliminate him was not made lightly, and it came as part of a renewed focus on taking out figures associated with terror networks, as documented by the *Washington Chronicle*'s earlier expose of Operation Black Lotus. For Bakshi, it was more than just another mission—it was about finally closing a dark chapter that had haunted the families of Flight 182's victims for nearly four decades.

Malik's Life in a Fortress

Surrey's South Asian community was no stranger to security concerns. Even before the bombings, extremist elements had existed on the fringes of its diaspora. Malik had built a successful business empire, spanning everything from real estate to media. Despite his controversial past, he remained an influential figure in the Sikh community. His wealth afforded him the best security technology money could buy—motion sensors, bulletproof glass, and a team of well-trained bodyguards who monitored his every move. Malik's paranoia was not unfounded; he had received numerous death threats over the years, some linked to families of the Air India bombing victims who never believed his claims of innocence.

The Ratpack had monitored Malik for weeks, analysing his routine, looking for patterns, and finding potential gaps in his security. It was Heracles, a seasoned operative within Lucifer's team, who led the efforts to identify these vulnerabilities. Heracles was known for his methodical approach and had previously orchestrated complex operations with unerring accuracy. Yet, Malik's case presented an unusual challenge. For all the team's expertise and resources, penetrating the multi-layered defences surrounding him would require not just skill but an extraordinary level of ingenuity.

The first plan to eliminate Malik involved using a sniper. Surveillance had shown that Malik had a nightly habit of heating milk before bed, a ritual that took place in his kitchen at precisely the same time each night. The window facing the kitchen provided a fleeting opportunity for a clear shot. Heracles scouted the perfect location—an abandoned building nearby that offered a direct line of sight into the kitchen window.

The sniper Ghost, an expert marksman known for his ability to make long-distance kills, was brought in through a series of untraceable intermediaries. On the night of the operation, he set up his Ruger precision rifle chambered for the .338 Lapua magnum cartridge and waited patiently for Malik to appear. Ghost had already used his range finder and adjusted the sights on the night vision scope on his rifle; there was hardly any wind. The timing was precise, and the sniper's finger tightened on the trigger as Malik moved into the kill zone. But just as he was about to fire, the sniper detected something that had not been visible during the recon—tiny, nearly invisible titanium wire mesh embedded within the glass. A shot would be unlikely to penetrate the window cleanly, and any deflection could potentially injure someone else in the house. Ghost eased his finger off the trigger and swiftly unloaded and dismantled his weapon, and the mission was aborted.

This failure forced the team to regroup and rethink their approach. The aborted sniper attempt revealed not just the robustness of Malik's security but also his paranoia;

it was clear he had taken exceptional measures to ensure even a brief exposure would not endanger him. A more innovative approach was needed—one that did not rely on breaching the fortress walls directly.

Lucifer, Heracles, and the team reconvened to assess other options. It became clear that the challenge lay not only in the strength of Malik's physical defenses but also in his guarded routine, which left few moments of vulnerability. They began to focus on his movements outside the house, particularly when he drove his Tesla. The vehicle itself was a fortress on wheels, with bulletproof windows and an AI-based threat detection system that could notify Malik of suspicious activity nearby. However, the complexity of such systems also presented potential weaknesses.

After days of analysing footage and tracking Malik's routes, Lucifer noticed that the Tesla's high-tech features did not account for the one threat that could still strike unexpectedly: a close-range hit while in motion. If Malik's car was moving at a predictable speed on a predictable path, a skilled shooter could execute what the team termed an 'open kill'—a tactic involving a shooter making a calculated shot with the intent to escape quickly before security could respond.

However, the open kill would not be easy. To pull it off, the Ratpack would need someone on the ground in Surrey, someone who could set the stage for the shooter by creating a distraction or diversion. It was here that Lucifer identified a local hoodlum, Bobby, with a reputation for street violence, who could be discreetly contacted and used to stage an apparently random attack on Malik's car.

The local hoodlum was hired to carry out what appeared to be a crude assassination attempt while Malik was driving. The instructions were simple: fire a few shots at Malik's car and then disappear into the night. The real plan, however, was for this diversion to create just enough chaos and confusion to give the sniper the opportunity to make the kill while security personnel were distracted.

On the day of the operation, the team coordinated everything down to the last detail. The hoodlum received a burner phone with explicit instructions, and the sniper took position at a location along Malik's regular driving route. The timing had to be perfect; Malik's Tesla was equipped with a system that could alert him to any active threats, so the diversion had to be executed when he was passing a particular stretch of road with limited escape routes.

As Malik's car approached the designated area, Bobby emerged from an alley and fired two shots at the car's side windows. The Tesla's onboard system reacted instantly, sealing off the cabin and alerting Malik's bodyguards. While security reacted to the diversion, Ghost, positioned on an elevated position overlooking the street, loaded his Ruger precision with a custom-made bullet forged out of depleted uranium metal high-velocity round capable of piercing through the Tesla's supposedly bulletproof windows.

In the crucial few seconds following the diversion, Malik's car accelerated as the bodyguards attempted to manoeuvre him out of danger. But Ghost was prepared for this, having anticipated the car's trajectory in the moments following the shots fired by the hoodlum. With calm precision, he tracked the vehicle and fired a single shot. The round shattered the window and struck Malik directly in the chest. The Tesla swerved, lost control, and crashed into a nearby lamp post. Ghost realigned his sights and pumped in two more bullets through the top of Malik's head and it split open like a smashed watermelon

Amid the chaos, the hoodlum made his escape, disappearing down an alley and slipping into a prearranged safe house. The sniper disassembled his weapon and evacuated the area using a route meticulously planned to avoid detection. Within minutes, news began to spread about the fatal attack on Ripudaman Singh Malik.

The reaction to Malik's death was immediate and intense. Within hours of the explosion, the Canadian Prime Minister's Office issued a strongly worded condemnation of the incident, vowing to investigate the circumstances surrounding the killing and whether foreign covert assets were involved in an act of violence on Canadian soil. The incident provoked sharp criticism not just from Canada but also from Pakistan, which called the killing an example of India's 'lawlessness' and disregard for international norms. Pakistan's Foreign Ministry accused India of pursuing a policy of 'extrajudicial executions' beyond its borders, demanding that international bodies impose sanctions on India to deter such practices.

The media seized on the possibility that Malik's death could be the latest in a series of targeted killings linked to Operation Black Lotus, further straining diplomatic relations. The *Chronicle*'s headline stories became the subject of heated discussions on major news networks, with pundits debating whether India was indeed behind the recent string of high-profile assassinations. Despite the absence of concrete evidence connecting the government directly to the Fallen Angels' operations, the optics were difficult for New Delhi to manage.

Amidst the chaos, voices in international human rights organizations demanded investigations into India's alleged involvement in extrajudicial killings. Amnesty International and Human Rights Watch both issued statements calling for a United Nations inquiry into what they described as a 'pattern' of suspicious deaths among individuals associated with anti-India terror activities. The mounting pressure placed India on the defensive, even as domestic support for Operation Black Lotus—and for Col Bakshi's controversial approach—appeared to grow among certain segments of the Indian populace.

The Indian government found itself in a precarious position. The prime minister, already grappling with a fallout from the *Washington Chronicle*'s revelations, was wary of the diplomatic repercussions that would come from being linked to Malik's death. On one hand, abandoning covert operations could be perceived as a sign of weakness, a move that would embolden adversaries. On the other, doubling down on denials would risk aggravating already tense relations with Western nations, particularly Canada, whose soil had been the scene of the most recent incident.

Internally, the government convened high-level meetings to discuss its response. The national security advisor argued that any formal acknowledgment of ties to the Fallen Angels would not only be diplomatically disastrous but could also jeopardize the covert assets' safety. The home minister, meanwhile, contended that denying involvement and distancing the administration from Bakshi, as had been the strategy thus far, might no longer be sufficient to contain the narrative. The prime minister listened to both sides, but his focus remained on managing public perception and mitigating international condemnation.

The strategy eventually settled upon was one of plausible deniability, coupled with a strong domestic narrative emphasizing the nation's right to defend itself against threats. The government issued carefully worded statements condemning Malik's killing while reaffirming India's commitment to the rule of law and its opposition to extrajudicial actions. At the same time, influential political voices began to appear on talk shows and opinion columns, subtly suggesting that while the methods may be controversial, there was an underlying justice to the targeting of those linked to acts of terrorism against India.

However, the killing of Malik did little to dispel the growing mythos surrounding Lucifer and his team. In fact, the operation, with its theatrical diversion and sniper's precision, only served to enhance the legend. Public opinion was increasingly polarized; some celebrated the incident as a long-overdue reckoning for a man who had escaped justice, while others lamented the implications for democracy and international law.

As the international community debated the implications of Malik's killing, a different discussion unfolded within India. For many, the revelations about Col Bakshi and the Fallen Angels were met with a mixture of admiration and unease. While there was discomfort with the notion of extrajudicial killings, there was also a belief that India had long been a victim of cross-border terrorism, and traditional diplomatic approaches had failed to deliver justice for the victims of such attacks. For some, Bakshi represented a necessary evil—someone who operated in the shadows to achieve what conventional mechanisms could not.

Television debates became arenas for passionate arguments, with commentators and former military officials weighing in on the ethics of such operations. Supporters argued that the state's first responsibility was to protect its citizens, and if that meant resorting to unconventional tactics, so be it. Critics, on the other hand, questioned the morality of extrajudicial killings and the implications for democracy and human rights.

The mystique surrounding Col Bakshi only grew as the story of Lucifer and his Fallen Angels continued to dominate the headlines. Social media buzzed with speculation about the group's next target, with some even suggesting that the operations had become a war of attrition against those who threatened India's peace. The persona of Lucifer had taken on a life of its own

The fallout from Malik's death marked a new chapter for Operation Black Lotus. The assassinations carried out under Bakshi's command, though shrouded in plausible deniability, had begun to reveal a pattern. The world was waking up to the reality that a highly capable, clandestine group was targeting individuals linked to anti-India activities, operating beyond borders and without regard for national sovereignty.

The message from Lucifer was clear: no fortress, no matter how fortified, was immune from the reach of retribution. And as the team turned its attention to the next target on their list, one thing was certain—the hunt was far from over.

21

The Viper aka Ajay Rao

Ajay 'Viper' Rao was once the embodiment of duty and courage, a special forces operative from Maharashtra known for his rapid deployment capabilities and razor-sharp instincts. He had been the tip of the spear in countless covert operations, executing high-stakes missions with a cold precision that earned him a sterling reputation among his peers. Yet, his career came to an abrupt end when a high-profile mission went disastrously wrong. What should have been a textbook extraction turned into a bloody ambush, and the blame was laid squarely on Viper's shoulders. He was dishonourably discharged without a pension, scapegoated for the failures of his superiors, and cast out from the brotherhood that had once been his life. The bitterness from that betrayal had never left him. It lingered, festered, and slowly transformed his allegiance.

Now a lone wolf, Viper carried out his own kind of justice, hunting down those he deemed responsible for the debacle that ended his career. But beneath the surface of his quest for revenge, there was a deeper resentment—a disdain for the entire system that had abandoned him. This contempt made him the perfect target for those who sought to exploit his anger. Yet, the question of whether Viper was a traitor like Judas, or merely following a script written by Lucifer himself, remained shrouded in uncertainty.

Viper's decision to leak the details of Operation Black Lotus to *Washington Chronicle* journalist Tom Harrington and Rizwan Siddique was not made lightly. The operation had been a carefully guarded secret. It was a mission that existed in the shadows, beyond the reach of governments and bound by no legal oversight. But to Viper, there was a burning need to pull that mission from the darkness and thrust it into the blinding light of international scrutiny. The reasons for this could be seen through two conflicting narratives—either as an elaborate strategy deployed by Lucifer himself or as the actions of a man driven by greed and resentment.

Lucifer was known for his unconventional strategies, often embracing chaos as a tool to further his objectives. In that sense, Viper's disclosure of Operation Black Lotus could be seen as a deliberate move, designed to leave a lasting impact. To the Fallen Angels, their mission was not just a series of covert assassinations but a statement of defiance against terrorism, a reminder that justice would not be deterred by borders or bureaucracy. The leak ensured that their exploits would not be forgotten, that their story would live on, that their actions would echo through the halls of power even as the world tried to bury the truth under layers of political deniability. Perhaps Viper, in his own twisted loyalty to Lucifer, believed that leaking the details was an act of devotion rather than betrayal.

However, a darker motivation lay beneath the idealistic veneer of exposing the truth. Viper had been approached by an unknown international intelligence source, an entity with deep pockets and even deeper agendas. He was offered USD 3 million, a sum that would buy him more than just comfort—it would buy him power. The source was not interested in just bringing down Lucifer or his team; they sought to leverage the information to manipulate the Indian government. The leaked details would provide a means to exert pressure on India, forcing it to align with American geopolitical interests, to weaken its growing relationships with Russia and China, and to bend to the will of those who saw themselves as masters of the global order.

The decision to accept the offer was not as straightforward as it seemed. Viper's motivations were a volatile mixture of loyalty and disillusionment, profit and purpose. On the one hand, the money offered him a way out of the life of a discarded soldier, a life that had given him nothing but betrayal and hardship. On the other hand, his connection to Lucifer ran deep, and part of him wanted to believe that by exposing Black Lotus, he was honouring the mission's true spirit. If the world had to know of the Fallen Angels' crusade, it was better to reveal it through the words of a journalist than to let it fade into obscurity.

For Viper, the betrayal was not just of Lucifer but of the myth that had been built around him. The mystique of a commander who fought in the shadows, whose exploits were known only to a few, and whose wrath fell upon those who had inflicted terror on the innocent—this myth was now at risk of unravelling. As details emerged about the assassinations of Muzzamil Khan, Sajid Mir, Sukhdool Singh, and Ejaz Ahmed Ahangar, they took on a life of their own, fuelling debates, outrage, and speculation.

Yet, amid the media frenzy, there remained no definitive evidence linking the Indian government to these covert operations. That was Viper's insurance policy—Black Lotus, as revealed, was a private endeavour led by a court-martialled officer-turned-private military contractor. The story would implicate but never condemn, providing just enough room for deniability.

As the international community reacted to the leak, Viper watched with a mix of satisfaction and trepidation. He had set the stage for a confrontation that would test the resolve of world powers and shift the balance in covert warfare. India found itself under pressure from the U.S., Canada, Pakistan, and the Maldives, each demanding answers and accountability for the extrajudicial killings exposed by the *Washington Chronicle* article. The Indian government's swift denial of the allegations only added fuel to the fire, with opposition parties and activists demanding transparency and an inquiry into the matter.

The betrayal of Ajay 'Viper' Rao sent shockwaves through the Ratpack. It was not just the act of leaking details about Operation Black Lotus to *Washington Chronicle* that left them stunned but the calculated precision with which Viper had exposed their activities. For a man who had fought side by side with them, taken lives, his defection felt like a knife in the back. Worse still, Viper's betrayal threatened to unravel the entire covert operation that they had so painstakingly built and kept in the shadows.

The news reached Lucifer during a quiet night at the Mauritius safehouse. He was reviewing the team's next target when a secure message came through: Viper's information had made its way to the desks of Tom

Harrington and Rizwan Siddique. The details were too precise to be dismissed as rumours, and the damage was potentially catastrophic. With a clenched jaw, Lucifer called for an emergency meeting.

For Lucifer, the Judas-like betrayal by Viper, or so it seemed, did not spark outrage or surprise. In his world, loyalty was not eternal; it was forged through a constant cycle of necessity and expedience. If Viper's actions were indeed driven by a desire to cast light on their mission, then Lucifer's acceptance of the situation could be seen as a strategic move to embrace the chaos, to use the storm that Viper unleashed to cloak the team's next steps. And if Viper had betrayed him solely for money, then perhaps Lucifer had anticipated even this—that Judas was always there, lingering in the shadows, just waiting for his thirty pieces of silver.

Gathered in the dimly lit operations room, the mood was a mix of anger, disbelief, and an underlying sense of betrayal. Heracles, one of the team's senior members, broke the silence first. 'I can't believe Viper would do this. He had every reason to hate the same people we were hunting. Why would he throw it all away? For money?'

Lucifer's gaze swept over the room, taking in the expressions of his team. They had all fought for a cause, not for fame or fortune but because they believed in avenging the innocents who had fallen to terrorism. For one of their own to turn against them was not just a betrayal of trust but an attack on everything they stood for.

'Let's not jump to conclusions,' Lucifer said, his voice cutting through the tension. 'We need to know what Viper told them and why. If he leaked our operations, he knows the risk. The question is whether he did it on his own, or if he was manipulated.'

In New Delhi, the corridors of power buzzed with an uncharacteristic urgency. News of the leak had set off alarm bells in the Prime Minister's Office, the Home Ministry, and the NSA's headquarters. Top officials scrambled to assess the extent of the damage and whether the revelations would jeopardize India's security interests abroad. The prime minister, sitting with his closest advisors, demanded answers. 'Is there any indication that this leak was orchestrated by Lucifer himself?' he asked, his brow furrowed in deep concern. 'Or has one of our most valuable assets gone rogue?'

Home Minister Dinesh Patnaik, visibly troubled, added, 'If Viper was bribed or coerced, it could be a sign that there's trouble within the Fallen Angels. We need to know if Lucifer is still in control of his team.'

NSA Aditi Mehra weighed in, her tone grave. 'If Lucifer was involved, it could mean he's using the leak as leverage. Perhaps he wants something—immunity, funding, or a clean slate for him and his team. On the other hand, if Viper acted independently, it might mean the Fallen Angels are falling apart. We can't rule out the possibility that Viper was approached by a hostile intelligence agency seeking leverage over us.'

Back at the safehouse, the members of the team were still grappling with the reality of Viper's betrayal. Raven leaned forward, her expression thoughtful. 'Maybe he was disillusioned. We've been pushing hard, sometimes crossing lines even we thought we wouldn't. Viper always had a moral compass, as twisted as it was. What if he couldn't stomach what we were doing anymore?'

Lucifer's eyes narrowed. 'We were all aware of the stakes from the beginning. Viper isn't someone who suddenly grows a conscience and leaks classified information to foreign journalists. He knew exactly what he was doing. The question we need to answer is whether he did it for money, out of fear, or if there's a bigger game in play.'

Heracles interjected, 'And what if Lucifer is right? What if Viper was manipulated? We need to find out who got to him and what they promised.'

Meanwhile, in the *Washington Chronicle*'s newsroom, Tom Harrington and Rizwan Siddique were still dissecting Viper's revelations. The leak provided enough tantalizing details to piece together a rough outline of Operation Black Lotus, yet there were glaring gaps in the narrative. Lucifer's name came up frequently, as did the names of the Fallen Angels, but there was no direct evidence linking the Indian government to the covert operations. Tom wondered aloud if the leak was part of a larger strategy. 'Is it possible that Lucifer himself sanctioned this leak?' he mused. 'To control the narrative, maybe. If he knows we don't have hard evidence, he might be using the attention to send a message.'

Siddique shook his head. 'Or it's a diversion,' he suggested. 'Maybe Viper is setting us up for something, or Lucifer is playing a deeper game than we realize. Either way, there's more to this story.'

The real reason behind Viper's betrayal remained elusive, even as Lucifer and his team tried to piece together the truth. Was it greed that drove him to sell out his team, or was it a deeper sense of bitterness and disillusionment? Had he become a Judas among them, willing to trade loyalty for thirty pieces of silver, or was he coerced by powerful forces playing a game far above their heads?

Lucifer, however, was not willing to rest until he had answers. He convened another meeting, this time with only his most trusted operators. 'We need to find Viper,' he said with cold determination. 'Before anyone else does. If he's gone rogue, he's a liability. If he was coerced, we need to know who pulled the strings.'

Ghost, still visibly angry, asked, 'And if we find him?'

Lucifer's expression was unreadable. 'Then we decide if he's still one of us. Or if he's just another target.'

Leila spoke up, 'I'll reach out to our sources, see if anyone has seen or heard from him. But if Viper has gone underground, he'll be hard to track.'

Lucifer nodded. 'Find him. And find out who bought his loyalty. I don't believe Viper did this for money alone. There's something more sinister going on, and we need to know what it is before it's too late.'

As the team dispersed to begin their search, the spectre of Viper's betrayal lingered. Whether it was an act of greed, a cry for justice, or part of a grander design, one thing was clear: the hunt for Viper would be as relentless as any other mission they had undertaken. And when they found him, the truth behind his betrayal would come to light—whatever it may cost.

In the aftermath of the leak, Viper vanished into the world's dark corners, hunted by those who saw him as a traitor, and sought by those who saw him as an asset. Whether his actions would be remembered as those of a Judas who betrayed his master or as a loyal disciple who followed his leader's unspoken command remained a question that only time could answer. For now, Viper was a man without a country, without a cause—except, perhaps, for the one he had unknowingly served all along.

22

The Hunt for Paramjit Singh Panjwar

The next target for Lucifer and his Ratpack was Paramjit Singh Panjwar, a notorious Khalistani terrorist who had long eluded Indian authorities. As the leader of the banned Khalistan Commando Force (KCF), Paramjit had left a trail of violence, terror, and separatist propaganda in his wake. His involvement in the illegal training of terrorists, drug and weapons smuggling into Punjab, and a series of deadly attacks, including the high-profile assassination of General Arun Vaidhya, had made him a deserving target.

Paramjit Singh Panjwar was a name that sent shivers through the intelligence community in India and evoked anger among the families of his countless victims. For over three decades, he had been a looming shadow in the world of terrorism, particularly in the context of the Khalistani separatist movement. His list of crimes was extensive and brutal, revealing a man deeply committed to a violent agenda that spanned continents.

Paramjit first came to prominence as a key conspirator behind the 2010 twin bomb blasts in Patiala and Ambala, high-profile acts of terrorism that left scores of civilians dead and hundreds more wounded. These attacks were seen as attempts to destabilize the state of Punjab and spread fear among the populace. The sophistication of the bombings pointed to an individual who had not only deep logistical networks but also significant financial backing. These explosions were designed for maximum casualties and to send a message of defiance against the Indian state, reigniting memories of the bloody days of the Khalistani insurgency in the 1980s and 1990s.

But perhaps the most infamous act associated with Paramjit was his involvement in the assassination of General Arun Vaidya. As the chief of army staff during Operation Blue Star in 1984, Gen. Vaidya was instrumental in ordering the military operation to flush out heavily armed militants holed up inside the Golden Temple in Amritsar. The operation, while successful, resulted in significant casualties and collateral damage, deeply offending Sikh sentiments. For this, Gen. Vaidya was marked for death by Khalistani extremists. In 1986, just two years after the operation, Gen. Vaidya was assassinated in Pune, with subsequent investigations revealing that Paramjit had played a key role in orchestrating the killing. His involvement cemented his status within the Khalistani movement as a man willing to go to any lengths for the cause.

The 2009 murder of Rulda Singh, the head of the Rashtriya Sikh Sangat, added another dark chapter to Paramjit's legacy. Rulda was known for his vocal support of integrating Sikhism with the nationalist ideology of the Rashtriya Swayamsevak Sangh (RSS), a stance that made him a prime target for extremists. The attack on Rulda was ruthless, designed to send a chilling message to those who dared to oppose the separatist cause. While Indian authorities suspected Paramjit's involvement, evidence was hard to come by, and he continued to evade justice.

Paramjit's reach extended beyond mere assassinations and bombings. Over the years, he had evolved into a key figure in the nexus of terrorism, drug smuggling, and arms trafficking. The KCF had deep connections with Pakistan's Inter-Services Intelligence (ISI), which provided him with a sanctuary and resources to carry out his operations. Reports indicated that he was actively involved in smuggling arms and narcotics into Punjab using unmanned drones, a method that not only demonstrated his ingenuity but also posed a significant challenge to Indian law enforcement. The drones carried payloads of drugs and weapons, which were then picked up by local operators. The smuggling racket funded his terrorist activities and also contributed to the worsening drug epidemic in Punjab, which had claimed thousands of lives.

Paramjit's life of crime led him across borders and into various safe havens. In 1994, he fled India and sought refuge in Pakistan, where he found support from sympathizers of the Khalistani cause and allies in the ISI. In Pakistan, he was not merely in hiding; he was operating with a significant degree of freedom, raising funds for Babbar Khalsa, a banned separatist organization, and coordinating activities aimed at reigniting the Khalistani insurgency in India. His efforts were particularly focused on Western countries with a significant Sikh diaspora, where he found both financial support and recruits for his cause.

Despite his long list of transgressions, Paramjit had a knack for escaping justice. In December 2015, he was arrested in Portugal following an Interpol red corner notice issued at the request of the Indian government.

This arrest was seen as a significant victory for Indian intelligence and a step closer to bringing him to justice for his numerous crimes. However, the euphoria was short-lived. The Portuguese authorities, citing legal technicalities and concerns over his safety if extradited, turned down India's plea for extradition. Once again, Paramjit slipped through the fingers of the law, and he returned to Pakistan where he resumed his activities with renewed fervour.

For Lucifer, Paramjit Singh Panjwar was a target that checked all the boxes: dangerous, influential, and seemingly untouchable. Eliminating him would not only strike a significant blow to the Khalistani terror network but would also send a clear message to those who believed they could continue to attack India from abroad with impunity. The Ratpack began gathering intelligence on Paramjit's movements, and their efforts soon bore fruit. The target had become complacent, believing that his notoriety and political connections would protect him.

It was Heracles who first learned of a potential opportunity. Paramjit was scheduled to attend a private gathering at a hotel in Lahore. The meeting was supposedly a low-key affair, organized under the pretence of discussing a business deal but, in reality, serving as a front for smuggling negotiations. Heracles briefed the team, explaining that the location provided a rare chance to strike in a setting where security would be lighter than usual. Lucifer agreed, knowing that the window of opportunity could close at any moment if the target changed his plans or heightened his security.

Lucifer summoned his team to a secure location for the briefing on the mission. Heracles, the team's intelligence expert, began by outlining Paramjit's profile, detailing his movements and recent activities. 'We've been tracking Panjwar for months now,' Heracles explained, his voice steady but intense. 'He operates out of Lahore, using a series of safe houses, and moves with a convoy of armed guards. He's been active in drugs and weapons smuggling, using drones to infiltrate our borders.'

Jezebel, the team's logistics and support specialist, interjected, 'He's a slippery one. Our window of opportunity is small. We need to hit him when he's vulnerable, and we've identified the perfect moment: he's set to meet with some of his contacts at a hotel in Lahore.'

Lucifer nodded thoughtfully. 'Any chance we can use this meeting to our advantage? Turn his paranoia against him?'

Heracles responded, 'That's already the plan. The woman leading the operation on the ground is someone who lost her son in one of Panjwar's orchestrated attacks. She's motivated, and her contacts have provided valuable intel on his schedule. Her role is crucial in guiding the team into position.'

The operation was to be conducted by a group of handpicked operators who, under the cover of hijabs, would blend seamlessly into the urban landscape of Lahore. Raven, Leila, and Dove—their height and slender build had been key factors in their selection to ensure they could convincingly pass as local women—would work with Yasmin, who lost her son and the other handpicked local women operators. Dressed in hijabs, they would take their positions around the parking lot of the hotel where Paramjit was scheduled to meet with his contacts.

The night before the mission, the tension in the safehouse was palpable. The team reviewed the plan repeatedly, aware that a single mistake could jeopardize the entire operation. Heracles provided final updates on the logistics, while Lucifer reiterated the importance of the mission's success. 'Panjwar isn't just a terrorist; he's a symbol for a lot of dangerous people. Taking him down means more than eliminating one target—it disrupts a network. It's a strike at the heart of the ideology that keeps these movements alive.'

Jezebel took a deep breath, her tone resolute. 'The team on the ground is ready. The local assets are in place. We have our escape routes mapped out and contingency plans if things go sideways.'

Lucifer gave a curt nod. 'Then let's make sure they don't.'

The hotel parking lot in Lahore was bustling with activity. It was mid-afternoon, and guests moved in and out, unaware of the operation unfolding around them. A black SUV pulled up near the entrance, and out stepped Paramjit, flanked by two bodyguards. They scanned the area with practised eyes, their expressions impassive. To them, it was just another routine stop—one of the many meetings Paramjit attended to keep his network operational.

A group of women in hijabs stood near a *paani poori* stand, seemingly engaged in casual conversation while eating the tart snack. They were anything but ordinary. Each had been trained to move with precision, to avoid detection, and to execute the plan without hesitation. As Paramjit and his guards approached the entrance, one of the hijab-clad women subtly touched the device hidden in her sleeve, signalling the others.

In a coordinated movement, the women sprang into action. The first operative, Leila positioned closest to Panjwar, drew a concealed weapon and fired two rapid shots into the terrorist's chest. The sound of the suppressed gunfire was barely audible over the ambient noise. The other operators followed suit, despatching the bodyguards with lethal efficiency. The entire assault lasted no more than a few seconds, but it felt like an eternity.

Amid the chaos, Yasmin who had led the hit team to Paramjit took a moment to look down at the man who had caused so much suffering. Her face remained hidden behind her veil, but her eyes told a story of grief and justice. She said nothing, but her presence was a silent testament to the consequences of Paramjit's actions.

The operators quickly retreated followed by the 'owner' of the *pani poori* cart who had been part of the team all along, leaving behind a pile of dead bodies and an unattended stall moving with practised speed to the getaway car parked a short distance away. Within moments, they had left the scene, disappearing into the labyrinthine streets of Lahore.

News of Paramjit Panjwar's death spread rapidly. The initial reports cited a targeted assassination, with some sources speculating that rival factions within the Khalistani movement were responsible. Others hinted at the possibility of a state-sponsored hit, though there was no concrete evidence to support the claim. The Pakistani authorities, caught off guard, scrambled to contain the fallout. As usual, there was no trail leading back to Lucifer or his elite operators.

At the safehouse, Lucifer watched the news unfold with his team. 'A job exceedingly well done, ladies,' he said. 'We are not just fighting terrorists; we are dismantling the myth that these men are untouchable.'

Heracles, still monitoring the situation from his laptop, glanced up. 'The Pakistani media is pointing fingers in all directions. There's talk of internal strife among Khalistani groups. No one suspects us. Not yet, at least.'

Lucifer leaned back, his gaze thoughtful. 'Good. Let them think we're rattled or that we've been forced into hiding. The assumption that we'd stop after being exposed only adds to our cover.'

Jezebel nodded, 'They don't realise we've adapted. As long as they believe we've gone underground or been spooked by the media, it gives us a tactical advantage.'

Heracles added, 'We'll use that to our benefit. The misdirection buys us time and freedom to operate. Of course, we will strike again when they least expect it, and by then, it'll be too late for them to react.'

Lucifer's expression hardened. 'Let them keep guessing. It keeps us a few steps ahead. They'll never see us coming.'

Jezebel exhaled, the tension slowly ebbing from her body. 'One more target down. But there will be others. There always are.'

Lucifer's gaze was distant as he considered their next move. 'There will be,' he agreed.

As the men and women of Operation Black Lotus began preparing for their next mission, the memory of Paramjit's demise served as a reminder of the dangerous game they were playing. For every victory, there was the looming threat of discovery, of betrayal, and of enemies who would stop at nothing to hunt them down. But for Lucifer, it was all part of the mission—to protect his country from the shadows, no matter the cost.

23

ISI Bounty on the Fallen Angels

The success of Operation Black Lotus had stirred a hornet's nest in the corridors of power across the globe. For Lucifer and his team of covert operators, every mission achieved was a victory against terrorism and a step deeper into the shadows. Now, their enemies were beginning to circle, eager to find a way to dismantle the team that had evaded capture and even exposure despite the *Washington Chronicle*'s revelations and persistent international scrutiny.

After the high-profile elimination of Paramjit Singh Panjwar, a shift occurred within the Pakistani intelligence apparatus. The ISI, embarrassed by the frequency and precision of Lucifer's operations against their proxies, decided to take the fight directly to Lucifer and his team. An order was issued to neutralize the threat by any means necessary. They put out a lucrative bounty, reaching out to private military contractors and freelance intelligence operators, some with murky allegiances, to track down the Fallen Angels and eliminate them.

The offer was unprecedented in scale. Several mercenaries and former intelligence operators known for their skills in counterinsurgency and covert operations were contacted. The ISI also reached out to various intermediaries within the network of global private military contractors, offering significant rewards for any leads or assistance that could help pinpoint the location of Lucifer or any of his team members. While the ISI engaged these external covert assets, they also activated a more dangerous, closer threat—a deep-cover asset within the Indian intelligence network itself.

The asset was known by the code name 'Chahat'. Her identity had been hidden well, an operative embedded so deep that even the highest echelons of the Indian intelligence community had no suspicion. Chahat was cultivated over the years, working quietly and strategically to rise within the ranks, earning the trust of key officials and gaining access to sensitive operations and personnel data. She had been kept dormant but now her role would be critical. Her mission was clear: monitor Lucifer's operations, uncover his location, and relay the information to the ISI so that a Pakistani Black Ops team could be despatched to eliminate him.

Lucifer sat in his dimly lit office, poring over the latest intelligence reports. His instincts told him that the recent success of Operation Black Lotus would provoke retaliation. However, even he had underestimated the extent to which their enemies would go to find them. Jezebel, his trusted lieutenant, entered the room with a stack of documents.

'There's chatter,' she began. 'The ISI is upping the ante. They're offering a bounty to private military contractors. The buzz is all over the network. We've also intercepted some signals suggesting that they've activated assets within India.'

Lucifer's gaze remained fixed on the documents in front of him. 'And Chahat?' he asked without looking up, his voice calm but with an underlying tone of concern.

'That's where it gets complicated,' Jezebel replied, taking a seat across from him. 'We've known for a while there's a leak somewhere high up. Our source confirmed that someone matching Chahat's profile has been active in the intelligence circles, digging around for our whereabouts. But there's no definitive trace.'

Lucifer leaned back, his eyes narrowing. 'Chahat has been a ghost for years. The fact that there's a hint now means she's probably more active than we thought. The ISI must be desperate, which means we're doing something right. But if we don't identify her soon, she'll have our heads delivered on a platter.'

Heracles, the team's tech expert, joined the conversation through a secure line from his offsite location. 'We can start running diagnostics on internal communications,' he suggested. 'Cross-referencing metadata from the files Chahat might have accessed could give us some clues.'

Jezebel shook her head. 'It's not that simple. If we start probing too deeply, it'll tip Chahat off that we're onto her. The last thing we need is to spook her into hiding or, worse, speeding up her timeline.'

Lucifer nodded in agreement. 'We need a more subtle approach. We'll lay some false trails. Feed bits of misinformation and see which ones resurface. If Chahat bites, we'll know.'

As they strategized, across the border in Islamabad, the ISI was already laying the groundwork for its next move. With Chahat relaying critical data, the agency had set up a task force of elite Black Ops personnel, trained specifically for high-value target eliminations. They would be despatched as soon as Chahat pinpointed a location or identified a weak link in Lucifer's operations. The ISI's leadership was not willing to take any chances—this team had been granted authority to neutralize any member of the Fallen Angels, even if it meant collateral damage on Indian soil.

Meanwhile, Tom Harrington and Rizwan Siddique were still pursuing the story of Lucifer and Operation Black Lotus, despite the media frenzy subsiding in the wake of the exposé. The two journalists had kept in touch with Viper, the informant who had initially provided them with the explosive details. Viper's information had dried up since then, but Tom was convinced there was more to be uncovered.

'Something doesn't add up,' Rizwan said one afternoon as they went through old notes. 'We know Viper was close to Lucifer. Why would he betray them so publicly unless it was part of some larger plan?'

Tom leaned forward, his brow furrowing in thought. 'The way I see it, there are only two options: either Viper did this on Lucifer's orders to use it as a bargaining chip, or there's trouble within Lucifer's Ratpack. Either way, we need to find out who's pulling the strings.'

Unbeknownst to them, Chahat had also been keeping a close eye on Viper. The ISI had instructed her to establish whether Viper was indeed still aligned with Lucifer, or if he could be turned as a secondary source of intelligence. Chahat was methodical in her approach, using a mix of cryptic messages and indirect contacts to probe for weaknesses in Viper's loyalty. If Viper could be leveraged further, it would add an additional layer of pressure on the Fallen Angels.

As days passed, Lucifer began to notice subtle changes in the behaviour of those around him. Small inconsistencies in communication protocols and unexplained absences hinted at a leak. The pressure began to mount, with Heracles running exhaustive digital sweeps and Jezebel initiating discreet background checks on personnel. But even with all their precautions, it felt as if the net was slowly tightening around them.

Jezebel voiced what they had all been thinking. 'If we don't take Chahat down soon, we might not get another chance. The ISI is too close.'

Lucifer's eyes hardened with resolve. 'Then we find her, and we cut off this serpent's head. But we do it our way—quietly, without raising an alarm. Chahat may be the ISI's asset, but she's on our turf now.'

They knew that they were not just facing an enemy outside their borders but also one hidden within. The hunt for Chahat had begun, and for Lucifer and his team, this was a mission for survival; it was also a test of their loyalty, resolve, and the bond they had forged through countless battles. As the ISI intensified its pursuit, the Fallen Angels prepared to face an invisible adversary whose next move could be the difference between life and death.

24

ISI Strikes Back at Lucifer

The chase for Lucifer and his team was heating up, with the ISI determined to make its next move count. Chahat, the deep-cover asset within the Indian intelligence network, had finally zeroed in on Dev 'Inferno' Choudhary, an explosives expert whose unorthodox techniques had earned him a formidable reputation. Inferno had been a vital part of Lucifer's operations, providing the firepower needed for some of their most daring missions. But now, he was about to become a target himself.

Chahat knew how to exploit weaknesses. She had carefully studied Inferno's profile—his interests, habits, and vulnerabilities. Inferno was a loner by nature, a man who sought solace in his craft and had little room for relationships in his life. The few people he trusted were within the tight circle of the Fallen Angels, but even they knew that Inferno kept much of his personal life to himself. Chahat decided to use this isolation to her advantage, opting for a more subtle approach to lure him out.

She contacted him through a secure Telegram channel, using a profile that she had meticulously crafted over several weeks. Her online persona was that of a like-minded explosives enthusiast who shared his passion for the art of demolition. She engaged him in conversations about techniques, theories, and historical military operations that relied on sophisticated explosives. Their exchanges gradually moved beyond the technical and into the personal, as Chahat—under the alias 'Pari'—began to introduce a flirtatious undertone to their chats. She played her role perfectly, presenting herself as an adventurous woman who shared Inferno's interests and admired his work.

As their online relationship deepened, Inferno found himself intrigued. The conversations with Pari were a welcome distraction from the tension of his missions and the constant danger he lived in. Chahat carefully escalated her approach, using charm and subtle seduction to reel him in. She began to suggest that they should meet in person to take their connection to the next level. The location she proposed was Dubai, a place where Inferno had some legitimate business contacts, which made her invitation seem less suspicious.

Eventually, she made the offer that would seal Inferno's fate. 'Why don't we meet in Dubai?' she wrote one evening. 'I'll be there for a few days on business, and I'd love to finally meet you in person. We could share ideas, maybe even have a little fun.'

Inferno hesitated at first, but the combination of professional interest and the promise of personal excitement was too tempting to resist. After some persuasion, he agreed. Chahat had chosen Dubai for its neutral ground and the ease with which she could coordinate the ISI's operations there. She set up the rendezvous at the London Crown Hotel in Bur Dubai, a location popular with international business travellers, where their meeting would not draw attention.

As Inferno arrived in Dubai, Chahat's plan was already in motion. She had been coordinating with a team of ISI agents who were stationed in the city, awaiting her signal. Their orders were clear: neutralize the target swiftly and quietly. Chahat checked into the London Crown Hotel under a different name and sent Inferno a message confirming their meeting time. Everything was in place.

Inferno entered the hotel lobby, scanning his surroundings as a precaution. Even though he was off-duty, years of covert operations had taught him to always be alert. The hotel was bustling with activity, its guests a mix of tourists and business travellers. It seemed like the perfect cover. He took the elevator up to the room number Chahat had given him.

When he knocked on the door, it opened slightly, and Chahat stood there, a smile on her face. 'Pari?' Inferno asked, just to be sure.

'Yes, it's me,' she replied, stepping aside to let him in. 'I'm so glad you came.'

The room was dimly lit, and as Inferno entered, he noticed that it seemed overly quiet. Chahat walked over to the minibar, offering him a drink. 'Let's have a toast to new beginnings,' she said, pouring two glasses.

Before Inferno could respond, there was a sudden movement from the shadows. Two men emerged from behind a partition in the room, and Inferno's instincts kicked in too late. The ISI operators, dressed in plain clothes to blend in with the hotel's environment, moved with practised precision. One of them was armed with a silenced pistol, while the other carried a syringe filled with a powerful sedative.

Inferno reached for the knife strapped to his leg, but Chahat was quicker. In one swift motion, she kicked the knife out of his hand. The next second, the ISI agents were upon him. He managed to land a punch on one of them, but the other drove the syringe into his neck, releasing the sedative into his bloodstream. The room began to blur, and the last thing Inferno saw was Chahat's cold, emotionless gaze as he collapsed to the floor.

The ISI agents worked quickly to make it look like a case of natural causes. They placed Dev's unconscious body on the bed and staged the scene to resemble a heart attack. With Chahat's help, they wiped down the room for any traces of a struggle. Within minutes, they left the hotel through different exits to avoid raising any suspicion.

Chahat stayed behind for a few moments, watching Inferno's lifeless form lay there. She felt a pang of guilt—he had been a formidable adversary, someone she might have respected under different circumstances. But sentiment had no place in her line of work.

The air was crisp and cool in the narrow bylanes of Masoodpur as dusk fell, casting long shadows across the crowded streets. Farah 'Tempest' Kaur had chosen to stay at the Indira Inn International under a false name, as she always did. With her background as a communications specialist and a master of deception, she knew the importance of anonymity and discretion. Over the years, Tempest had crafted a web of false identities and safe houses, each one more nondescript than the last. However, her measures were not enough this time. The net Chahat had cast over the Fallen Angels was slowly beginning to close in.

Unbeknownst to Tempest, Chahat had tracked her movements through a combination of digital surveillance and information gleaned from her contacts within the intelligence community. It was not an obvious trail, but rather a mosaic of small details—a call here, a credit card transaction there—that allowed Chahat to triangulate her location in Delhi. Once Chahat had forwarded the information to the ISI, the agency activated a team of operators to trail Tempest and wait for the right moment to strike.

The operators shadowed Tempest with expert precision, following her as she made her way through Delhi's bustling streets, blending into the crowds and disappearing when necessary. The team leader, posing as a street vendor, observed Farah as she stopped briefly at a small café. She appeared to be just another visitor, sipping tea and scrolling through her phone. But to the trained eye, there was a wariness in her movements—a quiet vigilance that spoke of someone accustomed to being hunted.

As Tempest left the café, the operators followed at a distance, keeping to the shadows. Her destination was the Indira Inn International, a small hotel that sat on a crowded street lined with shops and stalls. It was the perfect place for an ambush. Once she neared the hotel, the agents began closing in, positioning themselves along her path.

Tempest walked briskly, glancing occasionally over her shoulder. She had noticed a man loitering near the entrance of the hotel, a sight that made her instinctively reach for the small knife she kept concealed in her sleeve. But before she could react, a figure emerged from a nearby alleyway and rushed toward her. The attack was swift—almost clinical. A glint of steel flashed in the dim light as the knife drove into her side.

Tempest gasped, her body stiffening in shock. She tried to twist away, to reach for her own weapon, but another agent grabbed her from behind, covering her mouth to stifle any scream. The knife struck again, sinking into her abdomen with brutal precision. The attackers released her just as quickly, allowing her to fall to the ground. One of the agents reached down and rifled through her bag, pulling out her wallet to make it appear like a robbery had gone wrong. They disappeared into the alley before anyone could react.

Tempest lay on the cold pavement, her breaths coming in shallow gasps. She tried to scream for help, but all that came out was a ragged whisper. As her vision blurred, she felt life draining from her, the pain becoming a distant echo. She fought to stay conscious, to gather her thoughts, but darkness quickly overtook her.

When the news of Inferno and Tempest's deaths reached Lucifer, the Ratpack was gathered at one of their safe houses, a remote villa on the outskirts of Pune. The atmosphere was already tense, but the announcement sent a chill through the room. Heracles was the first to react, slamming his fist on the table. 'How did they find them?' he demanded, his voice laced with frustration. 'We were careful. We were always careful.'

Jezebel's expression hardened. 'It's Chahat,' she said, her voice steady. 'It has to be. She's closing in on us. We need to find her before more of us fall.'

Lucifer, who had been silent until now, spoke up. 'The ISI made this look like a random robbery in the case of Tempest and natural death in Inferno's case, but we all know better. They're not just trying to kill us; they're trying to send a message. They want us to know that they can reach us, even in the heart of our own cities.'

Heracles gritted his teeth. 'We should have gone after Chahat sooner,' he growled. 'We've been too reactive, letting her dictate the terms of engagement. That ends now.'

Jezebel nodded in agreement. 'We'll hunt her down,' she said, her eyes narrowing with resolve. 'And when we find her, we'll make sure the ISI knows what happens when they come after one of us.'

Lucifer's gaze was distant, his mind already racing through the possibilities. He knew that Chahat's intelligence network was formidable and that their chances of flushing her out would be slim without a solid plan. 'We have to approach this carefully,' he said. 'If we move too aggressively, she'll slip through our fingers. We need to set a trap—lure her out using the information she thinks she's piecing together.'

The team agreed, and the planning began in earnest. They would lay a series of false trails across the country, each one meticulously crafted to suggest the whereabouts of the team's remaining members. The hope was that Chahat, desperate to maintain her credibility with the ISI, would attempt to follow these trails. And when she did, Lucifer and his team would be waiting.

Meanwhile, in Islamabad, the ISI operators celebrated their small victory. Dev Choudhary and Farah Kaur had been key members of the Fallen Angels, and their elimination had weakened the team, at least in the eyes of the agency's leadership. They believed that the psychological impact of her death would disrupt the Fallen Angels' cohesion, causing paranoia and mistakes.

But Chahat was less convinced. As she reviewed the details of the operation, a nagging feeling crept into her mind. Tempest's movements had seemed almost too predictable, as though she had been laid out like bait. And Lucifer was not known for making things easy. If she had indeed been a decoy, then Chahat's position was now more precarious than ever.

She sent a coded message to her contact at the ISI, urging them to proceed with caution. Lucifer was cunning, and his next move would undoubtedly be calculated for maximum effect. If Chahat underestimated him, she would become the next casualty in a deadly game of cat and mouse.

Back in India, as the team prepared for their next move, the memory of Inferno and Tempest lingered like a dark cloud over the team. Her loss was a stark reminder that even the most careful plans could unravel in an instant. But for Lucifer and his team, this only fuelled their resolve. They had come too far to let fear dictate their actions. Now, they would turn the tables on their pursuers and remind the world why they were called the Fallen Angels.

Chahat leaned back in her chair, the dim light of her office flickering as she scrolled through the reports cluttering her computer screen. The atmosphere was thick with tension, but she thrived in such conditions. Her position within the ISI as an asset embedded in the Indian intelligence network was precarious, but she was determined to make it work. She knew that the stakes were higher than ever; the Fallen Angels were no longer mere shadows. They had become a formidable force, and now, with Tempest's elimination, the ISI was racing against time to neutralize them before they could retaliate.

As she pieced together the information gathered through her sources, a chilling realization struck her. Much of the intel she had been using to track Lucifer and his team was derived from the CIA. The American intelligence agency had been quietly monitoring Lucifer's activities since the inception of Operation Black Lotus. Their interest stemmed from their growing concern of India's assertive military actions against terrorism and the potential destabilization of the region.

The CIA had planted informants and technology across South Asia, keenly observing any unusual patterns in the movement of individuals associated with Operation Black Lotus. The shared intelligence was like gold dust—precise and actionable, allowing Chahat to navigate the labyrinth of information with relative ease. It was also a double-edged sword; the CIA's involvement complicated her position, making her operations more conspicuous to both her own agency and the Fallen Angels.

Chahat's contacts within the CIA had provided her with crucial leads, pointing out specific meetings, financial transactions, and even whispers of plans that revealed Lucifer's strategy. With this information, she had successfully narrowed down the possible locations of Lucifer's remaining team members.

During a recent briefing with her CIA contacts, Chahat had received a cryptic warning. 'Keep your eyes open,' one of the agents had advised. 'Lucifer is smart, and he'll know someone is on his tail if you're not careful. Don't underestimate his capabilities.'

'Don't worry,' Chahat had replied, a confident smirk on her face. 'I'm already one step ahead.'

She knew the game she was playing. Using CIA intel made her operations more effective, but it also put her in a precarious position. If the CIA ever suspected her loyalty was wavering, it could cost her everything. She had to maintain her cover, appearing as an indispensable asset to the ISI while deftly relaying information to her handlers in the United States.

However, she also knew that Lucifer and his team were resourceful. They had already proven that they could adapt and strike back when cornered.

With this in mind, Chahat meticulously planned her next move. She would use the intel from the CIA to create a trap for Lucifer, feeding him false leads that would draw him out into the open. It was a risky gambit, but one that she believed could pay off handsomely. The goal was to disorient his team and create chaos, making it easier for the ISI to take decisive action.

She compiled the information into a comprehensive report, highlighting the locations of recent sightings of the team members and speculating on their possible next moves. She knew she had to act quickly; the window of opportunity was closing, and any slip-up could jeopardize everything she had worked for.

As she sent the report to her superiors at the ISI, she felt a surge of adrenaline. The clock was ticking, and she was determined to outsmart Lucifer. With the CIA's resources at her disposal and her instincts guiding her, she was ready to escalate the conflict, set the trap, and, hopefully, turn the tide in favour of the ISI.

But deep down, she wondered: How long could she walk this fine line before the truth caught up with her? The implications of her actions weighed heavily on her conscience, yet the thrill of the chase was irresistible. In this deadly game of espionage and intrigue, only time would tell who would emerge victorious.

25

Lucifer Strikes Back

In the shadows of the bustling streets of Kathmandu, the hunt for Lal Mohammad had reached a critical point. The Indian intelligence agency, R&AW, had been pursuing him for years, tracking his every movement and trying to gather enough evidence to justify an operation. Lal was a man shrouded in controversy, notorious for his connections with the infamous Dawood Ibrahim and his alleged involvement in a web of anti-India activities, including counterfeit currency operations and even uranium transactions. His ties with the ISI further complicated matters, making him a priority target for Indian intelligence.

In Nepal, Lal had found a temporary sanctuary. The political landscape there allowed him a certain level of immunity, especially after the government granted amnesty to various individuals for political reasons. This development, however, didn't sit well with RAW or its covert assets. An officer working within the Special Bureau of Nepal Police noted, 'Despite our efforts to monitor him, we couldn't do much without solid grounds for arrest. The amnesty left us with our hands tied.'

As information about Lal's daily routine came through various channels, the team led by Lucifer felt they finally had an opportunity. Heracles, the tech wizard and strategist of the team, meticulously analysed Lal's travel patterns and lifestyle choices. 'Lal Mohammad rides his bike to his garment factory every morning at precisely eight. If we can intercept him on the road, it'll be a clean hit,' he announced, a glint of determination in his eyes.

The plan began to take shape. Lucifer gathered the handymen, Ghost, Zaid 'Falcon' Ahmed, and Tariq 'Grim' Iqbal, a specialized team trained for speed and stealth. Their slender builds made them the perfect choice for a motorcycle operation. Dressed in unassuming clothing, they blended seamlessly into the chaotic urban landscape. 'We'll ride in pairs,' Lucifer instructed. 'Speed is our ally, and anonymity is our armour. We approach from the north; we need to get close enough to take him out without raising suspicion.'

On the day of the operation, the handymen prepared their motorcycles. Each bike was equipped for the task: one carried a large bundle of cloth, making it look like a delivery vehicle. The streets of Kathmandu were alive, and the handymen manoeuvred effortlessly through the morning traffic, synchronized like a well-oiled machine.

As they approached the garment factory, Heracles signalled from the control centre. 'He should be leaving any minute now,' he communicated to the earpieces each member wore. 'Get ready.'

The clock struck eight and, just as anticipated, Lal rode out of the factory's parking lot, the familiar roar of his motorcycle slicing through the morning air. The handymen had positioned themselves a few blocks away, their breathing slightly elevated in anticipation of violent action.

As they revved their engines and closed the distance, an unsuspecting Lal was none the wiser. In a seamless manoeuvre, they pulled alongside him, the bundle of cloth serving as the perfect disguise. Without hesitation, they opened fire with their Uzis. Bullets tore through the air, striking Lal's motorcycle and causing him to lose control momentarily.

Lal was tough, a survivor, and as he regained his composure, he instinctively ducked and swerved, trying to take cover behind a nearby parked vehicle. But the handymen were relentless. They split up, one taking the left and the other the right, flanking him with precision.

'Keep pushing!' Lucifer's voice crackled in their earpieces. 'Don't let him escape!'

The street erupted into chaos as pedestrians scattered in panic, screams echoing around them. But the handymen remained focused, their mission clear. They followed Lal who was trying to evade them by hiding behind a large delivery truck.

'Cover me!' Grim shouted as he moved closer, firing his weapon again.

The sound of gunfire rang out, mingling with the city's cacophony. Lal tried to scramble to safety, but he was no match for the speed and determination of the handymen. With a flanking manoeuvre they cornered him.

'Game over, Lal,' Falcon growled, stepping forward with his Uzi machine pistol.

With nowhere to go, Lal raised his hands, frustration and fear flashing across his face. 'You think you can kill me and walk away? I'm untouchable!'

A chilling laugh erupted from Grim. 'You should have thought about that before siding with terrorists.'

Before Lal could respond, the handymen moved in swiftly, finishing the job as the sun continued to rise above the cityscape. Their mission complete, they vanished into the growing shadows of the bustling streets, leaving behind nothing but confusion and chaos.

Back at the safe house, Lucifer sat in front of a wall covered with photos and maps, detailing each of the Ratpack's operations. The latest success against Lal Mohammad was a significant blow to the ISI and the network supporting anti-India activities. He felt a surge of satisfaction as he relayed the news to his team.

'Another one down,' he said, leaning back in his chair, his fingers steepled beneath his chin.

Jezebel nodded in agreement. 'This will rattle the Khalistani factions and their supporters. We've taken out a key player who had the potential to orchestrate more attacks.'

Lucifer smirked. 'Let them think it's infighting. It keeps them distracted. What we need to focus on now is the fallout. Lal had ties with ISI and Dawood Ibrahim. This could provoke a reaction from them. We have to be ready.'

Lucifer leaned forward, his expression serious. 'We need to keep an eye on our next targets. The ISI will not take this lightly. They'll want to make an example of us. We can't afford to be complacent.'

Just then, the sound of a message alert broke the tension. Heracles read the notification, his brows furrowing. 'It's from our contact within the CIA. They've caught wind of something brewing in the ISI. They're preparing for a counter-operation against us.'

Lucifer's eyes narrowed. 'So they suspect us. We need to tighten our security and ensure our movements remain hidden. If they're planning something, we must strike first.'

The team exchanged glances, the gravity of the situation weighing on them. They had become more than just a covert operation; they were now targets. Lucifer knew they had to act swiftly and decisively to ensure their survival.

'Let's regroup, reassess our intel, and prepare for whatever comes next,' Lucifer ordered. 'We've struck back, and now it's time to be on the offensive. We're not just fighting for our lives; we're fighting for the future of our country.'

As they began to discuss their next steps, a sense of unity enveloped the team. They were no longer just individuals on a mission; they were a force to be reckoned with, and together, they would continue to strike back against those who threatened their homeland.

26

The High-stakes Meeting

The mood in the conference room in the Prime Minister's Office was sombre yet charged with urgency. The air was thick with tension as the senior officials of the Indian government gathered to address the escalating situation surrounding Operation Black Lotus. Prime Minister Ashok Singh sat at the head of the table, flanked by his key advisors—Home Minister Dinesh Patnaik, Intelligence Bureau chief Rajesh Khanna, R&AW chief Devendra Joshi, and National Security Advisor Aditi Mehra.

The stark fluorescent lights illuminated their grave expressions, reflecting the weight of the decisions that lay ahead.

'Gentlemen, and Aditi,' the prime minister began, his voice steady but strained, 'we are at a crossroads. The recent eliminations, particularly of Lal Mohammad, have stirred the pot in ways we anticipated but are still trying to fully comprehend. The ISI will retaliate, and we need to be prepared for that.'

Dinesh, a man known for his no-nonsense approach, leaned forward. 'We've already lost two members of Lucifer's team. Each death escalates the conflict, and with every action, we are inching closer to an all-out war fought in the shadows. The public is starting to question the morality of our operations. Extrajudicial killings are not just a talking point anymore; they're becoming a crisis.'

Rajesh interjected, 'The media is relentless, and there are increasing demands for transparency. We must find a way to communicate our objectives without compromising our strategies. If we continue to lose operators, it will create a perception that we are floundering in this conflict.'

Devendra, ever the strategist, stroked his chin thoughtfully. 'We are operating in a highly charged atmosphere. The killing of Lal Mohammad, despite his criminal background, raises ethical questions. The ISI is using this narrative against us, painting us as a rogue state that resorts to assassination instead of diplomacy. We must control the narrative.'

Aditi, who had been quietly listening, spoke up, her voice laced with urgency. 'The reality is that we are in a street fight, and the ISI has been relentless in its attempts to destabilize us. We must keep our operators hidden and our strategies covert. The disappearance of Viper has left us vulnerable, and we must be cautious. They may be trying to infiltrate our network, which means we need to tighten our internal security.'

The prime minister nodded, absorbing Aditi's points. 'Agreed. We must reassess our intelligence capabilities. The CIA is watching us closely, and they are in contact with Viper, who is proving to be a liability. If he reveals anything about Operation Black Lotus, we will face dire consequences.'

Dinesh leaned back in his chair, his brow furrowing. 'But can we afford to pull back? Operation Black Lotus has gained significant momentum. Eliminating key figures like Lal Mohammad sends a clear message to our enemies, but the collateral damage is becoming concerning.'

Devendra replied, 'We are not just fighting against individuals; we are combating ideologies. Every terrorist eliminated is one less potential attack on our soil. However, we need to strategize carefully. Our next moves must be calculated, and we cannot afford to lose more operators.'

Rajesh chimed in, 'And we must consider our allies. The growing unrest among our international partners about our methods could turn them against us. We need to provide them with a justification for our actions—proof that we are not acting recklessly.'

Aditi crossed her arms, her gaze piercing. 'The PM's office needs to craft a narrative that highlights our commitment to national security while addressing human rights concerns. We must convince the public that every life lost in this war is a step towards a safer India.'

The prime minister leaned forward, clasping his hands. 'We need to understand the ISI's next move. We know they are looking for revenge, especially after the deaths of their covert assets. It's crucial that we get ahead of their plans. Rajesh, I want your teams to intensify surveillance on known ISI operators within India and abroad.'

Rajesh nodded, taking notes. 'We can make use of our contacts in allied agencies to monitor their communications more closely. They will undoubtedly be sharing their plans for retaliation.'

Devendra added, 'We should simultaneously increase our focus on the Khalistani factions in Canada and the UK. If they coordinate with the ISI, they could launch attacks that might catch us off guard.'

Dinesh leaned back, reflecting on the broader implications. 'And we need to consider the possibility of retaliatory strikes. If they hit us hard, we will be compelled to respond, escalating the conflict further. We need to maintain a balance between offensive actions and diplomatic channels.'

Aditi raised an eyebrow. 'How far are we willing to go? We've already committed to a hardline approach with Black Lotus. We can't afford to show weakness, or we might embolden not just the ISI but also the terrorists operating within our borders.'

The prime minister took a deep breath, weighing the ramifications of every word. 'We need to project strength, but we have to also ensure that our operations do not draw us into an unmanageable conflict. We have the upper hand with Lucifer and his team, but they cannot become a liability. Their operations must be contained, and we need to ensure their loyalty.'

Rajesh cleared his throat. 'We might consider using disinformation strategies to create confusion within the ranks of the ISI and Khalistani groups. If they think we are targeting different leaders or factions, it could disrupt their plans and allow us to strike effectively.'

Dinesh nodded. 'That's a valid point. If we can make them distrustful of their own, we can buy ourselves time. But we need to ensure that the information we release is credible enough to create real doubt.'

Devendra raised a finger. 'Let's also remember that while we can control the narrative externally, we must maintain internal cohesion. If our covert assets feel isolated or suspect infiltration, we could face a catastrophic breakdown in communication and trust.'

Aditi added, 'This is why we need to reassess our internal communication lines. The remaining members of Lucifer's team need to feel secure, or we risk losing their trust, especially after Viper's betrayal. They should be prepared for anything.'

The prime minister looked around the table, the gravity of the situation weighing heavily on them all. 'Our objective is to protect India's sovereignty and security at all costs. We are at war, albeit one fought in the shadows. We must remain one step ahead of our adversaries while ensuring we do not become the very thing we oppose. This is not just about survival; it's about securing our future.'

The meeting progressed with intense discussions about strategies and contingencies. The stakes were high, and the atmosphere was filled with a sense of urgency as they reviewed intelligence reports and updated their operational protocols. Each member of the team understood the delicate balance they had to maintain: projecting strength while ensuring that their covert operations did not spiral into a full-blown war.

As the sun began to set, casting long shadows over the conference room, the prime minister called for a wrap-up. 'We will reconvene in two days. Until then, keep communication lines open and maintain vigilance. The next move is crucial, and it's imperative that we remain united.'

With that, the officials filed out, their expressions grim but resolute. They were all aware that the battle was far from over, and the struggle against the ISI and terrorism would demand not just intelligence and strategy but also an unwavering commitment to their cause.

In the days that followed, the atmosphere across the intelligence community buzzed with tension. The news of Lal Mohammad's elimination had sent shockwaves through the underworld, but it had also ignited fear and fury within the ranks of the ISI. The vulnerability of their operators was becoming increasingly apparent, leading to a flurry of communications and counterstrategies among their network.

Meanwhile, Lucifer and the Fallen Angels remained focused on their mission, undeterred by the chaos surrounding them. Despite the losses they had endured, the team was more determined than ever to stay one step ahead of their enemies. Lal's killing was not just a tactical win; it was a demonstration of their resolve.

Back at the safe house, the team gathered to reassess their operational strategies. The atmosphere was tense but charged with a sense of purpose.

'Lal's death has created a vacuum, and vacuums are dangerous,' Lucifer began, addressing his team. 'We must capitalize on this chaos and dismantle their networks while they're scrambling to respond.'

Jezebel interjected, 'We need to identify the next potential targets. The ISI will look to retaliate quickly, and we can't allow them the initiative. We must work with our contacts to gather intelligence on their movements.'

Heracles, still tapping away at his laptop, chimed in, 'I've been monitoring their communication channels, and there's been a noticeable uptick in chatter among Khalistani operators. They're scared and looking for a leader to fill the void left by Lal.'

'Good,' Lucifer said, his eyes gleaming with determination. 'Fear is our ally. Let's leverage it. We need to plant misinformation that will create distrust among them. If we can make them second-guess each other, we'll weaken their resolve.'

The team nodded in agreement, understanding the gravity of their mission. They were operating in a dangerous game, but one that was essential for the safety of their homeland.

As the team delved deeper into their plans, they knew that the ISI was not just a faceless enemy; it was a network of individuals with resources and motives that ran deep. They had to be vigilant and prepared for any retaliatory measures.

27

The Silent Strike

In the shadows of Birmingham, a city pulsing with energy and history, Avtar Singh Khanda was unaware that the noose was tightening around him. Khanda, a prominent Khalistani terrorist and the main handler of Amritpal Singh, a radical pro-Khalistan separatist and now Member of Parliament, had made a name for himself by conducting radicalization training classes aimed at Sikh youth. Under his guidance, many were being indoctrinated and trained in the assembly of improvised explosive devices (IEDs), leading to fears that a new wave of violence could emerge from the diaspora.

In the dimly lit safe house on the outskirts of Birmingham, Lucifer convened a meeting with his team. The room was filled with tension and determination as they discussed their next target. The recent successes against Lal Mohammad and other high-profile figures had emboldened them, but they also understood the risks involved.

'Khanda is a dangerous individual,' Lucifer began, his voice low but commanding. 'He is not just a figurehead; he is actively radicalizing young minds, and if we don't neutralize him, we risk a new wave of terrorism aimed at India.'

Heracles, the tech-savvy member of the team, nodded in agreement. 'Surveillance has revealed that he frequently visits a small café near the Guru Nanak Gurdwara in Birmingham. If we can watch him closely, we might find an opportunity to strike without escalating the situation.'

Jezebel chimed in. 'We need to exploit his routine. But this time, we should consider a different approach. If we can't use firearms or explosives, we need to think outside the box.'

'Poison?' Leila suggested. 'Something subtle that can evade immediate detection.'

Lucifer considered this. 'Yes. Something that mimics a natural occurrence—a medical emergency. Blood clotting agents could work. If done right, it would look like a natural health crisis, leaving no trace of foul play.'

As the team mapped out their plan, they initiated surveillance on Khanda. Heracles worked diligently to monitor Khanda's movements, using a combination of surveillance cameras, informants, and social media tracking. The risk was high, but the urgency of the situation demanded action.

For days, they shadowed Khanda, learning about his patterns, his haunts, and the people he interacted with. He often held training sessions at various gurdwaras, rallying support for the Khalistani cause.

'He has become a martyr in the eyes of many,' Heracles reported during one of the strategy sessions. 'If we can eliminate him, it could destabilize the Khalistani movement significantly.'

As they prepared for the operation, they discovered that Khanda had developed a routine of visiting a local café every afternoon, where he often ordered freshly squeezed juice.

Under the cover of darkness, the Ratpack began their operation. Armed with a concoction of a blood clotting agent that would be undetectable in the juice Khanda loved, they positioned themselves near the café.

Jezebel and Lucifer disguised themselves as local patrons, sitting at a table where they could observe Khanda without raising suspicion. Meanwhile, Heracles coordinated from a distance, monitoring the situation through a concealed camera.

As Khanda entered the café, he was greeted warmly by the staff, oblivious to the storm brewing around him. He ordered his usual juice, a vibrant orange concoction that he relished.

Lucifer's heart raced as they watched him take a seat at the table. The plan was simple yet effective.

Jezebel and Lucifer continued to chat casually, their demeanour relaxed. Khanda's attention was entirely on his phone, posting updates about his training sessions and plans for the next demonstration against the Indian High Commission.

Moments later, Khanda's juice arrived. He raised the glass to his lips, taking his first sip.

Jezebel and Lucifer got up from their table. She pretended to stumble, and fell with a squeal just after crossing Khanda who instinctively looked back. At the same time Lucifer emptied the syringe into the orange juice. He then helped Jezebel up and the couple left.

After a few minutes, Khanda seemed to lose focus. He glanced around, his brow furrowing as if sensing something was off.

'What's wrong?' one of the waiters asked him

'Just a little lightheaded,' Khanda replied dismissively, waving his hand. 'I'm fine.'

However, within moments, his demeanour shifted dramatically. He clutched his stomach, the colour draining from his face. 'Something's not right,' he muttered, looking around frantically.

'Sir?' the waiter queried, concern etching his features.

Khanda stumbled to his feet, knocking over the table. 'I ... I need help!' he gasped, his voice barely a whisper as he collapsed onto the floor.

The café erupted into chaos, patrons rushing to assist while others pulled out their phones to record the scene.

As emergency services arrived, Khanda was rushed to City Hospital Birmingham, but the damage was done. The blood clotting agent had done its work silently, and within days, Avtar Singh Khanda was declared dead from what authorities would later classify as a sudden medical emergency—an unexplained case of cardiac arrest.

In the days following his death, the news reverberated throughout the Khalistani community. Khanda's followers were incensed, demanding answers and blaming the Indian government for what they perceived as an assassination. His martyrdom would only further fuel their radicalization efforts, but to the team it was another success for Operation Black Lotus.

Back in their safe house, the team gathered to review the operation.

Heracles leaned back in his chair, his eyes shining with triumph. 'The impact will resonate. Khanda was a key figure, and his absence will create a power vacuum among Khalistani groups.' The others nodded and there were some high fives thrown.

With Khanda's elimination, the Fallen Angels had struck another blow against the Khalistani movement. But in the shadows, the ISI was already plotting its next move, and the conflict was far from over. The game of cat and mouse continued, with lives hanging in the balance and the stakes rising ever higher.

The death of Avtar Singh Khanda in Birmingham sparked a firestorm in the UK. As an influential figure among the Khalistani diaspora and a vocal advocate for Sikh separatism, his sudden demise did not go unnoticed. The initial reports of suspected poisoning and his subsequent death led to an outcry from pro-Khalistani groups and Sikh advocacy organizations, which accused the Indian state of orchestrating a targeted assassination on British soil.

The UK government found itself in a precarious situation. On the one hand, they had to address the concerns of the Sikh community, which demanded a thorough investigation into Khanda's death and decried what they saw as a violation of British sovereignty. On the other, intelligence reports linking Khanda to radicalization activities, including training Sikh youth in assembling IEDs and holding classes at gurdwaras in Birmingham and Glasgow, complicated the narrative. These revelations indicated that Khanda was not merely a political activist but a facilitator of violent extremism.

The British Home Office ordered a high-priority investigation into Khanda's death, and law enforcement agencies coordinated with MI5 to gather more information. There were questions raised about the security breach that allowed an assassination to occur in a major UK city, raising concerns about potential foreign intelligence operations being conducted on British soil. The foreign secretary also reached out to his Indian counterpart, seeking explanations and expressing concern over the implications for diplomatic relations.

However, behind closed doors, there was a different conversation. Several UK intelligence officials were not entirely surprised by Khanda's fate, considering his increasing involvement with extremist networks. His participation in tearing down the Indian flag at the Indian High Commission in London in March 2023 and subsequent anti-India activities had placed him on the radar. British authorities had struggled with balancing concerns of national security with the right to free speech and political activism. Khanda's death, while officially condemned, was seen by some as eliminating a problematic figure whose activities were becoming increasingly difficult to manage.

Khanda's killing and subsequent revelations about the involvement of a covert Indian unit known as the Fallen Angels sparked outrage from several international quarters. Human rights organizations and activists accused India of carrying out extrajudicial killings beyond its borders, setting a dangerous precedent for global norms. Some Sikh diaspora groups, particularly in Canada and the UK, organized protests and demanded justice for Khanda, labelling Lucifer and his team 'rogue agents' engaging in state-sanctioned assassinations.

Western governments, including the United States and the European Union, faced mounting pressure from civil society to condemn India's alleged use of covert operations to eliminate individuals who were deemed threats. Diplomatic channels saw increasing demands for India to cooperate with international law enforcement to investigate the incident thoroughly. There were calls to designate Lucifer and the Fallen Angels as terrorists under international law, urging India to arrest the operators and hold them accountable for their actions. Amidst this pressure, New Delhi maintained a stoic silence, with intelligence officials neither confirming nor denying the existence of the Fallen Angels or Operation Black Lotus. The international fallout signalled a growing rift between protecting national security interests and adhering to international legal norms.

28

Lucifer Finds ISI Agent Chahat

In the dimly lit safe house that had become their operational hub, Lucifer sat hunched over his laptop, the glow illuminating his face as he examined the files that had come into his possession. The chilling reality of Chahat's true identity weighed heavily on him. The ISI asset embedded deep within the Indian intelligence network had been living under the alias Pooja Yadav. But her real name—Rehana Tasneem Malik—was a revelation that could turn the tide of their fight against the ISI.

Her role in the shadows of Indian intelligence had been more than that of a mere informant; she had been a trusted member of R&AW, working directly under the command of Devendra Joshi, the organization's chief. This insider knowledge made her a significant threat, one that needed to be dealt with swiftly.

Lucifer's mind raced with thoughts of vengeance as he gathered the evidence, piecing together Chahat's connections and how deeply she had infiltrated their operations. The loss of Dev and Farah had ignited a fire within him, a relentless desire to eliminate anyone who had played a part in their deaths.

Lucifer paced the dimly lit room, his thoughts racing. He needed to speak with NSA Aditi urgently. Without hesitation, he sent her an encrypted message:

'Aditi, we need an urgent meeting. I have critical information regarding Chahat's true identity. The implications are immense, and it directly impacts our operations against the ISI. This isn't just about her role; it's about the entire infiltration network within our intelligence community. Time is of the essence. Please meet me at the safe house in an hour. We can't afford to waste another moment.'

His heart raced, knowing the gravity of what he was about to reveal. As he prepared to relay this critical information to NSA Aditi Mehra, a mix of anger and anticipation coursed through him. He had suffered two losses to his team and now he felt that fate had given him a chance to strike back.

'Aditi,' his voice taut with urgency, as she stepped into the room an hour later, his demeanour calm despite the brewing storm within him.

'What's going on?' Aditi asked, sensing the tension in the air.

'Chahat isn't who she claims to be,' Lucifer said, his eyes piercing through her. 'Her real name is Rehana Tasneem Malik. She's been living as Pooja Yadav and has been embedded in R&AW, working directly under Devendra Joshi.'

Aditi's brow furrowed as she processed this information. 'How do you know this?'

'I've got proof,' Lucifer replied, turning the laptop towards her. 'Documents, correspondence—everything ties back to her connection with the ISI. She's been feeding them information.'

Aditi scanned through the files, her expression shifting from curiosity to disbelief. 'This is huge,' she murmured. 'If this is true, she's a critical asset for the ISI, and we need to act fast.'

Lucifer leaned forward, the desire for vengeance was increasingly difficult to control. 'We should eliminate her now, make sure she can't betray us any further. She's the reason we've lost Dev and Farah. She must pay.'

Aditi took a deep breath, her mind racing with the implications of what Lucifer was proposing. 'I understand your anger, but we can't afford to act recklessly. Yes, she's a traitor, but if we kill her, we lose the opportunity to gather more intelligence about the ISI's infiltration into our ranks.'

Lucifer frowned, frustration bubbling to the surface. 'You want to interrogate her? After everything she's done? You know what she's capable of.'

'Precisely,' Aditi replied, her tone steady. 'By keeping her alive, we can extract vital information that could help us identify other assets within our intelligence community. We can't let personal vendettas cloud our judgement.'

'Prudence, Aditi?' Lucifer scoffed. 'Prudence doesn't bring back the dead.'

'I'm aware of the cost of this war, Lucifer,' she snapped, her voice rising slightly. 'But we have to think strategically. If we arrest her quietly, we can interrogate her without raising alarms. We can understand how the ISI operates, how they've infiltrated our system, and potentially dismantle their network from within.'

Lucifer's absorbed her words. She was right, but the prospect of leaving Rehana alive, potentially to betray them again, gnawed at him. 'And then what? We just let her go after that?'

'No,' Aditi said firmly. 'We let her face the consequences of her actions. We hand her over to those who put her in our system in the first place. The wolves who funded her treachery.'

Lucifer sighed, the fury simmering beneath his skin. 'You think they'll take her? You think they'll care about her betrayal?'

Aditi crossed her arms, her expression serious. 'They will. She's a liability to them now. They'll want to tie up loose ends. We use her as a bargaining chip to expose the deeper layers of the ISI's operations.'

'Fine,' Lucifer relented, though the fire within him hadn't extinguished. 'But I want to be involved in the interrogation. I want to know everything she's been doing.'

Aditi nodded. 'You'll have your chance. But for now, we need to move fast. We can't allow her to slip away.'

Within hours, a covert operation was set in motion to apprehend Rehana Tasneem Malik. Aditi coordinated with R&AW, ensuring that the arrest would be discreet and controlled. They aimed to intercept her as she returned to her apartment, a place that had become a hub for her intelligence activities.

As night fell, a small team of agents surrounded her building, their movements swift and silent. Lucifer remained on standby, his heart pounding in anticipation.

He was ready to confront her, to demand answers, and to extract a sense of justice for his fallen comrades.

'Remember, we need her alive,' Aditi reminded him as they waited in a nearby vehicle, the tension palpable.

'I understand,' Lucifer replied, though his thoughts were clouded with the desire for vengeance. 'But once we get her, she won't have the luxury of walking away.'

As the agents moved in, they saw Rehana exit her building, oblivious to the trap around her. The operation unfolded flawlessly; she was apprehended before she could react. Within moments, she was blindfolded and whisked away to an undisclosed location for interrogation.

Inside a dimly lit room, Rehana found herself tied to a chair, her hands restrained, and her face obscured by a cloth that left only her eyes visible. The atmosphere was thick with tension, and as the door creaked open, Lucifer stepped in, his presence commanding and intimidating.

'Rehana,' he said, his voice steady, 'or should I say Pooja? You've been a busy little bee, haven't you?' he removed her blindfold, and she squinted at the sudden exposure to light.

Rehana remained silent as she assessed the situation.

'You think you can intimidate me?' she shot back, her bravado intact.

Lucifer leaned closer, his gaze unwavering. 'You're the one who's in a precarious position. You've betrayed your country and your colleagues. You've cost lives.'

Rehana smirked, unflinching. 'And what do you plan to do about it? You think you can scare me into confessing?'

Lucifer's patience thinned. 'You're not in a position to make demands. You're going to tell me everything about your activities with the ISI, and you're going to do it willingly. If you don't, I can make your life very uncomfortable.'

'Threats don't work on me,' she replied defiantly. 'I've survived worse.'

'Let's test that theory,' Lucifer said, signalling to Aditi, who was observing from behind the one-way mirror. 'Bring in the others.'

A few moments later, the door opened again, and a group of the Fallen Angels appeared. Leila, Nisha, Raven, Dove, and Wraith entered, carrying a variety of tools that hinted at their intentions. Rehana's expression shifted as she realized the stakes had been raised.

'What do you want?' she asked, her bravado faltering.

'Just the truth,' Aditi interjected, stepping forward. 'You've been an asset for the ISI, and we want to know how deep your connections run. If you cooperate, perhaps there's a chance for leniency. If you don't ... well, let's just say we have ways to extract information.'

'Leniency?' Rehana laughed bitterly. 'Do you really think you can bargain for my life? I'm a traitor, remember?'

'No,' Aditi replied sharply. 'You're a survivor, and you can either help us dismantle the network you've been feeding or face the consequences of your actions. This is your chance to choose.'

The room was tense, the air thick with the weight of unspoken threats and hidden agendas. Rehana's eyes darted between Lucifer and Aditi, weighing her options.

'I won't betray my people,' she declared defiantly, though uncertainty flickered in her eyes.

'Your people?' Lucifer spat. 'You've betrayed them long ago. You're a pawn in a game you don't even understand.

The ISI is using you, and when they're done, they'll dispose of you like a used tool.'

'I know what I'm doing,' she retorted, a spark of defiance igniting within her.

'Is that so?' Aditi pressed. 'Then tell us about your operations. Tell us about the people you've been working with. This is your last chance to come clean before it gets messy.'

Rehana took a deep breath, the walls closing in around her. She could feel the tension simmering, and the realization hit her: this was no ordinary interrogation. They were playing for keeps, and if she didn't act fast, she might find herself on the receiving end of the consequences.

'Okay,' she relented, her voice steadying. 'But you have to promise me protection. I want assurances that I won't be discarded like a piece of garbage when I'm done.'

Lucifer's expression hardened, but Aditi stepped in, her voice steady. 'We can discuss terms, but first, you need to tell us everything you know about the ISI's operations in India, starting with your handlers.'

Rehana paused, weighing her words. 'I'll talk, but only if you can guarantee my safety. I have information that could bring down a lot of people in high places.'

Aditi exchanged a glance with Lucifer, who nodded, albeit reluctantly. 'Fine. But if you try to play us, you'll regret it. You have no leverage here.'

With a tense atmosphere hanging in the air, Rehana began to speak, revealing names and connections that sent shockwaves through Aditi and Lucifer. The web of deceit extended further than they had anticipated, with several politicians involved in orchestrating operations that spanned the globe.

'Farah was close to discovering the links,' Rehana admitted, her voice dropping. 'She had begun to connect the dots, and that's why they targeted her. They knew she was a threat.'

Lucifer's heart tightened at the mention of Farah's name. 'Who gave the orders?'

'Dawood Malik, Lashkar-e-Jabbar founder and the ISI operative,' she said, her eyes darting nervously. 'He's been coordinating with several politicians here in India. He's got his hands in everything—arms deals, funding for Khalistani groups, and the radicalization of youth.'

'And what's your role in all of this?' Aditi pressed, the tape recorder and the CCTV documenting every action and word.

'I was the link,' Rehana said, her expression shifting. 'I provided intel, connected them to the right people, and facilitated communications. They trusted me because I was on the inside.'

Lucifer leaned closer, the intensity of the moment sharpening his focus. 'How many others are involved?'

Rehana hesitated, the weight of the betrayal looming over her. 'There are several, but I don't know all their names. I can give you leads, but it will take time to piece everything together.'

'Time is something we don't have,' Aditi replied, her voice firm. 'You need to give us something concrete—names, locations, anything that can help us dismantle their operations.'

Rehana nodded slowly, her facade of confidence cracking under the pressure. 'There's a meeting happening next week at a safe house in Manesar, Gurgaon. High-ranking officials from the ISI and their Indian contacts will be there. If you can get in, you can gather enough evidence to expose them.'

Lucifer's heart raced at the thought of such a significant operation. 'And how do we know you're not leading us into a trap?'

'I swear, it's legitimate,' she insisted, desperation creeping into her voice. 'I want to get out of this mess, and the only way is to help you. I can't go back to them now; I'm a liability.'

'Then we'll set up an operation to infiltrate this meeting,' Aditi decided. 'But know this: if you betray us again, there will be no second chances.'

As the interrogation continued, Rehana spilled more information, revealing connections that would send ripples through the intelligence community. With every name and every operation she disclosed, the layers of the ISI's infiltration began to unravel.

Lucifer felt a mix of satisfaction and unease. They had finally unearthed critical intelligence, but the memories of Dev and Farah's sacrifices lingered in the back of his mind. Every piece of information Rehana provided brought them closer to justice, yet the thirst for vengeance still burned within him.

Once the interrogation concluded, Aditi looked at Lucifer, her expression serious. 'We have a plan, but it will require precision and stealth. We need to assemble a team to infiltrate this meeting and gather as much evidence as we can.'

'Count me in,' Lucifer replied, his voice steady. 'I need to see this through. I want to confront the ones responsible for Dev and Farah's deaths.'

Aditi nodded, recognizing the determination in his eyes. 'I understand, but we have to be smart about this.

We're dealing with dangerous people, and we can't afford to act on emotion.'

'I get it,' he replied, his resolve solidifying. 'But I'll do whatever it takes to bring them down.'

Over the next few days, the team worked tirelessly to plan their operation, gathering resources, and strategizing on how to infiltrate the ISI meeting in Delhi. As they prepared for the mission, Aditi kept a close watch on Rehana, ensuring she remained compliant and cooperative.

'Remember, you're a key player now,' Aditi said during one of their meetings with Rehana. 'If you try to double-cross us, there won't be a second chance. We'll make sure you end up back in the hands of the ISI.'

Rehana nodded, her face pale but resolute. 'I understand. I don't want to go back. I just want to be free of this nightmare.'

The day of the operation approached, and tension hung thick in the air. As they finalized their plans, Lucifer couldn't shake the feeling of impending confrontation. The stakes were higher than ever, and the ghosts of the past loomed large.

As the sun dipped below the horizon, casting shadows across the city, the Ratpack geared up for what could be a decisive blow against the ISI's network in India. With the information they had gathered from Rehana, they were ready to face the darkness head-on.

In his heart, Lucifer carried the memory of his fallen comrades, fuelling his determination to ensure that their sacrifice would not be in vain. The time for retribution was near, and he was prepared to unleash hell on those who had wrought chaos in his life.

But amidst the fervour of vengeance, Aditi's voice echoed in his mind, a reminder that strategy and caution were paramount. The battle was not just against the individuals who had caused pain but against a system that thrived on deception and betrayal.

As the night enveloped Delhi, the Fallen Angels prepared for the storm that lay ahead, ready to confront the shadows that threatened to consume them all.

29

Unfinished Business

The outskirts of Manesar, near Gurgaon, are far removed from the hustle and bustle of the city—a mix of industrial areas and farmlands, with hidden corners perfect for clandestine meetings. For Lucifer and his team, it was also the site of a critical operation, one that would determine the future of their mission. They were zeroing in on a meeting of high-level ISI operators and their Indian collaborators, including a well-known political figure—an Independent MLA from Punjab, Bahadur Singh. The intelligence suggested that these operators were planning the next wave of terror attacks across India, targeting major religious sites.

The information had come directly from Chahat, now securely under arrest, whose disclosures during interrogation had peeled back layers of the ISI's deep infiltration into Indian networks. Armed with this intelligence, Lucifer knew that the time for action was now. The operation to neutralize these threats was code-named 'Last Stand'.

Lucifer and his team moved under the cover of darkness. Heracles, ever the planner, had outlined a multi-pronged approach. They would hit the meeting with overwhelming force, while simultaneously deploying diversions to prevent backup from arriving. The team split into small units, spreading out to cover multiple escape routes, each agent carrying the weight of duty on their shoulders.

The compound where the meeting was taking place was heavily fortified. It sat on a piece of farmland that had been converted into a makeshift base, complete with high walls and a watchtower. It was dusk when the Ratpack made their move, breaching the perimeter using stealth and precision. Lucifer, Wraith, and Grim led the first assault team, while Ghost, Falcon, and Raven took the eastern flank, covering the exits.

The meeting itself was in full swing when they struck. Gunfire erupted as Lucifer's team breached the main building. The ISI operators, Adnan, Khalid, Rehman, Zubair, and Arshad, immediately responded, returning fire with ruthless efficiency. The compound became a cacophony of violence, bullets tearing through the air as both sides fought fiercely.

Wraith was one of the snipers and had taken up position to provide cover. From her vantage point, she picked off two operators, her aim steady. But as she shifted her position, a round from an unseen shooter hit her. She crumpled to the ground, the silence following her fall unnerving. Ghost ran to her and checked her pulse, finding none.

'Wraith's down!' Ghost's voice crackled over the comms.

Lucifer's heart sank, but he forced himself to stay focused. He charged forward, tearing through the chaos and unloading his weapon at the ISI agents. Arshad was hit in the shoulder, then the chest. He fell back dead.

The air was thick with gunpowder and desperation. The team moved with urgency, pushing back the ISI's defences, but the losses began to mount. Grim took a shot to the leg and fell, unable to find cover in time. Ghost and Falcon, attempting to rescue him, were caught in the crossfire. Falcon managed to drag Grim to safety, but a sudden explosion ripped through the compound, killing Ghost and sending Falcon flying. He landed hard and didn't move again.

Raven, who had been lying down suppressing fire, saw Zaid fall. She took off towards him, firing as she ran. But before she could reach his side, a stray ricochet found her. The force of the impact sent her sprawling. She lay still, the last light of dusk fading around her as she tried to suck in some air. The bullet had hit her Kevlar vest and a later examination would find two broken ribs.

Lucifer's world narrowed into a blur of rage and pain. He fought like a man possessed, cutting through the remaining ISI operators. The compound echoed with shouts and the crack of gunfire.

When the smoke finally cleared, five ISI agents—Adnan, Khalid, Rehman, Zubair, and Arshad—lay dead. Among the survivors, a shell-shocked Bahadur Singh was dragged out from the wreckage, his hands tied behind his back. His arrest would soon expose his close links to ISI operators and Khalistani extremists, shocking the political landscape in Punjab.

The battle had ended, but the war was far from over. The death of the Ratpack's members weighed heavily on Lucifer and Heracles as they regrouped to assess the fallout. The loss was bitter, made more so by the knowledge that Chahat's intelligence had been instrumental in setting up the ambush that killed their comrades.

NSA chief Aditi Mehra joined Lucifer in the debrief. 'This operation, despite the cost, has delivered a significant blow to the ISI's network within India,' she said solemnly. 'But we need to address what's next.'

Lucifer handed her a report. 'We've captured Bahadur Singh. His interrogation should lead us to more local assets, but there's more. During the firefight, we seized encrypted devices from the ISI operators. Our tech team is already working to decode the data.'

The initial results were staggering. Two ISI operators who had been captured alive, Shabbir and Aijaz, revealed that the agency's plans were far more advanced and insidious than initially suspected. They disclosed the existence of sleeper cells in India, collaborating not just with Khalistani groups but also with transnational jihadist networks like LeT and ISIS. Their most immediate goal was a series of high-profile attacks on Indian soil.

'Their targets include the Ram Mandir in Ayodhya, Akshardham Temple in Delhi, Siddhivinayak Temple in Mumbai, and other significant cultural landmarks,' Aditi relayed to Lucifer and Heracles. 'The terrorists planned to time these attacks one after the other, causing maximum chaos and panic.'

The decrypted data pointed towards a network of sleeper cells coordinated through encrypted Telegram channels. One of these channels, named 'Caged Parrot', had been used by Mohammed Shahnawaz, an ISIS operative, to recruit and indoctrinate young engineers in India, including his close associates Arshad Warsi and Mohammed Rizwan Ashraf. The group had been radicalized by a Maldivian woman posing as a humanitarian, raising funds for ISIS fighters and refugees.

Shabbir's interrogation had been especially revealing. He admitted that the Maldivian woman and her network were coordinating terror plots across South Asia, using religious cover stories to conceal their recruitment efforts. They had been raising money under the guise of helping women at the Al-Hawal refugee camp on the Syria–Iraq border, but the funds were being funnelled to support terror cells.

With this intelligence, Lucifer and the remaining team members mobilized for a rapid counterstrike. Their objective was clear: disrupt the sleeper cells before they could strike, and dismantle the communication networks that allowed them to function. They coordinated with the Delhi Special Cell and other security agencies, leading to a series of raids in the capital and surrounding states.

The first target was a safe house in Noida, believed to be the operational base for the ISIS-affiliated group in India. Lucifer led the assault team, breaching the building with a combination of tactical precision and brute force. Inside, they found weapons, explosives, and detailed plans for the attacks on the temples.

Shahnawaz, Ashraf, and Warsi, engineers-turned-militants, were apprehended in simultaneous operations across Delhi. Their arrests marked a significant breakthrough, as intelligence gathered from their interrogation led to further dismantling of ISIS cells operating within India.

As the dust settled, the arrest of Bahadur Singh caused ripples in the political landscape. His close connections to ISI agents and Khalistani extremists were made public, triggering outrage and demands for a crackdown on anti-national elements. The disclosure of how deeply these networks had penetrated Indian politics and society caused a reassessment of security measures.

For Lucifer and his covert assets, the victory was bittersweet. They had struck a blow against the enemy, but the cost had been high. The fallen members of the team were not just operators; they were family, and their loss would not be forgotten. Their sacrifice became the driving force behind the Ratpack's renewed resolve to hunt down every last agent of chaos.

Lucifer and Aditi's attention now turned to the larger network. The Maldivian woman behind the funding channel was still out there, as were other sleeper cells across South Asia. The captured ISI agents, Shabbir and Aijaz, continued to provide information under interrogation, revealing more about the link between ISI, LeT, and ISIS operators.

But there was a nagging question on Lucifer's mind: How many more Chahats were embedded in the system? He knew that as long as the ISI had informants and agents placed within India's intelligence agencies, their fight would remain a perilous game of cat and mouse.

As Lucifer geared up for the next phase of Operation Black Lotus, he understood one thing with certainty: the stakes had never been higher and there was no turning back. It was time to take the fight directly to those who threatened the very fabric of the nation, and the Ratpack would ensure that their fallen comrades' sacrifices would not be in vain.

30

Operation Black Lotus Continues

Operation Black Lotus was far from over; in fact, what had just concluded was only the first phase—a beginning marked by audacious strikes and calculated eliminations of key terrorist operators in Pakistan. Lucifer and the Fallen Angels had proven to be the sword of retribution, striking deep into the heart of the enemy's stronghold. Each kill had sent shockwaves throughout the global jihadist network, demonstrating that even in the shadowy world of terrorism, there was no refuge safe enough, no sanctuary distant enough, to escape justice.

The operation's second phase opened with a high-stakes mission targeting Dawood Malik, the elusive founder of Lashkar-e-Jabbar. Dawood had been a prominent figure in the terror network, with deep ties to Masood Azhar and other extremist leaders. His organization was responsible for numerous attacks on Indian soil, and he had long been one of the most wanted figures in counterterrorism circles.

Tracking Dawood's movements had been no easy feat; his life was shrouded in secrecy, moving between safe houses in North Waziristan. But intelligence gathered through a combination of electronic surveillance and human assets on the ground finally pinpointed his location—a fortified compound nestled in the rugged terrain of the tribal region.

The Ratpack launched a carefully coordinated strike. Under the cover of darkness, an elite sniper team was deployed to the area, positioning themselves at strategic vantage points. As Dawood stepped out of his compound, seemingly oblivious to the danger lurking in the night, a single suppressed shot cut through the stillness, striking him in the chest. It was a fully recovered Falcon who pulled the trigger. He took deep satisfaction in avenging the deaths of his friends Wraith and Ghost. Dawood's guards scrambled in panic, but it was already too late. The founder of Lashkar-e-Jabbar lay dead, his life's work dismantled in an instant.

With Dawood's death still reverberating through terrorist circles, Lucifer set his sights on Hanzla Adnan, a notorious operative and key conspirator behind the 2015 Udhampur attack on a Border Security Force convoy, which claimed the lives of two soldiers and left several others injured. The attack had been a brutal reminder of the constant threat that insurgent networks posed, and Hanzla's role as a central figure in planning and executing the operation made him a prime target for retribution. The intelligence pointed to his presence in Karachi, where he was reportedly coordinating future operations under the protective cover of a network of local sympathizers and criminal elements.

The operation to eliminate Adnan was not the usual brute force assault. Instead, Lucifer and the team opted for a more calculated approach, ensuring minimal collateral damage while sending a resounding message. A local informant, a shadow in Karachi's underworld, was recruited to attach a discreet tracking device to Hanzla's vehicle. The process took weeks, requiring patience and precision, as the informant had to blend seamlessly into the terrorist's daily environment without arousing suspicion.

With the tracking device in place, Hanzla's routine became a pattern, and the team monitored his movements, learning the ins and outs of his daily schedule. Intelligence reports indicated that he frequently visited a particular neighbourhood where his network's key operators were known to reside. This provided the perfect opportunity to strike. The plan was to intercept him at a traffic junction during one of his regular visits, ensuring that he was away from heavily guarded locations and surrounded by enough chaos to allow for a quick exit.

On the day of the operation, the tactical team positioned itself at strategic points along the route. Disguised as street vendors and passers-by, they waited for the signal. Hanzla's vehicle, a black SUV with tinted windows, slowed down as it approached the junction. The Ratpack moved with surgical precision. Two motorcycles boxed in the SUV from the right and the rear while a van swung directly in its path and slammed on its brakes.

Falcon and Heracles were the motorcyclists, and Lucifer was driving the van. Falcon and Heracles opened fire with AK 103 rifles while the SUV had rear-ended the van and stalled. They kept firing consistently, emptying their magazines and inserting fresh ones, thereby trapping the occupants in the SUV whose bulletproof windows were beginning to shatter under the sustained fire.

Meanwhile, Lucifer got down from the van and lobbed two phosphorous grenades with a seven-second delay fuse under the SUV. He swiftly got behind Heracles's bike and the two motorcycles sped away. Three seconds later, the SUV was engulfed in twin explosions and engulfed in white eye-searing flames, incinerating its occupants.

The operation's focus shifted to Maulana Raheem Ullah Tariq, a senior figure within the Jaish-e-Mohammed (JeM) and a close associate of the group's founder, Masood Azhar. Tariq was a key orchestrator behind cross-border infiltrations, playing a crucial role in funnelling logistics and resources to militants sneaking into India to carry out attacks. Known for his organizational skills and ability to evade security agencies, his elimination was deemed essential to disrupting the JeM's operational capabilities. Intelligence reports confirmed that he was based in Orangi Town, a densely populated area of Karachi, notorious for its labyrinthine streets that teem with militant hideouts and sympathizers.

The mission required both finesse and audacity, given the challenges posed by Orangi Town's chaotic environment. The team opted for a direct yet low-profile approach. Disguised as local street vendors, the operators blended into the bustling atmosphere, setting up near the mosque that Raheem was known to frequent for Friday prayers. The plan was simple but risky: strike as he exited the mosque, taking advantage of the crowded setting to facilitate a quick escape.

On the designated day, the team took up their positions well before the Friday prayer congregation began. The narrow lanes and crowded bazaar served as natural camouflage, allowing them to stay inconspicuous. As the prayer session concluded, a surge of people streamed out of the mosque, among them Maulana Raheem Ullah Tariq. Clad in traditional attire, he exchanged brief pleasantries with a few acquaintances before heading towards his vehicle parked nearby.

At that moment, the Ratpack executed their meticulously timed operation. One of the agents, who had disguised himself as a sherbet vendor, casually approached Raheem. In a flash, Shade produced a concealed handgun and, with deadly accuracy, fired two shots: one to Raheem's chest and the other to his head. Leaving absolutely no margin for error, Spectre shot the fallen Raheem twice more in the head and then the two fired random shots in the air to create confusion. The sound of gunfire pierced the air, and the atmosphere erupted into chaos as bystanders screamed and scattered in panic.

In the midst of the ensuing confusion, the Fallen Angels melted away into the crowd, leaving behind nothing but disarray and the lifeless body of their target. Within seconds, they disappeared into the maze of alleyways, abandoning their vendor disguises at prearranged locations. The entire hit took less than a minute, leaving local authorities struggling to make sense of what had just transpired. By the time law enforcement cordoned off the scene, there was little evidence to suggest who was responsible, except for the tell-tale signs of a professional execution.

For the Ratpack, the mission was a resounding success. It sent a clear message to the JeM and others who facilitated acts of terror: even in the most fortified strongholds, there would be no sanctuary from those seeking justice. Lucifer and his team knew that removing Raheem was another step towards dismantling a network built on violence and terror, a strike at the very heart of the machinery that perpetuated cross-border militancy.

Akram Khan Ghazi, a senior commander of the LeT, was not just a militant leader; he was a master recruiter and indoctrinator, responsible for radicalizing countless young men and sending them across the border into Kashmir to carry out terror activities. His sphere of influence spanned the volatile Khyber Pakhtunkhwa region, where his fiery rhetoric and promises of martyrdom resonated deeply. For Lucifer, neutralizing Akram was a crucial step in dismantling the operational chain that sustained LeT's cross-border terrorism. Intelligence efforts had been tracking Akram's movements for months through intercepted communications and a network of local informants, who risked their lives to gather crucial information.

The breakthrough came when intelligence confirmed Akram's temporary stay at a secluded farmhouse in the rugged terrain of Bajaur, a tribal district near the Afghan border. The farmhouse was a strategically chosen hideout, surrounded by steep hills and accessible only by a few narrow roads. Any large-scale assault, such as an airstrike, was immediately ruled out. Such an approach would have attracted unwanted international scrutiny and ignited a diplomatic incident. Instead, Lucifer opted for a more discreet and surgical operation: a night raid by a ground assault team.

The Ratpack began their preparations, studying the terrain and mapping out the compound's layout based on the information provided by local sources. They timed the operation for the early hours of the morning, when the darkness would provide cover and the guards would be at their least vigilant. As the moonlight faded, the team moved swiftly and silently through the rugged landscape, using the natural cover of rocks and trees to approach the farmhouse undetected.

Upon reaching the outer perimeter, the team breached the compound using silenced weapons to eliminate the guards posted at key positions. The initial gunfire lasted only seconds but was enough to alert the remaining defenders inside the farmhouse. As Lucifer's team advanced, a brief but intense firefight erupted, with Akram's men putting up a determined resistance. However, the Ratpack, highly trained for close-quarters combat, moved with lethal precision. One by one, the guards fell, leaving a trail of chaos within the farmhouse.

Amid the escalating firefight, Akram attempted to escape, making his way through a side door towards a storage room at the back of the compound. His attempt to flee was cut short when two Ratpack members flanked him, blocking his path. Realizing he was cornered, Akram drew a handgun, but it was a futile gesture. Before he could fire a shot, Heracles squeezed the trigger. A single, well-aimed bullet pierced Akram's skull, ending the life of a man who had sown terror for years.

As silence fell over the farmhouse, the covert operators quickly swept through the remaining rooms, ensuring no other threats remained. The entire operation had lasted just minutes.

There was one last thing to do before they left: to send a particularly violent message to a particularly violent group. Lucifer opened a three-foot-long box they had brought with them. The rest of the team waited at a distance and listened to the high-pitched mechanical whine as Lucifer went to work. It took him just under half a minute.

With the mission accomplished, they exfiltrated the area, leaving behind no trace of their identity. For Lucifer, the elimination of Akram Khan Ghazi was more than just a tactical success; it was a significant blow to the morale and operational capabilities of the LeT, sending a powerful message that even in the remotest regions, there was no escape from justice.

The next morning when the milkman entered the compound, he was greeted with the scene of a massacre. When he entered the main hall, he saw Akram's decapitated head on the centre table and a bloodstained chainsaw on the floor.

The death of Khwaja Shahid, known by his alias Mia Mujahid, was a necessity. Khwaja had gained notoriety as the mastermind behind the February 2018 attack on the Sunjuwan Army camp in Jammu, a bold assault that resulted in the deaths of several soldiers and crippling injuries to others. His role in planning the attack had made him a high-value target for the team and Lucifer had taken his pursuit personally. The Sunjuwan incident had not only been an attack on Indian soldiers but also a calculated attempt to destabilize the region and strike fear into the hearts of many. For Lucifer, this mission wasn't just about eliminating a terrorist; it was about targeted vengeance.

The trail leading to Khwaja had been elusive. Despite extensive efforts by various intelligence agencies, the man seemed to vanish and reappear at will, using his network of sympathizers to move between safehouses in Pakistan-occupied Kashmir (PoK). Each near miss only heightened

Lucifer's resolve. The intelligence gathered finally pointed to an abandoned building in a remote area of PoK, where Khwaja was believed to be temporarily hiding out. The location was a dilapidated structure, once used as a makeshift logistics hub for militants crossing into Kashmir.

The operation was as calculated as it was swift. Knowing that an open assault would raise the alarm and potentially give Khwaja a chance to slip away again, Lucifer opted for a quiet, close-quarters approach. A small team of operators infiltrated the area under the cover of night, evading the watchful eyes of local informants and bypassing security measures that had been put in place. The abandoned building stood isolated, with broken windows and walls covered with the scars of previous firefights—a fitting place for the swansong of Shahid's life.

Lucifer's team breached the structure with silent precision. Moving through the dark, decrepit hallways, they found Khwaja asleep in a corner room, but he awoke with cat-like reflexes through pure animal instinct. Khwaja reached for his AK47, but he was both outmatched and outgunned. The suppressed gunfire echoed faintly through the empty building as bullets tore into his body, leaving him slumped against the wall, his life extinguished in mere seconds.

With Khwaja's lifeless body lying on the cold floor, the Fallen Angels completed their final task. A note was pinned to his blood-soaked chest with a simple but powerful message: 'For Sunjuwan'. Those two words said more than any lengthy statement could; they were a declaration that justice had found its mark, that the blood spilled at Sunjuwan had not been forgotten. It was a reminder to others in the militant network that no matter where they hid or how long they evaded capture, retribution would eventually reach them.

As the operators withdrew from the scene, leaving no trace of their identities, the abandoned building fell silent again. By the time local authorities found Shahid's body, the Fallen Angels were long gone, their mission complete. For Lucifer, it was not just the end of a hunt; it was a promise fulfilled, a potent reminder that those who orchestrated terror would face their reckoning, no matter how long it took.

Next on Lucifer's list was Shahid Latif, a high-ranking JeM operative who had masterminded the 2016 Pathankot airbase attack, a brutal incident that left several security personnel dead and exposed significant vulnerabilities in India's defences. Shahid had long operated from across the border, coordinating terror activities and providing logistical support to militants in Kashmir. He believed himself untouchable within Pakistan, particularly in his home district of Sialkot, where he had gone to ground. His confidence was misplaced.

Lucifer's network of informants worked tirelessly, piecing together Shahid's movements and identifying patterns in his routine. The intelligence they gathered eventually led to a remote farmhouse on the outskirts of Sialkot, where Shahid was believed to be staying. It was a location he thought was safe, surrounded by fields and away from the scrutiny of the authorities.

The plan was clear: Shahid would be taken out with a single, precise shot, eliminating the need for a high-profile operation that could risk an international backlash. The sniper Falcon was positioned over 700 meters away, concealed in the rugged terrain that surrounded the farmhouse.

As dawn broke, Shahid emerged from the building, strolling confidently into the open, unaware that he had just a few seconds to live. Falcon took a deep breath and half exhaled, then in between heartbeats he found that snipers' sweet spot and gently applied a squeeze, his rifle an Israeli bolt-operated DAN .338 was geared with a six-ounce trigger pull, and he fired.

The shot echoed across the fields, its source untraceable in the early morning haze. Shahid collapsed to the ground, struck by a single bullet that pierced his skull. His death was instantaneous, a swift and silent conclusion to a life spent orchestrating terror. As blood pooled on the earth, it was clear that even within his homeland, surrounded by familiarity, Shahid was not beyond the reach of those seeking justice. As instructed by Lucifer and despite knowing it was a sure kill, Falcon fired two more bullets into his inert body.

As Lucifer quipped later, 'The first shot was sure but the next two made it certain.'

The elimination of Shahid Latif was more than just a tactical victory; it was a repetitive statement. Geography and borders offered no sanctuary to those who shed innocent blood, and the Fallen Angels' reach extended far beyond conventional limits. The operation demonstrated the capabilities of Lucifer's Ratpack, whose precision and timing were unmatched. With Shahid's death, JeM had lost a significant operative, and the terror network received yet another reminder that their actions would not go unpunished. For Lucifer, it was another step towards dismantling the machinery of terror, one body at a time.

Lucifer's covert operators continued their relentless campaign by targeting Mufti Qaiser Farooq, a close associate of Hafiz Sayeed and a key figure in the financial machinery of the LeT. Farooq had long played a critical role in coordinating funding for the group's operations, funnelling money through various channels to support training camps, arms purchases, and logistics. His expertise in navigating the financial underworld had made him an indispensable asset to the LeT's leadership.

Qaiser's elimination took place in Karachi, a city known for its sprawling urban landscape and dense population, which he believed offered some degree of anonymity and protection. However, Operation Black Lotus's apparatus had tracked his activities closely, gathering intelligence on his movements and financial dealings. When the opportunity arose, the Ratpack acted swiftly.

Qaiser was shot dead in a calculated strike that left little room for escape. The hit occurred on a busy street, blending into the chaos of Karachi's everyday life. The Fallen Angels vanished into the crowd, leaving behind a scene of confusion and a high-profile target eliminated. The operation was executed with precision, ensuring minimal collateral damage and avoiding drawing unwanted attention from local authorities.

The impact of Farooq's death was felt immediately within the LeT. His removal not only deprived the organization of a senior operative but also disrupted the flow of funds that kept its terror activities running. With a significant chokehold on the financial lifelines, the LeT faced considerable difficulty in maintaining its capabilities for large-scale operations.

One of the more audacious strikes in the Fallen Angels' campaign was the assassination of Ibrahim Kamaluddin, son of Hafiz Sayeed and a key architect of the 26/11

Mumbai attacks. Ibrahim had not only carried on his father's legacy of orchestrating terror but had also become a prominent figure in the planning and execution of future LeT operations. His familial ties to the notorious Hafiz Sayeed had long been considered a form of protection, granting him a level of security and freedom in militant circles that most could only dream of. That illusion of safety, however, was shattered when Lucifer's Ratpack turned their sights on him.

The operation was as bold as it was secretive. Ibrahim was abducted by unknown assailants in what appeared to be a meticulously planned operation. He had been travelling with a small security detail, but the ambush was swift and left no chance for a counterattack. In a matter of moments, he was whisked away, disappearing without a trace. The entire incident was carried out with such precision that even the LeT's extensive network of informants was left scrambling for answers.

Days later, Ibrahim's body was discovered in a remote area. It bore the marks of a brutal end; signs of torture were evident, indicating that his captors had interrogated him before his execution. A single gunshot wound to the head served as the final act in a calculated mission that had gone off without a hitch. The message sent by his death was unmistakable—no one, not even the son of LeT's founder, was beyond the reach of retribution.

The assassination sent shockwaves through the LeT's leadership ranks. Ibrahim Kamaluddin's death was more than just the loss of a senior operative; it was a symbolic blow that struck at the heart of the organization's power structure. For years, many in the LeT hierarchy had believed that family connections to Hafiz Sayeed would offer a shield against targeted operations. Ibrahim's death shattered that myth, instilling fear and uncertainty among the group's leadership.

Zahoor Mistry, one of the notorious terrorists involved in the 1999 hijacking of Indian Airlines flight IC-814, had been living a seemingly quiet life in Karachi. For years, he had managed to blend into the city's bustling environment, assuming his past crimes had faded into obscurity. He had participated in one of the most audacious acts of terrorism in Indian history, a hijacking that had left the nation scarred and forced to negotiate for the release of hostages in exchange for freeing dangerous militants. Yet, over time, Zahoor came to believe he was safe, that the world had moved on and his involvement had been forgotten. But Lucifer, the relentless pursuer of justice, had a long memory.

Lucifer's team had been tracking Zahoor for some time, piecing together fragments of intelligence that placed him in different locations across Pakistan. An anonymous tip provided the final piece of the puzzle, revealing his exact whereabouts in a modest neighbourhood in Karachi. The time had come to settle a score that had remained unresolved for over two decades.

The operation was planned with surgical precision. The aim was not just to eliminate Zahoor but to do so with the kind of swiftness and finality that would make clear no fugitive was beyond reach. The assault team moved in under the cover of dusk, utilizing the city's chaotic traffic and narrow alleys to their advantage. As Zahoor stepped out of a small shop, oblivious to the danger, the operators struck.

The entire operation took less than three minutes. Heracles and Lucifer emerged from the crowd and fired multiple shots, each finding its mark with lethal accuracy. Zahoor collapsed, his life extinguished before he could even comprehend what was happening. The team dispersed just as quickly as they had appeared onto the streets of Karachi, leaving behind a scene of confusion and a slain terrorist.

The elimination of Zahoor Mistry was not just another mission completed; it was an act of closure for the families and loved ones of the passengers aboard flight IC-814. It sent a powerful message to the perpetrators of terror—that justice, though sometimes delayed, would not be denied. For Lucifer, Zahoor's death was a reminder to those who believed they could escape their past. The Fallen Angels had not forgotten, and their reach extended far and wide, even into the heart of a city like Karachi.

31

The Cost of Retribution: International Tensions and the Fallen Angels

As the death toll of high-profile targets attributed to the Fallen Angels climbed, so did the international pressure on India to arrest Lucifer and his team. The clandestine operations carried out by this shadowy group had drawn the attention of human rights organizations as well as foreign governments. Accusations of extrajudicial killings began to surface, with critics claiming that the Indian government was turning a blind eye to the violations of international law. Prominent human rights advocates argued that the tactics employed by the Fallen Angels blurred the lines between justice and revenge, calling for accountability for their actions.

In response to the growing outcry, several Western nations, influenced by Pakistan's diplomatic manoeuvring, joined the chorus of voices demanding a formal investigation into the activities of the Fallen Angels. Pakistan seized the opportunity to portray itself as a victim of India's aggressive tactics, suggesting that the operations led by Lucifer were not only extrajudicial but also destabilizing to the entire region. Calls to designate the Fallen Angels as a terrorist organization intensified, with some Western nations aligning their policies with Pakistan's narrative. This growing coalition insisted that any state-sponsored action must adhere to the principles of international law, emphasizing that rogue operations could set a dangerous precedent.

Yet, within India, public opinion was far more complex. Many viewed Lucifer and his covert team as heroes avenging unspeakable atrocities—especially in light of the tragedies that had befallen civilians over the years due to terrorist attacks. For a significant portion of the population, the deaths of figures like Zahoor Mistry, Ibrahim Kamaluddin, and Mufti Qaiser Farooq represented not just a reckoning but a necessary response to a long history of violence. The narrative of justice resonated deeply, framing the Fallen Angels as vigilantes operating in a landscape where formal legal systems had often failed to provide redress.

In New Delhi, the government remained officially silent amid the mounting pressure. Officials were acutely aware of the delicate balance they needed to maintain in the face of international scrutiny. Publicly denouncing the Fallen Angels could alienate a significant segment of the populace that saw them as protectors rather than perpetrators. Unofficially, however, the Fallen Angels had earned a place in the annals of India's covert operations. Their actions were regarded as a testament to the nation's resolve in confronting the persistent threat of terrorism.

As the world watched, the second phase of Operation Black Lotus commenced with a resounding message: The war was not over. Led by Lucifer, the Fallen Angels regrouped to plan their next moves, knowing full well that the shadows held many more secrets, and their enemies had not yet been fully unmasked. The Fallen Angels understood that the stakes had been raised; their enemies would be more vigilant and their networks more fortified in response to the chaos left in the wake of the assassinations.

Lucifer remained undeterred. He gathered his closest advisors Heracles and Jezebel to strategize and evaluate their next targets. The overarching goal was clear: dismantle the networks that had perpetuated violence against Indian citizens and ensure that those responsible faced the consequences of their actions. The stakes were high, but the Fallen Angels were committed to their mission, fuelled by the belief that their work was essential for a safer future.

In the ensuing weeks, intelligence reports indicated the presence of several key terrorist figures in various locations across South Asia. The Ratpack began to methodically plan their next moves, focusing on high-profile targets that could send shockwaves through the terror networks. Each target was selected not just for their operational significance but for the symbolic weight their eliminations would carry. They knew they had to strike at the heart of the insurgency, demonstrating their reach and resolve.

As tensions mounted and the international spotlight turned ever brighter, the Ratpack remained committed to their operations. Each successful mission emboldened them, reinforcing their belief that they were engaged in a righteous battle against an unyielding enemy. Their network expanded, incorporating local informants who provided invaluable insights into the movements and plans of various terrorist factions.

But as their reputation grew, so did the scrutiny from international powers. A coalition of nations, alarmed by the surge of violence and the subsequent retaliatory strikes, convened to discuss a unified response. Sanctions were contemplated, and diplomatic channels buzzed with discussions about how to address what many viewed as a rogue element operating with impunity.

Despite the mounting pressure, the Ratpack forged ahead, driven by a singular focus on their mission. They recognized that the narrative surrounding their actions could be shaped to serve a greater purpose—one that went beyond revenge and entered the realm of justice. In the minds of their supporters, they were not just executing operations; they were writing a new chapter in the fight against terrorism.

Lucifer understood that the path ahead would be fraught with challenges, but he was resolute. Each life taken was a step towards restoring a sense of safety and security for the people of India. The fight was far from over, and with each operation, his Ratpack etched their legacy deeper into the fabric of the nation's history. Their mission was not just about retribution; it was about reclaiming a narrative that had long been overshadowed by fear and violence. In the shadows of South Asia, the Fallen Angels were determined to forge a new path—one where justice would ultimately prevail.

Ajay Meets Aditi

In a dimly lit room in a secluded location, the atmosphere buzzed with a mix of urgency and camaraderie. NSA

Aditi Mehra sat at a small table, her eyes fixed on a laptop displaying intelligence reports. She looked up as Col Ajay 'Lucifer' Bakshi entered the room. His demeanour was calm yet commanding.

'Ajay,' Aditi said, rising to greet him. 'Congratulations on the success of the first phase of Operation Black Lotus. The prime minister and home minister have both expressed their commendations.'

Ajay nodded, a faint smile crossing his lips. 'Thank you, Aditi. It was a team effort. Each operation executed flawlessly was a testament to the dedication of everyone involved.'

'They're thrilled with the results,' Aditi continued, her tone turning serious. 'However, you know there was never anything officially sanctioned about Operation Black Lotus. The government can't acknowledge our actions publicly, but the impact is undeniable. The fall of so many high-profile targets has sent shockwaves through terrorist networks.'

Lucifer leaned against the wall, arms crossed. 'I understand the delicate balance we must maintain. But we are not here for glory or accolades. We are here to ensure justice is served and to protect our nation from those who wish to harm it.'

'Still, it's hard not to feel a sense of accomplishment,' Aditi replied. 'We've taken down figures who've orchestrated unimaginable atrocities against our people. Their deaths have destabilized the networks and made a statement. But the international pressure is mounting. There are calls for accountability, and some are questioning our methods.'

'Let them question,' Lucifer said, his voice firm. 'When you're fighting a war in the shadows, there will always be critics. What matters is the outcome. Every life saved, every attack thwarted, and every criminal brought to justice—these are the measures of our success.'

Aditi took a moment to absorb his words, her expression softening. 'You're right, Ajay. But it's a heavy burden we carry. The lines we tread are not just tactical but moral.'

Lucifer stepped forward, his gaze steady. 'Once a soldier, always a soldier,' he said, a hint of nostalgia in his voice. 'I may not wear a uniform, but my mission remains the same. I fight for my country, for its people. It's in my blood.'

She smiled, moved by his unwavering commitment. 'You've always had that fire, haven't you? No matter the odds, you stand resolute.'

'And I will continue to do so,' Lucifer replied, his tone now laced with determination. 'The shadows hold many more secrets, and our enemies have not yet been fully unmasked. We have much work ahead of us.'

Aditi nodded, feeling the weight of their shared mission. 'We need to remain vigilant. The next phase will require even greater precision and coordination. We cannot afford to grow complacent.'

'I agree,' Lucifer said, straightening his posture. 'We'll gather intelligence, strengthen our networks, and identify the next targets. The fight is far from over, and I won't rest until we've dismantled their operations completely.'

To her own surprise Aditi stepped closer and hugged him, a gesture of affection and respect. 'Just promise me you'll be careful out there. We need you, Ajay.'

'I will,' he replied, his voice softening momentarily. 'But remember, this is a war. And in war, sacrifices are inevitable. We just have to make sure those sacrifices lead to victory.'

Aditi released her embrace, steeling herself for the challenges ahead. 'Then let's make that victory count. Together.'

Lucifer stepped back and reached into his jacket. 'There's just one thing I want you to do.'

Aditi's eyes opened wide.

A Toast to the Ratpack

That evening, Lucifer sat on the veranda of his secluded home, listening to the rhythmic crashing of waves on the distant shore, the sound blending with the wind's mournful song as it swept through the trees in his backyard. The night carried a quiet chill, but the whisky would soon warm his veins.

On the wooden table before him sat five shot glasses, lined up in silent tribute. One was for himself; the others belonged to Ghost, Tempest, Inferno, and Wraith—friends and comrades, each one lost to the dark paths they had all chosen. Their faces flickered in his memory, each bearing the scars of a life lived on the edge, where survival was a constant struggle and death was an uninvited companion.

He stood, walked to the corner cabinet, and retrieved a bottle of eighteen-year-old Glenfiddich—his personal favourite. Returning to the table, he uncorked the bottle and poured generous slugs into each glass, the amber liquid glinting in the dim light.

Raising his own glass, Lucifer stared into the night and spoke softly, 'To the fallen.' He drank deeply, the burn of the whisky a reminder that he was still here while they had become ghosts in the wind.

He had disbanded his Ratpack, knowing their paths would diverge across the world. Some would find new battlefields to serve on, while others might enjoy a life of peace and prosperity. Yet, a few would not be so fortunate, as the darkness they embraced would consume them—or perhaps, it had always chosen them. As they parted ways, he wished them luck, sensing their unspoken hope that the call to reunite would come sooner rather than later. In their eyes, he saw the unyielding loyalty, forged in war, that could never truly fade, no matter the distance between them.

Lucifer took his time over the drinks, savouring each sip as the past drifted in and out like smoke. Memories played their tricks—sometimes fading, sometimes sharpening with an unexpected clarity. But amid the haze, they affirmed relationships and revealed the signatures of those he had known so well. Hair pulled back into a ponytail, the way one sat astride a chair, the quiet moments before chaos—each detail belonged to someone, like a fingerprint of the soul. He toasted them individually, remembering their strengths, their flaws, and the fierce loyalty that bound them.

Call them what you will: dead soldiers, fallen angels, mercenaries, or fanatics. The labels never mattered; they were all shades of the same darkness. They didn't care, and neither did he. What they shared ran deeper than causes or allegiances, forged not through common ideals but by surviving together in places where hope had no place. They had walked through fire and shadows, embracing a destiny of their own making—or one that had been thrust upon them, indifferent to whether it led to glory or an unmarked grave.

Lucifer knew some were long gone, while others still wandered the world's battlefields, moving from one conflict to the next, trying to outrun the ghosts that followed them. But tonight, he drank to all of them—the living, the lost, and those who had left pieces of themselves scattered along the way.

He raised his glass to the night, feeling the weight of unspoken memories settle around him like a shroud. To him, they were more than comrades or friends; they were his Ratpack, a band of broken souls who had carved their own path through hell. They belonged to the darkness, and the darkness, in turn, belonged to them.

Epilogue

Dr Ananya Sharma was unwinding after a particularly rough day when the doorbell rang. As she opened the door, she was met with the unexpected sight of National Security Advisor Aditi Mehra smiling at her. The armoured car and security detail behind her emphasized the weight of her presence.

'Well, aren't you going to offer me a drink, girl?' Aditi asked, arching her eyebrows with a playful challenge.

Half an hour later, Dr Ananya found herself at her desktop, sipping on half a glass of Chianti, the warmth of the wine slowly spreading through her. She glanced at the sealed envelope Aditi had handed her before leaving, her curiosity piqued. Gently tearing it open, she unfolded the contents and began to read.

The first line alone sent a chill down her spine. It wasn't just a message; she had been summoned. As her eyes moved across the typed lines, the implications started sinking in. The words outlined a covert operation—one that would require her unique expertise. A sense of foreboding crept over her as she realized this wasn't just another assignment; it was a call to enter a world where moral lines blurred and loyalties would be tested.

Dear Ananya,

As I take a moment to reflect on the life I've led, the battles I've fought, and the sacrifices made, I feel compelled to share my thoughts and experiences with you.

For years, I have operated in the shadows, driven by a singular purpose: to protect my country from the existential threats that lurk around every corner. It is a calling that demands not only courage and resilience but also a profound understanding of the delicate balance between justice and mercy. The shadows may seem dark, but they are filled with the light of hope—the hope that comes from knowing that our efforts can and will lead to a brighter future for our children, women, and the elderly who call this land home.

As I write this letter, I am aware that our actions have drawn criticism from various quarters. Human rights organizations and advocates for justice have raised their voices against what they perceive as extrajudicial measures. While I respect the right to dissent, I urge those who question our methods to consider the context in which we operate. When the enemy uses civilians as shields and hides behind facades of normalcy, the rules of engagement become blurred. In the fight against terror, we must sometimes make choices that challenge our moral compass, but we do so with the knowledge that our ultimate goal is to protect the innocent.

In the face of increasing international scrutiny, it is vital for us to remain steadfast in our mission. Our resolve must not waver in the face of pressure; instead, it should strengthen our determination to eliminate threats that seek to undermine the fabric of our society. The Fallen Angels, my dedicated team, have made it clear that we are prepared to do whatever it takes to secure our nation's future.

I often find myself reflecting on the children of this country—their laughter, their dreams, their potential. We fight for them. We risk everything to uphold their right to a peaceful and prosperous life. I envision a day when they will inherit a nation free from the scourge of terrorism, where they can grow, learn, and thrive without the shadow of violence looming over them. That vision keeps me awake at night, pushing me to strive harder and fight longer.

I don't want to meet you because I am darkness, and you are light; we coexist but we are different. We feed off each other but we are self-sustaining—individually we are not perfect, but together, we don't have a future.

As we move forward, let us continue to stand united in our pursuit of peace and justice. Together, we can illuminate the path from darkness to light, ensuring that the ideals we cherish endure for generations to come. Let us work tirelessly to build a future where every citizen can live with dignity, freedom, and security. With unwavering resolve and profound gratitude,

Col Ajay Bakshi (Lucifer)
A Soldier for India

Ananya picked up her glass and walked onto the terrace, the cool autumn air brushing against her skin. The night sky spread above her, with the moon hanging low and the pale orange casting an ethereal glow over the quiet surroundings. She leaned forward, resting her arms on the guard rail, letting the calmness of the moment steady her racing thoughts.

But her mind kept drifting back to a man code-named Lucifer. He was a figure from the shadows, a name spoken in whispers among those who operated beyond the reach of conventional rules. Their paths had crossed only briefly, yet the encounter had left a lasting impression, a mix of fascination and wariness. Lucifer was known for his ruthlessness and skill as well as a kind of haunted quality, as if carrying burdens invisible to the world.

Ananya swirled the remaining Chianti in her glass, wondering what had drawn Aditi to mention him and the role he had played in the operation described in the envelope. She knew this wasn't a coincidence; his involvement hinted at something deeper, more dangerous. As the night deepened, a part of her wondered if their paths were destined to intertwine again, and what it would mean if they did.

Acknowledgements

Our sincere gratitude to the team of researchers—Kaydence Rodrigues, Kianna Rodrigues, and Sonakshi Datta—for their painstaking work.

About the Authors

Shirish Thorat is the author of four bestsellers, including *A ticket to Syria,* which has been adapted to the much-acclaimed web series *The Freelancer* on Disney+ Hotstar. His other noteworthy works include *The Scout: The Definitive Account of David Headley and the Mumbai Attacks, Twisted: A Profile of Indian Serial Killers,* and *Clay Horses*. He has had a career spanning three decades in law enforcement, anti-narcotics, anti-terrorism, and aviation security. He has also moonlit as a private military contractor. In his books, Shirish brings the knowledge and authenticity of a fly-on-the-wall professional. He is now semi-retired and lives in a small town in Delaware, USA.

Savio Rodrigues is a journalist and published author. With a deep-rooted interest in law, politics, religion, and spirituality, he pursues these subjects passionately. Savio's literary contributions are both prolific and impactful. His debut novel, *Karmic Ishq,* is a poignant exploration of the psychological effects of child sexual abuse. Co-authored with Amit Bagaria, his second book, *Modi Stole My Mask,* which documents India's struggle against the COVID-19 pandemic, is an Amazon bestseller. His third book, *The Path of Peace: Conflict Avoidance the Jesus Way,* also an Amazon bestseller, delves into themes of peace and conflict resolution. In addition to writing novels, Savio has to his credit a collection of poetry titled *Love of My Life*.